LOTTE SKALE
AND THE WYVERN HATCHERY

ASOLEENYA

Kullusk
Ceris
Endlor
Northern Ruins
Guldkem
Linnea's Sanctuary
Slokyl Ocean
Immorthial Forest
Akeltic Sea
Holan
Vroaevalon
Port Labree
Ruins of Urtica
Twisp
Gruik Territory
Etisa Sea
Shattered Islands
N
W E
S

LOTTE SKALE
AND THE WYVERN HATCHERY

1

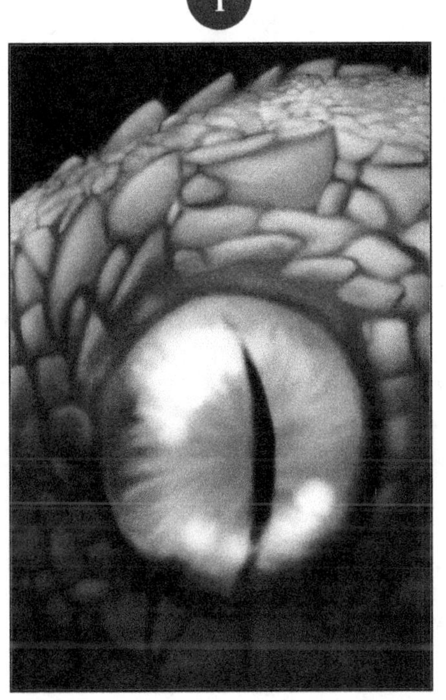

SHANNA P. LOWE

To Gordon and Morgan,

May life never clip your wings.

— S. P. L.

Contents

LOTTE SKALE

AND THE WYVERN HATCHERY

Chapter One
FIRST HUNT

Lotte Skale crouched next to the skeleton of Mrs. Gibbs beloved milking cow, half-submerged in blood-saturated mud. Deep scratches marred the bones and exposed the missing marrow. According to the woman, who stood crying next to Lotte in the middle of a fenced pasture, she had let the cow out of the barn earlier that morning, just as sunlight chased away the night. Sometime in the hour before Mrs. Gibbs had come out to milk her, the cow had already been stripped of its flesh.

Lotte shivered from the overwhelming stench of copper emitting from the carcass. She adjusted the thin scarf she wore over her nose. Beside her towered her father, Orm, curling a finger to his chin in thought. A fog shrouded most of their view of the pasture, only the faint outline of Mrs. Gibbs' cottage and barn visible behind them. Somewhere beyond the wall of gray was a lofty cliff to the forested plateau that stretched across southern Holan's coastline.

"Libby has been in my family for over ten years." Mrs. Gibbs dabbed her tears with the sleeve of her patchwork dress. "I have six children. It's only a matter of time before those blasted things go after one of them."

"I assure you we will track them down and guarantee they

never bother you and your family again," Orm said.

"You had better," she said. "Word around Twisp says you are the best at hunting pixies. I hope for all of our sake you live up to that kind of reputation."

"I would argue that we're hardly the best, but . . . " He trailed off, eyebrows furrowing together. He squinted at the ground for a moment and then bent over to retrieve a small lump from the mud.

Lotte knew what her father had found even before he wiped the object clean. He turned toward Mrs. Gibbs, outstretched his hand, and revealed the body of a pixie.

Mrs. Gibbs screamed and staggered backwards.

"The pixie is dead." Orm brought the creature close to his face for observation. "It can't hurt you now."

Lotte's father wore a hooded cloak and scarf, identical to her own attire, which covered most of his face. However, the narrowing of his brown eyes told Lotte that her father was concerned. She stood up and peered at the pixie in his fingers.

The creature resembled a fist-sized mosquito with a round body, translucent wings, and a needle snout with tiny, serrated teeth on the end. The pixie's bent arms descended into sharp, blade-like points. Yellow bulbous eyes dominated its head. Pixies were truly a horrifying sight. If Lotte had not handled them on a daily basis, she imagined her own reaction being similar to Mrs. Gibbs'.

"What do you see?" Lotte asked, as her father remained fixated.

"Look here." Orm whispered so only she could hear. He pointed toward the pixie's long snout. "Notice the red patch on the chin?"

Lotte squinted at the tinge of color where her father gestured. "That's not blood?"

"No," he said. "It's a marking. Study the wings — they are

wider and more rounded at the tips than pixies native to our region."

"Huh." Lotte could not tell. Then again, she was not a magical creature expert like her father. He noticed details no one else could.

"These are Eastern Desert Pixies, native to former Urtica," he said.

Lotte blinked in surprise. Urtica was once the capital of their neighboring country, Vroaevalon, before King Bouldermaul rose to power and created his Firewraiths — the nickname given to his chivalric order who, during the king's first year of reign, would slip into towns undetected before setting them ablaze. The ruins of Urtica were located in the Ka'Rok Desert, which was clear across the continent of Asoleenya and would require a month of heavy travel by horse to reach. Lotte was puzzled as to how a swarm of Eastern Desert Pixies had arrived in southern Holan.

"Did black market traders bring them?" she asked.

Orm shook his head. "Pixies are as common as rats and mice. They're hardly worth half a nebbin," he said, referring to the lowest value currency of their region, made out of whale bone and shaved into a disk-shaped bead. "No, Lotte — it's here for the same reason other magical creatures are appearing in our region from all over Asoleenya."

"Bouldermaul." Just whispering the tyrant king's name caused the hairs on Lotte's neck to rise. It seemed like most of the crippling problems in Asoleenya stemmed from his siege of the land, eleven years prior. In this case, his mad quest of eradicating anything magical was causing many creatures to relocate.

Lotte frowned in sympathy. She and her father were also refugees, having been driven from their home in Urtica due to the war.

Orm adjusted the leather satchel so that it sat on his belly. He rummaged through it until he found a hunting game pouch and carefully placed the pixie inside. After tightening the drawstrings, he slipped the pouch into a pocket on the inside of his cloak.

"We will dispose of the pixies by the end of the day," Orm said to Mrs. Gibbs. "I suggest you stay close to home and wait for word of our success."

Mrs. Gibbs nodded silently before turning and scurrying through the field and back to her home.

When Orm was certain they were alone, he pulled down his hood and tugged off his scarf, revealing the cluster of freckle-like birthmarks that covered his face. Unfortunately, his past role as an advisor to the former king of Urtica had made him a target for Bouldermaul and his Firewraiths. With the enemy aware of his face, he kept it hidden at all times. Lotte, who shared the same constellation of markings, also opted for a matching hooded cloak and scarf. If any of Bouldermaul's followers recognized them, the consequences would be dire.

Orm waved for Lotte to follow him and led her to the pasture's split-rail fence. He climbed over and approached the imposing cliff that materialized through the fog. They stopped at the base, and Lotte ran her hand up the rockface, causing dirt and small pebbles to shower onto her boots. Her father hummed and noted, "Too loose," under his breath before scanning the steepness of the cliff. Even with proper equipment, the vertical drop would prove impossible for them. There were stairs about two kilometers north, but they would lose the pixies' fresh trails if they wasted time looping all the way there and back.

"We'll have to use magic," her father said, and Lotte's heart thumped.

Orm searched his satchel, once again, and pulled out two

smooth oval stones. Deep blue veins glittered with light, and when he handed one to Lotte, an electric sensation warmed the palm of her hand. Manacore. The only inorganic material to exhibit magic. Helyaits shaved and melted manacore into various items, such as the runes Orm carried for hunts. Carved into stone was the helyait word for levitate.

"Do you remember the phrase?" Orm asked.

"*Sfavatt*," Lotte said, mimicking the coarse, guttural accent of their region's helyait dialect. The underwater race typically spoke in whines, whistles, and clicks; but on land, they created their own language to communicate with "landwalkers." Growing up among the helyaits, Lotte was almost fluent.

"Now the next part is *galm* — repeat after me, *sfavatt galm*."

Lotte did, knowing the phrase translated to "rise slowly."

"Helyait magic — the magic embedded in that rune — intertwines with their language. When you speak the phrase, you will activate the magic."

"I know how it works," Lotte said.

"Do you, now? Alright, prove it then."

Oh, she planned to. Her father acted as though she did not live in a town where magic was used on a daily basis. Clutching the rune to her chest, Lotte repeated the incantation.

The manacore pulsed, warming Lotte's hand. The briny stench of beached seaweed filled the air — the smell of helyait magic — and Lotte felt her body become weightless. Slowly, she floated until her feet dangled above Orm.

Her stomach churned. She was not used to being so far off the ground. Looking up, she gauged another twenty meters more. Lightheadedness clouded her mind, and she came to a stop, suspended in the air.

"Focus, Lotte. Remember my words — and *will* the magic with your mind."

Ignoring the rising panic, Lotte closed her eyes and blocked out the rest of the world. She whispered, *"Sfavatt galm,"* picturing herself moving up the cliff. Her body jolted gently, and she ascended. The moisture of the morning fog formed a layer of slick on her exposed cheeks, but as she rose higher, the air became slightly cooler and drier. Blinking, Lotte found herself breaking out of the fog. Soon, she reached the top of the cliff.

Lotte exhaled, *"Riv."* Stop.

She plummeted like an anchor, missing the ledge below. The rushing wind barely registered as she fell. An arm wrapped around her waist, eliciting a breathy *oof* from her lips. She looked up to see Orm smirking.

"Shall I finish explaining?" he asked.

Heart hammering in her chest, Lotte jerked a nod. She refused to look down, not wanting to contemplate what might have occurred if her father had not been right behind her. Fortunately, her father was either quick to react or had predicted her potential failure — most likely both.

Orm lifted them both to the top of the cliff.

"Amat to move forward. *Nerla* to lower." As he spoke, the magic reacted. Orm's boots touched the ground. "Then you use *riv.*"

"Thanks," Lotte said, pushing away from her father. Her legs quaked at her near death encounter.

They stood before a jungle dense with vines, leafy shrubs, and flowering fruit trees. Smells of sweet floral mixed with decaying vegetation and wet dirt, as the humidity layered everything with water droplets. Vibrant birds with hooked beaks tweeted from high branches, and cicadas droned from their hiding spots. Moss covered every inch of the forest floor, boulders, and the trunks of trees, like thick woolen sweaters.

"You will get the hang of hunting with magic soon enough," Orm said. He held out his hand for Lotte's rune.

She moved to return it, but froze as she noticed something different about the manacore. The bright veins from before had dulled.

"What happened to it?" she asked, lifting the stone up for him to see.

"The energy of magic is fleeting." Orm took the rock to inspect it. "Think of it like oil in a lamp — it eventually burns out."

"Will it ever come back?" Lotte asked. Only after she turned fourteen years old had Lotte's father taught her to use magic runes for hunting. Before that, her only experience was manacore torches and door locks, all of which she had never seen run out of magic.

"Not with inorganic material. There is no way for them to naturally rejuvenate the energy needed for magic unless you transfer magic from one source to another — such as a helyait infusing their magic into depleted manacore."

"Living creatures can replenish themselves, though." Lotte jabbed a finger in the direction of Twisp. "Helyaits don't run out of magic. They use it for everything."

Orm nodded. "They eat, drink, and sleep to renew their magic energy supply — as do other magical beings. Some can even absorb sunlight and heat for the same reason." He tosses the rune into the air and catches it playfully. "Shall we find the pixie nest, now?"

Excitement rose in Lotte's chest, a smile lighting her face. She eagerly trailed after her father into the forest. This was her first hunt. For as long as she could remember, she had wanted to participate with her father's captures of pixies. Yet, the rule was she must wait until she was fourteen years old.

Last week was her long-awaited birthday.

From its holder on his belt, Orm unsheathed a large knife with a broad blade and swiped an arc in front of him, cutting a path through the thick foliage. The process was slow, with leaves and branches constantly sliding off Lotte's hood. After the fifth attempt at adjusting it, Lotte gave up. No one was around, anyway, to recognize her and her father.

Orm swung one last time before a deer path split the forest. They followed it up a steep, rocky slope and down to a shallow creek where mosquitoes swarmed in clouds over their heads. Luckily, Lotte and her father had lathered their skin and clothes in a salve that deterred bugs from biting.

A grating animal call startled Lotte. She whipped her head upward just in time to witness a blue-feathered glider raptor gracefully soar over her, eventually landing on the trunk of a tree with sharp nails gripping the bark. It had a reptilian face — sharp and pointed, with smooth scales on the top of its head. However, its body resembled that of a bird, featuring a scaly tail that fanned out into colorful feathers at the end. Plumage on its underarms allowed for a brief distance of flight for the glider raptor.

The deeper they ventured into the jungle, the more peculiar creatures they encountered. They were only ten kilometers away from the Immorthial Forest, the abode of Asoleenya's most formidable and terrifying magical beasts. It was perilous for a mere human without any magical abilities to enter.

Orm halted his steps suddenly and thrust out his arm, causing Lotte to walk into his elbow. She shot him a confused look, wondering why they had stopped.

"Do you hear that?" Orm asked.

Lotte brushed her chin-length brown hair back behind her

ear. All she could hear were the typical jungle noises and the glider raptor squawking nearby. Giving her father a sideways glance, she wondered if he was imagining things. Orm brought his index finger to his lips and motioned for silence. He crouched down and tiptoed forward, and Lotte mimicked his movements.

The creek divided into two, and Orm followed the one that flowed into a stagnant pond. Vibrant ginger lilies emerged from long, broad leaves, which were taller than Lotte's father and obstructed her view of the forest as she crept toward the pond. After a while, Lotte heard the sound her father had mentioned earlier.

Buzzing. Like hundreds of large wasps.

Orm squatted down and grabbed a handful of mud, wiping it over his face and hands, before he held out a glob of the foul muck to Lotte.

"This will help mask your scent. Rule number one for dealing with pixies is to not alert them of your presence," Orm said.

"Got it." Lotte took the mud, hands trembling, and wiped it over every exposed part of her body. This was it! After all the waiting and begging, she was going to catch her first swarm of pixies. Any normal human would tell her she was crazy for wanting to go anywhere near the flesh-craving pests, but to Lotte, this was a rite of passage — proof she was just as useful as the rest of her extraordinary family.

"Keep your head down and stay absolutely quiet," Orm whispered. "Rule number two for dealing with pixies is not to alert them of your presence."

"That's the same as the first rule," Lotte deadpanned.

"Exactly."

She snorted, catching her natural instinct to roll her eyes. "How do we tell where we're going with all the ginger lilies?"

With their current visibility, they might accidentally step

onto the pixie nest.

In that case, Lotte and her father would be dead.

"That is a question answered by rule number three."

"Let me guess — don't alert the pixies of our presence."

"Close! But no."

Orm slid his satchel forward and extracted a large, lumpy velvet pouch. Something inside coiled and hissed. Untying the strings of the pouch and opening it up, a vibrant green wyvern slithered onto Orm's arm, wrapping its body around his wrist for support. The serpent creature, resembling a half-meter python with bony eye-ridges, stretched out two sets of feathered wings. One set extended a few inches past the wyvern's head, and the other protruded into legs from halfway down its body. At the end of its tail was a curled stinger, similar to that of a scorpion's.

"Always carry a tracking wyvern with you. That's rule number three," he said.

While wyverns looked like snakes, they were as smart as dogs and could be trained as such. Orm had done so with this particular wyvern.

Taking out the dead pixie from earlier, Orm held it in front of the wyvern's vented nose. Glut — the name they had chosen for him — inhaled the pixie's scent. His mouth snapped open, revealing two rows of serrated teeth, and lunged forward. Orm yanked his hand back.

"You were fed this morning!" he sounded exasperated.

Glut flickered his tongue with irritation. He coiled his body back and sprung again, attempting to eat the pixie. Lotte laughed when her father swatted the wyvern away. Perhaps Glut was not as trained as Orm claimed.

"Fly, you foolish thing!" Orm tossed the wyvern into the air.

With a hiss, Glut pumped his wings and rose until he was

higher than the tree canopy. The sun forced Lotte to squint as she tracked his movements. Soon, he was just a glimmer of green. Only a few meters ahead of Lotte and her father, Glut began circling. Orm grinned widely and nudged Lotte with his elbow. Glut had found the pixie nest.

"You know the way home from here, right?" Orm whispered.

"What! Why?" she exclaimed.

Her father ducked his head. "Too loud!"

"You promised I could hunt pixies once I turned fourteen." She spoke under her breath.

"We are not used to these pixies."

Orm risked parting the ginger lilies, giving them a small view of the pond. At least three dozen pixies zipped above the murky water. Mud mounds on the far bank peaked like skin boils, oozing with more of the pests. In those mounds were their young, born three to five in a litter. Only one sibling would survive — the rest eaten. They found the pixies' nest.

"I'm staying," Lotte reiterated.

Orm narrowed his eyes, irritation flashing across his face. "You agreed to abide by every instruction I gave you. If you cannot, then we will end this hunt early and forgo any future opportunities."

"But — "

"Lotte Skale, go home!"

Sharp chirps interrupted their argument. A pixie bumbled in their direction. Orm forced both of them flat on the ground, wriggling their limbs into the mud. Face down, Lotte pulled her cloak's hood on, closed her eyes, and held her breath. The whine of the pixie's wings grew closer before Lotte felt the wind of each beat hit her head. Her stomach lurched as if it might crawl up her throat.

A soft weight landed on her. She muffled a frightened cry as the pixie scuttled around, its needle beak prodding the fabric over her neck. The pixie lifted into the air and then dropped onto her back. It poked around more. Lotte's heart thudded so heavily in her chest that she was sure the pixie could hear it.

In her peripheral vision, a streak of green whizzed by. The pixie screeched as something heavier thumped against her spine. Glut. Relief flooded Lotte, and she carefully shook them off, rolling over and sitting up. She watched Glut bite the pixie while constricting around its gray body, stinger disappearing into its skin. Bones snapped, and the pixie fell limp. Glut's jaw unhinged, opening wide, and he gulped the pixie down. Lotte mentally thanked the wyvern for his impeccable timing.

Her father pushed himself up, and they locked gazes.

"Now is not the time to argue," he whispered.

After the close encounter, Lotte begrudgingly nodded.

Maneuvering onto all fours, she crawled backward while avoiding Glut, who worked the pixie down his long throat. When she was far enough away from the pond, Lotte stood. Perspiration from her forehead trickled down to her lips, collecting the pond scum on her skin, and she sputtered at the disgusting taste.

Lotte scowled one last time in her father's direction, and she stalked back the way they came. Her fists clenched with frustration. Orm was treating her no differently than before she turned fourteen years old — a child who could not hold her own.

Sullenly, Lotte traveled halfway to the cliff's edge before turning east and soon finding the boot-worn path that would lead her home. Through the trees, glimpses of the ocean glittered as the morning fog began to disperse. The cliff traveled along Holan's southern coast, and this particular section carved a deep crescent into the motherland.

Seabirds cawed, and horns blared from outside the bay. Lotte spotted Twisp floating on the water. A jetty more than a kilometer long connected to a rusted shipwreck converted into shops and lodging. If she squinted, she could probably make out specks of movement from helyaits and other locals.

A familiar buzzing noise stopped Lotte in her tracks. She held her breath and listened, noting that the sound was coming from not far ahead. The hairs on her arms rose as Lotte inched forward and pushed massive fern leaves out of the way. Her eyes searched the forest for the pixie.

There it was!

Lotte stifled an ecstatic gasp. A fat-bellied pixie was circling around a glider raptor nest in the trees. Judging by the two glider raptors screeching fervently from nearby branches, there must be hatchlings inside. The pixie was preparing for its next meal.

Lotte's lips twitched into a smirk, and she reached behind her back, where she kept a meter-long blowgun in a leather holster. It was made of cane, but the mouthpiece was carved from whale bone. From a canister clipped to her belt of pouches, she loaded a dart into the blowgun, waiting for the right moment. Attacking the pixie while it was airborne was useless, a sure miss. Patience was key. Lotte inhaled deeply when the pixie dropped onto the nest, an alarmed chirp coming from inside the woven dried grass. She placed the mouthpiece to her lips and exhaled hard. The dart was silent, but a hissing cry told Lotte she had hit her target.

Satisfaction replaced Lotte's earlier anger regarding her father's broken promise. She wished he were here to see it. Then she could rub her victory in his face, proving he had made a mistake.

Moving underneath the nest, Lotte squatted in the shrubbery and pushed around the ferns and vines until she came across the pixie's twitching body. She picked it up and rotated the pixie until she saw the underbelly. It had a red patch like the one her father had found by the remains of Mrs. Gibbs's cow. The pest must have wandered off from the swarm. Lotte removed the dart and tucked the pixie in her cloak pocket, patting the lump through the fabric.

As the high of adrenaline dwindled, Lotte realized something was off about her surroundings. The buzzing noise never stopped. In fact, the sound grew louder and began vibrating the leaves on the trees. Blood drained from Lotte's face. Without any hesitation, she sprinted in the direction of her home, leaping over warped logs and ducking under branches, lungs drawing desperate breaths. The buzzing followed her.

"Ouch!" Lotte cried. A sharp pain pricked her elbow. Looking over her shoulder, she saw a pixie looming mere centimeters away, followed by a swarm of at least fifty flesh-eating creatures. Was this a second swarm? Why were there so many?

THRAWP!

Lotte collided with the trunk of a tree and collapsed onto her back, her head bouncing on the ground. The spongy mulch thankfully cushioned her fall, but the initial impact left her stunned. Instantly, a swelling on her forehead appeared, and a sharp throb was excruciating. The pixies crowded her, punctures from their beaks on her exposed face and hands breaking her from her haze. They tore off morsels of flesh.

Lotte screamed and flailed her limbs, kicking her feet and propelling herself backward until her back hit another tree trunk. She dug her fingers into the furry bark, wailing from the endless barrage of pixies, and somehow she dragged herself to stand. Panic exploded through the pain. The pixies were eating her alive!

She began to run, telling herself, *Just make it home,* gritting her teeth together.

A pixie scuttled on her arm, and without looking, she yanked it off and hucked it behind her. Another one clung to her back, but there was nothing she could do. Half a second of hesitation could result in her demise.

The trees thinned, and the dirt path was replaced by a snake of large stones. Lotte entered a clearing with a massive glass dome structure, *The Aviary*, tropical foliage flourishing on the inside, the top twice as high as the forest canopy. A log cabin stood next to it, and vegetables grew in several raised beds out front. Along The Aviary was a shed, rabbit hutch, chicken coop, and a considerably smaller glass-dome structure no taller than her father. The compound was her home.

The sight of The Aviary sparked an idea in Lotte. To anyone else, it looked like an oversized greenhouse, but inside lurked the creatures that would be Lotte's only solution against the pixies. Racing to the entrance of The Aviary, she shouted *"alsum"*, the helyait word for "open," and touched her hand to the manacore door bolt. With a flash of light and a soft click, it unlocked, and Lotte pushed against the door with her shoulder. Groaning open, the corner caught on something inside, leaving the door open only a couple of inches wide.

"C'mon! C'mon!" Lotte shoved the door again.

She yelped as the pixies descended on her. In one last ditch effort, she kicked the corner that was stuck. The door swung open, and heat blasted her face. Lotte threw herself inside, her body splashing into warm, rancid mud. Out of pure instinct, she rolled to the side and under a wooden work table surrounded by stacks of metal pails and several rakes.

The pixies burst inside like a cork-popped wine bottle, zipping around the trees and shrubbery. Their movements were sporadic, and they seemed confused for a moment, likely due to the sudden shift in climate — but recovered fast and resumed the search. Lotte wavered and placed a hand over her mouth, praying for her plan to work.

Another movement joined the frenzied pixies, slithering along the tree branches and on the grounds. It was quiet and calculated, with slivers of vibrant scales flickering between leaves. Just as a pixie landed in front of the workbench, its yellow eyes reflecting a petrified Lotte, the air current shifted. Dozens of shimmering bodies and feathered wings exploded from every crevice in The Aviary. Wyverns of all colors and sizes clashed with the pixies, jaws snapping them out of the air and thumping them to the ground. They constricted the pixies to death.

An orange wyvern with red stripes caught the pixie that had found Lotte, its stinger thrusting into the pixie's chest and injecting venom. No longer in immediate danger, Lotte crawled on her belly out from underneath the worktable and towards the open door. Wyverns dropped all around her head. Outside, the heat of The Aviary made southern Holan's air cool and less suffocating than it normally was. Lotte exhaled with relief and scrambled to her feet, bellowing as she yanked the door shut.

She trapped the pixies inside.

Chapter Two
THE EGG

Fresh water — check. Clean moss bedding — check. A small yet plump wyvern curled in a wooden nest box, work-ing her jaw over a pixie body — also check. Lotte slid the glass panel shut on a two-meter-long enclosure mounted on a wall shelf. She stood in a deep hallway with three rows of similar enclosures stretching down to a workstation, stocked with gloves, masks, glass vials, and handling sticks. A powerful earthy smell permeated the air, signaling the presence of over forty wyverns temporarily inhabiting what Lotte and her father called *The Broody Room.*

Next to her was a trolley carrying the supplies needed to clean out the enclosures. Wiping the sweat accumulating on her freckled forehead, careful not to disturb the bandage taped to her left cheek, Lotte moved on to the next broody wyvern.

"Sixty eggs!" Orm called from the next hallway. "That's the most — *whoa!* The mother almost bit me!"

Lotte snickered, picturing the wyvern lunging at her father with frightening speed. Despite Orm having bred wyverns for years, aiming to replenish populations lost due to Bouldermaul's terror on Asoleenya, he always acted dramatically when the wyverns showed hostility toward him.

The wyverns in The Broody Room were all carrying eggs,

some just beginning their gestation period, while others had already laid. The enclosures provided safety and easy access to food and water without any competition. Orm would count each wyvern's clutch of eggs, removing the unfertilized ones, before assessing the health of the mothers. If they showed signs of illness, such as malnourishment or dehydration, he would remove their clutches, place the eggs in a special incubator in their basement, and allow the mothers to heal. Healthy wyverns were permitted to hatch their young before both they and their offspring were released into either The Aviary or the wildlife sanctuary Lotte's mother managed in an unclaimed territory west of Endlor.

"Easy, mama," Lotte cooed at a bright yellow wyvern, resting in a corner with her wings tucked into her side. Her flickering tongue stopped, the fork poking out of her lips. Her body tensed.

Recognizing the signs, Lotte sidestepped as the wyvern whipped its tail toward her face, skillfully avoiding the stinger. When the wyvern retreated, Lotte took a thin blanket from her trolley and gently covered the wyvern's body, avoiding the risk of adding another injury to the dozens she already bore from the pixies. Lotte proceeded to change the water bowl and bedding, collecting excrement, feathers, and any shedded skin. She saved the byproducts for her father, who would later use them in brewing potions.

When finished, she offered the wyvern a pixie, and it was nipped from her fingers. She repeated the process, over the next hour, with the other inhabited enclosures until she reached the end of the middle row, lifting the bucket of old water off the trolley and pouring it down a drain in the floor. She returned all her supplies to the workstation and peeled the gloves off her sweaty hands.

A few cuts marred her skin, resembling more like cat

scratches than anything else. They were nothing compared to the small gouges missing from the flesh of her back, requiring a special healing salve that her father made using the wyvern byproducts. There was not enough for all of her wounds, so they focused on the major ones. Another batch of salve was brewing in their kitchen.

"I'm done for the day!" Lotte announced.

She received no response from Orm.

"Did you hear me? Or did one of the wyverns actually bite you?" She headed to the next hallway, identical to the one she cleaned, except for the type of wyverns housed: Lotte dealt with the non-venomous wyverns, while Orm handled the venomous ones. They divided them into two separate, parallel hallways.

Yet, when Lotte arrived, her father was nowhere to be seen. His cart was left unattended, and the eggs he had collected were gone. Perhaps he was placing them in the incubator?

The entrance to The Broody Room, marked by a pair of double swinging doors, led to a stout passage that connected their bedroom doorways and the basement. Voices drifted from the kitchen at the end, leading Lotte to suspect they had a visitor. It was not uncommon for helyait healers to seek her father's potions. However, when she entered the kitchen, a peculiar guest sat at the table, catching her by surprise.

Two massive horns protruded from a bull-like, shaggy head, scraping against bundles of dried herbs hanging upside down from the rafters. Instead of feet, hooves shifted on the wooden floor, each as large as Lotte's head. He wore a beige robe over his mountainous, furry body, occupying most of the already cramped space.

"Greetings, Lotte," the *aksman* gave a curt snort, rattling his nose ring. "I have not seen you since you were a leg-wobbler at the old hatchery in Urtica."

That was news to Lotte. She was sure she would remember meeting an aksman. Then again, she was three years old when Bouldermaul chased everyone in Urtica out of their homes. Any time before their current hatchery was a blank space in her memory.

"What is your name?" Lotte asked him.

"I am Vodynn of the Firehoof Herd. I've known your father since he was younger than you are now," he said.

"Is this true?" Lotte turned to Orm, but she received no response. "Father?"

Orm remained motionless in his seat, eyes wide and mouth slack with unmasked shock. Lotte followed his gaze to the table, where a mound of cloth formed a nest around the largest egg she had ever seen. The oblong shell was dark blue with grainy emerald spots. Lotte reached out to touch it, but her father snapped out of his stupor and snatched her wrist.

"You'll spread your scent on it!"

Lotte frowned at his harsh tone. She wriggled her hand free and rubbed her skin. Her father's grip left marks, luckily already fading.

"What is it?" she asked, voice cracking. Her father's reaction unsettled her.

"A basilisk egg," Vodynn said.

Lotte froze, breath catching in her throat.

"Why did you bring it here of all places?" Orm demanded. He covered the egg with the cloth, careful not to touch it.

"I figured you would know what to do with it," he said. "You raise wyverns, after all."

"Comparing a wyvern to a basilisk is like comparing a mouse to a crocodile. Basilisks are completely out of my area of expertise."

"You could bring it to Lienna."

The mention of her mother's name caused the hairs on

Lotte's arms to rise. She scrambled across the kitchen for the metal-trough bathtub under the pump sink, flipped it upside down, and dragged it to the table. Since it had always been her and Orm, they only had two chairs. She sat on the tub and leaned toward the basilisk egg, listening to her father's conversation intently.

It had been years since she had last seen her mother. Lienna and Lotte's four older half-brothers lived in the sanctuary, working to restore all endangered species affected by Bouldermaul. Traveling there took four to six months on horseback — too long for Orm and Lotte to leave the hatchery unattended. The only connection Lotte received was through letters, about twice a year. She yearned deeply for her mother.

"I'm in the peak of egg season. My wyverns aren't prepared for my prolonged absence, and the person who delivers my wyverns to the sanctuary won't be here for another few months," Orm said.

Vodynn huffed, a hot mist escaping his nose. He opened his mouth to speak, but a movement caught everyone's attention. The egg rocked side to side under the covers. Lotte felt a mix of amazement and dread.

When the rocking stopped, Orm dragged a hand through his hair before pinching the bridge of his nose and sighing. "You should have left the egg where you found it."

"And let it hatch, grow up, and terrorize my herd? Absolutely not."

"Then you should have killed it!"

Lotte whipped her head toward her father, taken aback by his words. Her parents had dedicated their lives to protecting magical creatures — Orm with his wyverns and Lienna with her sanctuary — so hearing her father suggest such a violent solution astonished her.

"Our beliefs prevent us from killing the innocent," Vodynn

said icily.

Orm threw his head back and guffawed, "Innocent!"

"Basilisks are not evil. They are hungry by nature, requiring a vast amount of sustenance to survive. You would not blame a cat eating a mouse."

"Cats are not eight-ton beasts destroying entire villages!"

Lotte piped in. "Are basilisks that dangerous?"

The kitchen fell silent. Vodynn shifted, his chair creaking under his tremendous weight. He lowered his head so that he was eye-level with Lotte, and she crinkled her nose at the smell of his breath — fermented grass and fruit.

"There is a universal understanding of why most who enter the heart of the Immorthial Forest never return," Vodynn said. "Creatures beyond your worst nightmares thrive under its sprawling canopy. Basilisks are one of them."

"That doesn't explain why basilisks are so dangerous," Lotte countered. "Many people consider wyverns nightmarish, but only a handful of species are actually harmful to anything larger than pixies. The rest are practically harmless."

Orm cut in. "Basilisks are apex predators. Scratch that — basilisks are *the* apex predator of the Immorthial Forest. Not only are they expert hunters, with thousands of years of evolution perfecting their speed, intelligence, and jaw strength; but basilisks are also venomous and possess magical properties not fully known or understood. Death is inevitable if a basilisk catches your scent." He paused and then glared at Vodynn. "This is why bringing the egg here was a mistake! How did you even find our hatchery in the first place? I have not seen or spoken to you since we fled Urtica."

"Rumors of Orm Skale's hatchery and the potions you brew have reached my herd from helyaits passing through nearby waters. It was not hard asking around and learning of your location."

Orm's body tensed, face paling. "There goes our hatchery being a secret," he muttered.

"How did you find the basilisk egg?" Lotte intervened before her father worked himself up even more.

"Bounty hunters," Vodynn spat, stomping a hoof on the ground. His fists clenched as he continued. "They stumbled upon our settlement and tried luring away our young. We disposed of them swiftly and found the basilisk egg in their belongings."

She gasped. "Why would they try and take your herd's young?"

"Bouldermaul rewards anyone who captures and turns over those of magical nature. This is not the first time my herd has dealt with his followers. Just last season, our night patrol spotted Firewraiths scouting less than a league from our herd. We left the next day."

Lotte frowned sadly. "I bet that was hard."

"Hard, in the sense that we were unprepared for a swift departure," he explained, "but we are nomadic, and our settlements are temporary. We had no more of an attachment to that location than others."

Lotte glanced at the egg once more, her mind processing everything she had learned in this conversation. The answers she received sparked even more questions, but before she could voice them, her father spoke.

"You must take the egg north to Lienna," Orm said to Vodynn.

"I cannot leave my herd for that long. I already risked traveling for three days here."

"Then, you should have traveled three days north instead and left the egg in the Immorthial forest!"

Vodynn narrowed his eyes. "I will pretend you did not suggest an incautious task."

"Dramatics are unbecoming of you," Orm said.

"Nor is your unwillingness to help an old friend."

Orm snapped his mouth shut, rapping his knuckles against the table. Lotte held her breath as he mulled over his decision. She surprised herself by wanting him to go. Adventures like this do not happen often. Plus, she had a letter for her mother that she had written just after her fourteenth birthday, expressing that she was now old enough to venture into the sanctuary for the first time, not just the camp built for visitors outside its protective walls. However, Lotte understood her father's dilemma. Who would take care of the hatchery?

"I could do it," she whispered as the idea hit her.

Orm heard this. "You are *not* traveling by yourself across the country with a basilisk," he exclaimed.

"No, not that." Lotte shook her head. "I could manage the hatchery while you deliver the egg."

"For months on your own? I think not."

"There are ships that stop at Twisp before traveling to northern Holan. It takes under two weeks. Then, it would be a couple days on foot to the sanctuary."

"That's more than a month in total of me being away! We have over one hundred and fifty wyverns currently residing in our compound. That's way too many for you to manage on your own."

Lotte bristled. "I've lived with wyverns my whole life. One hundred and fifty wyverns may sound like a lot, but most of them are in The Aviary. Other than daily water changes and weekly feedings, they're self-sufficient. As for the mother wyverns inside, I already take care of half of them on my own."

"What about the venomous wyverns?" Orm demanded. "You have not done those on your own. And what about hunting for food?"

Lotte rolled her eyes. "If I can handle a swarm of pixies like I did this morning, then I can certainly handle hunting more. After the two swarms we found today, along with chicken eggs and rabbits, we have enough food in the ice chest to last a couple of weeks. We could probably store even more if we hunt one more time before you leave."

"Today you were lucky," Orm said. "Luck doesn't constitute a job well done."

"I had a strategy!" Sort of. When Orm had bandaged and cleaned her wounds, she explained how she ran into the second swarm and led them to the wyverns. She left out, of course, the use of her blowgun that she had whittled herself and practiced with for years. He would twist the story and say that she alerted the pixies because of her presence. Chances were they would have noticed her even without her successful shot.

"Even if I could travel by ship, the journey taking a month, I'm not comfortable with leaving you unattended for that long."

"I can check in with Healer Aklea once a day," Lotte mentioned, referring to the helyait who traded with them the most — a family friend at this point. His clinic was in Twisp, and the last time Orm left Lotte alone — for three days — she had met with Healer Aklea in the evenings for dinner.

"For so long? That's highly inconvenient."

"Not if you explained the situation to him." Lotte's voice rose, growing more frustrated with her father. Was she honestly that incompetent? "Say we just took the basilisk egg to the edge of the Immorthial Forest and left it there. What would happen?"

Orm paused, obviously knowing the answer but not wanting to admit it. He stood, chair legs scraping the floor, and paced back and forth in the small space between the table and the front entrance.

Vodynn, who had been silent during their entire exchange of words, fixed his pleading brown eyes on Orm. "Basilisks are native to the heart of the Immorthial Forest, around what many call Fern Lake, where their prey are large enough to sustain their massive sizes. If not for the local townsfolk, then consider the ecological disaster a basilisk will have on the environment in this area."

"You would use *ecological disaster* against me," Orm muttered.

"The egg is likely to hatch before you reach the north," the aksman said. "There is no one I can trust outside my herd to handle such a terrifying and delicate situation, except you."

Orm stopped in front of a window, his back facing Lotte and Vodynn. He scanned the jungle surrounding their compound, deep in thought. Lotte chewed her lower lip, foot jiggling with anticipation. Her eyes darted between her father and the basilisk egg.

It moved again.

"I should kill the blasted thing, but . . . " Orm trailed off.

"But?" A breath caught in Lotte's throat.

Orm spun around, a hard look plastering his face. "We prepare the hatchery immediately."

Chapter Three
A Clandestine Quest

Emerick Hammerthorne pretended the harsh smoke billowing from the burning homestead did not suffocate his breath. He drew his sword and pointed it at the man kneeling before him, sneering at the rune necklace dangling under the coward's bloodied beard. Even without the blatant use of magic against him during their altercation, the necklace itself provided sufficient evidence to prosecute the man, his sniveling wife, and children. But the Firewraith apprentice felt generous today and, instead of killing them, chose their home and barn as his target.

"How do I know you are telling the truth?" Emerick pressed the tip of his blade against the man's jugular, drawing blood as he forced him to look up.

"I s-swear on m-my 'ife," the man sputtered, two front teeth broken behind his swollen, busted lips. "Da town i'nt far from here. I-It float' on da w-water."

"A floating town?" Emerick raised an eyebrow.

The man sensed his disbelief. "Da town w-was buil' by h-helyaits — used an ol' H-Holan naval ship."

The Firewraith hummed at the mention of the underwater race. Though he had never come across one in person, he devoted a substantial portion of his studies to races notorious for their unlawful use of magic. He was prepared for the helyaits' mastery of elemental water magic.

Emerick glanced behind the man to his wife and kids. "Would you wager your family's lives on the information you gave me?"

"Yes," he said without hesitation. "It's c-called Twisp."

"Twisp." Emerick tested the unfamiliar name on his tongue. The town must have been newly erected, perhaps after His Highness saved Vroaevalon and the rest of Asoleenya. Another part of becoming a Firewraith meant spending years memorizing maps — countries and their settlements, ports, and military compounds. Twisp was either too small to make it on Holan's map, or it was new. Knowing how thorough His Highness was about understanding their enemy, Emerick had a feeling it was the latter.

"You claim Twisp is two kilometers north from here? On the water of the bay? A dock leads to the town?" He squinted toward the Slokyl Ocean, east of the homestead and past a long grassy field abundant with palm trees. The warm, teal water glittered with sunlight as it gently lapped the white-sand beach. A beautiful sight, but Emerick could not discern a town constructed out of a floating naval ship. A cliff trailed along the southern Holan coast — the homestead and beach resided at its base — and curved sharply toward the ocean, blocking his view of anything north.

"Yes! Please, I swear on our lives," he said, then coughed violently. After spitting up bloody phlegm, he added, "You'll f-find what you are l-looking for there."

Emerick lowered his sword until it caught on the necklace with the rune made of manacore, a sour taste in his mouth at the reminder of why he ventured two months — half at sea and half on horse — from Guldkem to southern Holan. He was looking for a potion, a magical one. This mission went against everything His Highness had taught him, which is why no one but his stepfather knew he had come.

They were desperate.

In one swift flick, he cut the necklace with his sword. He bent over as it thumped against the ground, shivering at the unnatural warmth enveloping his fingers when he confiscated it. He slipped the necklace into his pocket.

"I'll be back if you're wrong," Emerick warned.

Stepping away from the man, Emerick returned to his gray horse, Bones, who was tied to a tree along the road in front of the homestead. Out of the corner of his eye, he watched the wife scramble to her husband's side, sobbing into his bruised shoulder. Emerick snorted when the man told her to fill pails of water.

Flames taller than trees crackled and consumed their house, soot trickling down like snow. Even from this distance, the heat was scorching. He had been thorough when setting the building ablaze.

Emerick wiped the ash off his saddle before he hoisted himself up, adjusted the reins in his left hand, and clicked his tongue. His heels kicked into Bones' side, urging the horse into a canter. The movement made Emerick's chainmail armor rattle, and his sword clanked in its sheath, against his back.

Sweat formed along his hairline, dripping from the uneven strands of his normally shaved hair. He underestimated the heat and humidity of southern Holan. His home, Guldkem, never reached these temperatures even in the midst of summer. It stayed relatively cool all year long, with blizzarding winters that often seeped into what should be spring. Emerick would have taken off his armor if it did not prevent magic from touching him.

As he traveled the road, his mind drifted to his stepfather and the conversation that initiated this journey. *"We must save your mother, even if we must resort to . . . "* Brok had trailed off, ducking his head, too afraid to say "magic," as if a pyre would materialize suddenly under his feet. Originally, the notion of going against the core of their beliefs — engaging in such malevolent practices — elicited laughter from Emerick. He had walked out of their home without another word, ignoring his stepfather's woeful begging, and attended a month-long training session with no contact.

Until one day, he had received a letter from Brok.

Your mother is dying.

Around the bend, a bay carved into the land. An abnormal cloud of fog formed a mushroom on top of the water, too dense and symmetrically shaped to be natural, but as he squinted, Emerick could make out support pillars of a dock. If the man had told the truth, Twisp must be hidden here. He scanned the fog for any movement, then the beach and grassy fields. No one was in sight. His free hand still inched toward the hilt of his sword. He readied for a counterattack in case helyait guards launched an assault from the water.

Emerick pulled the reins of his horse and slowed him to a stop. He dismounted and led Bones to the start of the dock, tying him off to a pillar. A carving in the barnacle-infested wood caught Emerick's attention, and he trailed his fingers along it. They were characters of the helyait language, and while Emerick did not understand them, he recognized they were one of two main dialects found in Asoleenya's waters.

Drawing his sword, Emerick stepped onto the dock and felt a slight sway underneath his boots. He proceeded into the fog. Soon, the entire world muted to gray, and Emerick could only hear the lapping of waves and smell the salt and algae. He walked for what felt like a kilometer. His cautious steps increased to impatient strides. He had yet to cross paths with anyone, nor pick up any voices or other noises that typically accompanied towns, just an eerie silence that told him he was alone.

The end of the dock appeared while Emerick was midstep, and he stumbled to keep himself from falling into the bay. Fighting helyaits on land was manageable, but fighting helyaits in the water . . . Emerick could admit he had no chance.

Panting from surprise rather than exertion, he peered into the brackish water. Like the fog, it seemed abnormal — obsidian black with no visibility into its depth, contrasting greatly from the pristine waters outside of the bay. Magic was definitely at work here. While the man from the farm told the truth, he fibbed about one major detail: The town made from a naval ship was not floating; it was underwater.

This could very well be a trap.

Emerick's body tensed, and he spun around with a growl. He studied the water for signs of threat. Still, nothing so far. He took several deep breaths to calm the anger from being tricked. Allowing emotions to influence logic gave opponents the upper hand.

He needed to put as much distance between himself and the water as possible. He shuffled forward, eyes locked on the water, slowly backtracking the planks of wood. Each step lasted longer than the ones before it. He finally saw the silhouette of Bones tied to the post, and he exhaled with relief when his boots hit land. Like a veil pulled over his eyes, the fog opened up to the beach and cliff face of Holan's coast.

The further from the bay, the safer it was for Emerick. He untied his horse and crossed the beach to the grassy field, stopping in the middle to search for shelter. Other than tall grass, there was nowhere for anyone to hide. Enough time had passed since leaving the burning farm that the man and his family could have alerted local authorities of Emerick's presence.

The top of the cliff posed the most threat, along with the helyaits in the bay, giving anyone who could be up there the higher ground. He surveyed for sentient life or significant movements in the heavy foliage, though the absence of any immediate activity did not necessarily mean no one was present. He sniffed the air for magic.

Depending on the type, magic could smell of brimstone, cedar, or even a sickly sweet fennel stench that could suffocate a room. Unfortunately, the air was too saturated with scents of the sea for Emerick to tell. He need not worry, though, as his armor would protect him from magic. It was guards with weapons, mainly archers, that concerned him.

A glint of light flashed from above the jungle canopy, too high for someone lurking in the branches. A breeze parted the leaves enough to reveal a glass roof. It was quite peculiar with its rounded top, reminding Emerick of an emporium. And now that he was paying attention to that area, he spotted a trickle of chimney smoke.

He wanted to investigate the strange building, but he knew climbing the cliff here was dangerous. He would be helpless if an enemy attacked. Mounting Bones again, he kicked him into a trot and traveled the crescent curve of the cliff until he passed the north bend and the bay was out of sight. There were plenty of spots on the cliff that Emerick found suitable for climbing. However, nestled beside a sluggish waterfall trickling down into a crevice that cut into the cliff face, there was a staircase carved into the stone, zigzagging its way to the cliff's summit. Emerick felt elated with his luck!

Halting at the waterfall, Emerick tethered his horse to a grassy patch beside a pool of water using a lead rope and pitch from the saddle's travel bags. Bones dipped his head and drank greedily.

"I will return soon." Emerick rubbed Bone's neck, plucking

off leaves and twigs from his mane.

Checking the lead rope's knot one more time, Emerick began his ascent. Spray from the waterfall slickened the mossy steps, and Emerick gripped grooves in the cliff face to stay balanced. With no railing, slipping meant serious injury. The higher Emerick rose, the more that fact unnerved him.

Emerick allowed himself a break once he reached the top. From this point, he could see several kilometers of Holan's coastline in all directions. The endless blue of the Slokyl Ocean left Emerick breathless. Unfortunately, the inhabitants of the country tainted its magnificence. He glanced down at Bones once more before he continued his investigation of the glass-roofed building.

The jungle was lush and too dense for one to simply walk through, but a worn path through the foliage cut away by some type of blade told Emerick this route was used often. Soon, a log cabin in a manmade clearing appeared through the trees. The home was three times as long as it was wide, and a glass dome towered on the other side — easily four stories tall. This was definitely what he spotted in the field at the base of the cliff.

Emerick crouched low so he blended with the ferns, and he crept closer to the buildings. Eventually, the clearing forced him to abandon his cover. He passed a compost pile and an outhouse before reaching the side of the cabin.

He ducked under the windows as he silently came around front. Rows of raised vegetable beds filled the clearing. A rooster crowed from a coop on the far side, next to a rabbit hutch.

Emerick found it rather coincidental that he had not encountered anyone in Twisp, and now, he was faced with this peculiar compound. He held onto the corner of the cabin and waited for signs of the person or family who lived here, but his impatience swelled, and his feet marched on their own toward the cabin's front door. He was running out of time. He needed the potion weeks ago.

Emerick delivered three firm knocks before pressing his ear against the door. He heard no hushed voices or creaking floorboards. Had they overlooked his knocking? Or were they hiding? He was certain someone was inside, given the smoke lazily spiraling out of the smokestack. He knocked again, this time with more force.

Nothing.

He tried the door handle, delighted to find it unlocked. He pushed the door open. The room was dim, shutters drawn closed, but sunlight filtered from behind Emerick and revealed a rather plain kitchen — a wood stove centering the space, flanked by a hand-pump sink and a simple kitchen table. A short hallway led to multiple other rooms, one with double doors.

Emerick eyed the closed doors, withdrew his sword, and stepped further into the cabin. He pressed his hand on the smoldering stove and noted heat seeping through his gloves. Whoever had doused the fire had done so in a hurry. They were hiding.

He froze at a movement in the rafters above. Through hanging herbs, the massive body of what appeared to be a white snake slithered along the beams, its head dangling down and watching Emerick with blue eyes. His body tensed, a scream catching in his throat. He stumbled backward, dropping his sword. If there was one thing he hated more than magic, it was snakes.

Emerick spun around to escape the cabin, but something sharp impaled his neck. This time he did howl. Had the snake bitten him? He brought his hand to the pain and was surprised when his fingers met a long needle.

A dart, he thought grimly.

Pinching the protruding end, Emerick yanked it and hissed. He glared at the blood staining the tip. He was lucky it had not hit his jugular.

A wave of dizziness caused his legs to tremble, and he leaned heavily against the doorway. He momentarily forgot about the snake in the rafters as his heart picked up pace and his vision tunneled. His mind began to drift, detaching from his body.

The dart was laced with some sort of poison — a fast one. In that moment, he regretted listening to his stepfather. This was most certainly karma for going against His Highness and seeking a magical cure.

Knees buckling, Emerick collapsed onto his stomach. He blinked hard, eyelids growing heavier, and knitted his brows together when a pair of boots landed next to his head. His attacker had used the rafters to hide and, most likely, the snake as a decoy. The last thing he recalled before his eyes shut for a final time was a cloaked figure crouching over him.

Chapter Four
ORM'S DEPARTURE

Over the next two days, Lotte and her father prepared for his month-long trip. A week would have been ideal, but as the basilisk egg rocked more and more with each passing hour, Orm's luck of reaching the sanctuary before it hatched was running thin. They smoked enough fish to last him a few weeks, as well as stocked his bags with fermented vegetables from their pantry, and then dusted off his old bedroll and travel shelter. The main challenge was setting up the hatchery so Lotte could manage it on her own.

"Distill the wyvern skins for one hour. Any more or less time will affect the hydrosol's potency. Feathers take closer to two hours." Orm placed long strips of skins into the pot of a clay alembic, heating on the wood-burning stove in the kitchen, before pouring in steaming water.

Standing beside him, Lotte held out the alembic's head. "You know I've extracted wyvern essence with you hundreds of times, right?"

"With me, yes. Without me, I can count the times on one hand." He placed the alembic's head onto the pot and adjusted the spout above a ceramic bowl on the ground. Over the next few hours, the water vapor would rise and condense on the cooler lid, forming droplets that would trickle down the spout and into the bowl, producing the wyvern essence ingredient valued in many potions.

The effects of wyvern essence depended on the breed. The skins they brewed in the cauldron were from Endlor Blue Strikers, native to the snowy peaks of the Ferock Mountains. Their essence was an ingredient in a potion meant for reducing fever and swelling. Healer Aklea requested three batches, and in return, the helyait arranged a ship to transport Orm and the basilisk egg.

Lotte refrained from rolling her eyes when her father continued his regurgitated lesson, but she paid attention nonetheless. Never brew wyvern byproducts older than two days. Skins boil with skins, and feathers boil with feathers. Unless brewing a specific potion, do not mix the byproducts.

"Some potions require extract specifically from skins, and some require just the feathers. It has to do with the potency and the cellular composition of the byproducts."

"I understand," she said.

Orm beckoned Lotte to the table where glass vials, metal funnels, and ladles surrounded a bowl of essence that had distilled overnight and finally cooled. Together, they bottled the extract and placed them in a special slotted travel case.

After an hour, Lotte stepped back to observe their work, but the back of her boots hit something hard, and she fell backward. *"Oof!"* Her teeth clicked together when she landed on her rear. Large, scaly body wriggling underneath her legs, a nine-meter wyvern with milky scales lifted her dinner-plate-sized head, traveled up Lotte's chest, and nuzzled her chin. She was as thick as a tree trunk and weighed over one-hundred-and-thirty kilograms. Unlike other wyverns, she had four mounds of scarred flesh where her wings had once been. Her stinger, too, had sadly been removed.

"I'm sorry, Nilka!" Lotte said, stroking behind the wyvern's head. "I thought you were still in my bedroom."

Nilka was the oldest of all the wyverns at the hatchery. She was also the wyvern who Orm had the longest, rescued when she was a hatchling from the hands of bounty hunters. As the only wyvern allowed in their living quarters, bound to the ground due to her injuries in previous captivity, Lotte grew up with Nilka slithering under her blankets on cold nights, sunbathing nearby while she practiced her blow darts, and in general, acting as her shadow.

"Better let her outside to hunt," Orm said. "She can find her own food for a few weeks."

One of the benefits of being such a large wyvern was the lack of predators.

Lotte stood up and brushed dirt off her pants. "C'mon, Nilka, follow me." She beckoned toward the front door. The wyvern followed obediently, and once outside, she zipped off to the woods. Nilka always came back.

"Now, let me show you how to handle the venomous wyverns," Orm said, once Lotte returned.

This time she could no longer hide a scoff. "You showed me yesterday!"

"It doesn't hurt to show you once more."

"Father!" She exclaimed. "Even before the basilisk egg, I've watched you a million times. Plus, this is nowhere near my first time handling the venomous ones."

"It is alone." He paused, eyes narrowing. "And this will be your first time handling Scorn."

Lotte snapped her mouth shut. Nervousness fluttered in her chest, and the hairs on her neck rose. She swallowed thickly and nodded. "Perhaps you can run me through *his* care, again."

"Thought you might say that." An amused grin spread across Orm's face, before he washed his hands in the sink and went to collect all the gear they would need.

Between their home and The Aviary, tucked away and locked with some of helyiats' strongest magic, was an identical glass dome enclosure except only a fraction of the size — equivalent to Lotte's bedroom. Unlike The Aviary, the inside mimicked the Ka'Rok Desert: mounds of red sand covering the ground, flowering cacti growing in clusters, and large flat stones providing perfect sunbathing spots. A sign nailed next to the door read *DO NOT ENTER.*

The glass was dry and clear, giving Lotte a near-perfect view inside, yet she could not pinpoint Scorn's iridescent black scales and red underbelly. He must have buried himself in the sand.

Orm brought Lotte to the side of Scorn's enclosure where a peep door connected to a mounted platform, holding his food and water tray. A dry, hollow log gave the wyvern a makeshift ramp to the platform. Like Nilka, black market traders harvested Scorn's wings and stinger. His days in the sky ended decades ago. However, Scorn was still the deadliest wyvern in all of Asoleenya.

"Put these on." Orm held out blacksmith welding gloves.

Lotte did so without hesitation.

He lifted up a long set of prongs, snapping them together dramatically, and whispered the helyait word *"alsum."* The lock on the peep door clicked, and Orm revealed the small opening.

"Always use prongs to grab the water bowl, never your hands." He demonstrated as he spoke. "Though his stinger has been removed, he still has fangs. They are two inches long and can penetrate leather gloves."

"Why use them if they don't work?" Lotte raised a brow.

"Peace of mind." Orm dumped the water on the ground and scrubbed the bowl with a cloth. When he deemed it clean enough, he refilled it with his canteen and returned it to the enclosure. "In all seriousness, though, the gloves will protect you from his scales if he accidentally rubs his body against you."

"Th-That's good, I suppose."

If his bite was not fearsome enough, Scorn's scales were toxic enough to melt flesh. Lotte seriously questioned when her father had said a basilisk was scarier. She had a feeling that Orm was being biased.

Her father shut the peep door and relocked it. "See? Short and sweet."

"Define sweet," Lotte quipped, squinting through the glass for movement.

Orm chuckled. "I will clean his sand tonight, so you won't have to enter his enclosure while I am gone. Just like every other wyvern, fresh water twice a day and food once a week."

"Yes, Father."

The next day, the ship arrived to take Orm. He staggered out of their home with a massive pack on his back, bedroll and folded shelter restrained on the top. His beloved satchel bulged from the basilisk egg.

Lotte stepped into the early morning sunshine, carrying another bag for him. Her chest swelled with anticipation. While she understood how difficult the month ahead was for both of them, she was actually excited for him to leave. This marked not only his trust in her but also an unspoken acknowledgment that she was old enough to handle adult responsibilities. Last night, she added this to the letter for her mother which Orm would deliver.

Orm stopped in the middle of the compound, staring around as though it was his last time ever seeing it.

"The hatchery will be here when you return," Lotte said, bluntly. "We should hurry before the boat leaves without you."

He nodded, and they headed toward a thin strip of jungle

that separated the compound from the cliff's edge. Once past its dense foliage and mossy trunks, Lotte had a perfect view of Twisp. A long jetty connected the beach to a capsized ship missing most of its hull and all of its paint and markings to rust and barnacles. The exposed inside was renovated with scrap metal to form shops and lodging, a wooden platform wrapping the wreckage site. Manacore pillars towered along the perimeter of the town. Helyait runes carved into their veiny surface and created a magic field that kept the ship afloat.

On the far eastern end of Twisp, a double-mast sailboat, moored to the platform, rocked gently against the lines keeping it from drifting out to sea. That boat would carry Orm to a former city in northern Holan, left in ruins after Bouldermaul's siege but still used as a marker by the little population left in the country. From there, Orm would travel west via river with a helyait guide, reaching the sanctuary after a few days of journeying. He would have to be cautious of Bouldermaul's naval patrols, which were unusually prominent along the Endlor coast.

The cliff eventually dipped into a deep crevice, and a fast-flowing creek sprayed over the edge and formed a waterfall. Steps carved into the cliff, providing Lotte and Orm a route to the land below. When they had first settled in the hatchery, Orm built a ladder to access Twisp, but as his potions drew in money, he hired some locals to chisel out stairs. While it still needed a railing, no one had fallen from the stairs since they were constructed.

When Lotte and her father arrived at the beach and neared the dock, a familiar voice echoed from the water. A young helyait glided toward them. He possessed a sleek, hairless head adorned with bright blue stripes that originated from his forehead and extended down his spine, contrasting with his greenish-gray skin. Slits on the sides of his neck — gills — flared open. He had another set on the sides of his ribs.

The helyait grinned at Lotte, revealing sharp teeth, and hauled himself onto the dock. He stood as a bipedal helyait with webbed feet and a spiny dorsal sail running down his back, enabling him to move effortlessly through the water. He blinked his large, black eyes, adjusting them to the air. His slightly muscled body and lower regions, discreetly hidden by his anatomy, were visible. He wore only a belt with storage pouches, similar to Lotte's own, and a strap that clipped a spear to his back. His nose was the most human thing about him, allowing him to breathe on land.

"Father sent me. We look forward to hosting Lotte," Remi said, his accent crisp and formal sounding.

"I'm just checking in at dinner time. No hosting needed," she replied.

Orm nudged her with his elbow. "We are incredibly grateful for your and Healer Aklea's hospitality."

Remi bowed his head before gesturing that they continue to their destination. This time, Orm set the pace, and Lotte followed, the dock teetering slightly under their feet. Remi slowed until he walked next to Lotte. Although they were the same age, the young helyait's shoulders were at her eye level. He was only a few centimeters shorter than Orm.

Remi leaned over and whispered, "I have a new relic from training to show you."

"Yeah?" This piqued Lotte's interest. "Is it something you found while exploring a ruin site?"

"Yes, I have it in my sleeping chambers." He gestured toward the water where the rest of Twisp resided. Only a third of the town surfaced on the bay.

Lotte hummed, lowering her voice even more. "I thought *Idateori* apprentices were forbidden from removing relics from ruin sites."

After completing primary school, helyait teachers assigned the students apprenticeships. Remi was studying to become an *Idateori* — which translated in Lotte's native tongue to "theory knight" — a researcher of the sea with missions and physical training similar to a standard helyait knight. Remi specifically investigated the origin of his people and magic, exploring the remains of ancient underwater civilizations and collecting relics. He often liked to ramble descriptions to Lotte, which she did not mind. He was the only person in town who actively sought her out — the closest person she had to a best friend.

"Normally, we are not. However, this one is not of helyait origin. In fact, it looks like something that drifted from a shipwreck near the expedition site. I doubt anyone will notice it missing. The relic may not be ancient, but from what I have read about human weaponry, it is from quite some time ago — over two hundred years old," he said.

Lotte glanced at her father, making sure their conversation was still private. "When can I see it?"

"Tonight, after dinner," Remi said, giving another toothy smile.

Twisp bustled with helyaits when Lotte arrived, all with features similar to Remi. Two levels of shops made of scrap metal occupied the missing hull, sitting wall to wall, with a hallway splitting the businesses and leading further into the shipwreck. Ladders interconnected the top level with the lower level, though a crank lift at one end of the rows was available for trolleys and folks who needed an alternative to climbing.

As they passed through, waving at those who greeted them by name, Lotte caught whiffs of pickled sea berries and smoked fish, as well as the melodious whistle of an ocarina playing a mellow tune. One shop sold spears like Remi's, and another offered woven baskets and fish netting. Two bunk rooms were available for travelers who wanted to stay the night, maintained by a circuit of volunteers.

They rounded Twisp's perimeter platform toward the far end of the town where the two-mast sailboat docked. It was painted silver with blue trimming, and the sails featured the local helyait emblem, a pearl in front of two crossed spears. A line formed of humans and helyaits waiting to board, each with bags, and some pushing wagons of goods and small livestock. Blocking the ramp leading up to the boat were the captain, a yellow-striped female helyait who Lotte recognized as Pesha, and two town guards flanking her sides. Pesha, along with the other adult helyaits, stood considerably taller than the humans with sharply defined muscles.

Orm entered the line. He slipped off his heavy luggage, turned to Lotte, and frowned.

"If something goes wrong, Healer Aklea and Remi will assist you," he repeated for the dozenth time that morning.

"I know what I'm doing," she said.

"Follow the schedule I created for you, and always wear gear when handling the venomous wyverns."

"We have gone through all of this!" Lotte groaned. "Father, you should be more worried about your journey and the basilisk egg hatching, not me."

Orm chuckled and bent down to kiss the top of her head. "I'll always worry about you more than myself."

Lotte swallowed, feeling the immensity of the situation. Her father was leaving her. While he would be back in a month, this was the longest they would have ever been apart from each other. His departure brought memories of her mother — correction, the lack of memories. Lienna's absence festered in the back of Lotte's mind. Why were her half-brothers allowed to live in the sanctuary, but not her?

What if Orm decided to stay at the sanctuary? The thought was impossible. His life was dedicated to the hatchery and, of course, Lotte. But that did not stop it from briefly flickering through her mind.

Eyes tearing up, Lotte flung herself forward and hugged her father around his midsection. She inhaled his scent, leather and wyverns. Lotte knew she was overthinking. She wanted him to go, in the first place, yet she could not help buy worry.

"I will be back before you know it," her father promised.

The sailboat embarked an hour after Orm boarded. A small crowd of locals had gathered and waved goodbye to the departing ones, a somber anticipation fueling the atmosphere. It was not every day that a captain risked her vessel for an impromptu trip up north, not in the era of Bouldermaul. Lotte stood on the edge of Twisp until the sailboat was a speck in the distance, the sun centering the sky. A warm breeze wafted through the gap between her hood and scarf, and she closed her eyes to mentally wish her father the best of luck.

And that he delivered her letter.

Remi's arm brushed against hers, bringing her mind back to the present. He had stayed with her the entire time, sensing her need for quietness but still providing her support with his physical presence. Lotte was grateful for the helyait.

"I should return to the hatchery," she said, turning around and heading back the way she came.

Remi called after her, "Dinner will be at sunset!"

The next two days were a blur of water changes, counting wyverns, and cleaning enclosures. Lotte missed the first night of dinner, as well as Remi's relic, too caught up with the volume of work. A knock at the door had woken her up that night, and Remi appeared with a plate of food and a reminder to check in the following evening . . . which she forgot again.

It was not necessarily her fault, she decided, especially due to her close encounter with Scorn, who had hidden near the peep door and lunged at Lotte when she tried changing his water bowl. She screamed when he had gotten mere millimeters from her gloves and dropped the bowl. Unfortunately, it clattered off the platform and into the sand below. There was no way in Asoleenya that Lotte would ever go inside Scorn's enclosure, so she retrieved a new bowl and waited for the grumpy wyvern to move before finishing her task. Her father could tidy up Scorn's enclosure when he got back.

On the third morning after her father's departure, waking up to the rooster's piercing crows, Lotte debated leaving the warmth of her bed and the comforting pressure of Nilka curled around her body. Her muscles ached terribly, and her head felt stuffy. Lotte wondered if she was coming down with a cold or if she was simply overworked.

Wriggling out from her covers, Lotte stretched her back and neck before she dressed in her usual attire and left for the kitchen. She scarfed down bread smothered with pickled seaberry spread for breakfast, guzzled down two large glasses of water, and left her dishes in the sink next to a dirty cauldron she had used to brew a heat resistant potion. The portioned vials lay on the table, and Lotte gathered them into a basket and headed for the front door.

"I'll be back soon!" she called out to Nilka.

Twisp was still waking up when Lotte crossed the dock. Merchants were opening their shops, and the hot food vendors were lighting fires under their cooking pots. The town lacked its usual chatter, replaced by loud yawns and gentle waves. Though the sun had barely risen, the day was already hot, and Lotte guessed southern Holan was reaching the peak of its dry season.

She headed down the hallway into the belly of the converted shipwreck toward Healer Aklea's clinic. Inside, it was dark, as each manacore torch only provided a lazy orb of light from its holder, dangling from the ceiling. The rusted metal walls of the interior creaked and groaned eerily, echoing every footstep, breath, and drip of water. Smells of rust and creosote saturated the cool air. With the ship on its side, doors to rooms and hallways in the former cabin were below Lotte's boots; however, the helyaits had built wooden flooring to ensure smooth and even access. According to Remi, plaques on the doors revealed the origin of the ship—a royal naval vessel from Holan's former monarch.

At the end of the hallway, sunlight filtered through a gaping hole in the roof and onto a flourishing flower box. Next to it was the door to Healer Aklea's clinic. Lotte entered without knocking, shutting the door loud enough to announce her presence. The clinic was one room with three beds divided by curtains, a manacore pillar for warmth during the rainy season, and dozens of cabinets on the far wall containing all of Healer Aklea's medicines and equipment. Bunches of dried herbs and flowers hung from the ceiling in effort to freshen the old ship odor.

For a moment, Lotte thought she was alone in the empty clinic, but the curtains blocking one bed rustled, and a helyait emerged. Healer Aklea had the same skin coloration as Remi, but he was less vibrant and had thin streaks of yellow between each stripe. He wore a belt similar to Remi's, as well, and purple cuffs around his wrists that identified him as a healer, a revered position amongst the members of his pod.

"Ah, Lotte! I had just sent Remi to fetch you," Healer Aklea said.

"We must've passed each other without realizing," she said.

"You missed two nights of checking in." His voice grew stern. "Your father will not be pleased."

"It won't happen again." Lotte held out the basket of vials. "These are made from Pagos Lava Wyverns. Father mentioned you were running low on cooling potions, so I brewed some."

Healer Aklea plucked one vial and studied its contents. "Yes, helyaits require the potion if they wish to exist on land, as well as foreign travelers who are not accustomed to this region's climate. I am afraid heat exhaustion and even loss of consciousness has been a daily occurrence, as always during this time of the year."

"Will this be enough? I can make more."

"This is fine for now." Healer Aklea grasped the basket's handle and brought it to a counter next to a wash basin, under his cabinets. Turning to face Lotte, he clasped his hands together. "Good news — Remi's mentor granted him extra time off so he may assist you at the hatchery."

Lotte huffed. Why did everyone think she needed help? She was perfectly capable of handling the wyverns herself. She was fine with Remi providing her company, but she did not need assistance.

"It also helps that this week is what landwalkers call a *holiday*," he continued.

"Which holiday?"

"The Passing," he explained. "The transient helyait pods begin their migrations."

"Oh, that's right!" Lotte snapped her fingers, remembering. "It's tradition for you to make baskets full of food and goods and give them to the transient helyaits."

Healer Aklea nodded, "And in return, they will provide us goods collected during their travels."

"Father gets some of his ingredients for potions this way," she said. "I wish I had known earlier, and I could've prepared a basket and a list of ingredients like Father always does."

"Given the circumstances regarding the basilisk egg and your father leaving unexpectedly, I had assumed The Passing would have slipped both of your minds." He moved toward the back of the clinic, opening the largest of the cabinets. Inside was a reed basket handmade by Healer Aklea and, quite possibly, Remi — filled with various manacore runes and vials of potions that Lotte recognized as ones she and her father had made. Reaching into the basket, Healer Aklea pulled out a piece of parchment and showed it to Lotte. "I prepared this in advance based on what Orm has requested in the past. I will give it to Remi's mother who is among the transient pods."

"Thank you!" Lotte squinted as she read off the items on the list. "You always do so much for us."

"The hatchery and Twisp have a symbiotic relationship. One needs the other to thrive. The potions you and your father make allow helyaits to venture into climates and territories that would otherwise harm us," he said.

"And your ingredients let us make the potions that keep our hatchery alive," Lotte said.

"Exactly, symbiotic." Healer Aklea smiled, shutting the cabinet. "I've known your father for quite some time. We both served as advisors for the former king of Vroaevalon — he for magical creatures, and I as the ambassador of our region's helyaits. I cannot help but feel grateful that he chose our pod to form an alliance with, helping replenish what was lost due to war. I'm also grateful for you, who will continue his legacy."

Lotte ducked her head, feigning a blush. "All we do is take care of wyverns."

"In a world that views magic as evil, acceptance and under-standing are more valuable than any form of priceless stone or manacore."

"I feel like there's a lesson you are trying to teach me here," she deadpanned.

He chuckled. "You two bring us hope for the future of helyait-and-human coexistence."

Lotte scratched the back of her head, feeling awkward about the praise and trust the helyait showed her. "We appreciate you, too. The hatchery wouldn't even exist without your supply of building materials."

"Then let us continue this balance of camaraderie by allowing Remi to assist you with the hatchery. I can sense you want to prove yourself, but the sea is dangerous for a lone fish. Only in numbers do they turn the tides on their predators."

Lotte pinched her lips together, a flicker of irritation seeping through the appreciation she felt from the helyait's words. Had her father put Healer Aklea up to this? Had their entire conversation been a tactic of persuasion, or was this simply his opinion based on helyait tendencies — living in pods and working together as one?

"I'll ask Remi for help if — "

Distant shouting cut their conversation short. Lotte and Healer Aklea blinked at each other, listening intently, before they moved to the front door. Looking around, they found no one present in the hallway. The panicked voices continued, though, coming from the main part of town.

"I'll see what's going on," Lotte said, taking off.

"Wait!" Healer Aklea called after her. "I would much rather it be me who goes to investigate!"

Lotte ignored him. She raced out of the haul of Twisp, only slowing down when she spotted a crowd gathering where Twisp and the dock connected. Helyait guards breached the waters and joined the group, spears in hand. As Lotte approached, she heard whispers of gossip.

"Did you hear what the girl said?"

"A Firewraith attacked her home!"

"She lives on the farm south of here, correct?"

"QUIET!" a guard bellowed.

Lotte had not realized how fast her heart was beating until everyone fell silent, each beat a drum in her ears. A voice behind her called her name, and she turned to find Remi jogging toward her. Stopping on the outskirts of the crowd, his mouth parted as he craned his neck for visibility.

"It is Annsley Gibbs, I believe, the youngest daughter of the Gibbs family," he said, and the blood drained from Lotte's face.

The guard who silenced everyone spoke to his partner in the language helyaits invented for land — spoken too fast for Lotte to understand — before he raced to the town's edge and dove into the water. Hysteria washed through the townsfolk, and people scrambled to find shelter. After eleven years of peace, with only a few close calls that mostly involved Bouldermaul's military ships passing by, Firewraiths had discovered Twisp.

Lotte remained, wanting to see poor Annsley Gibbs.

"What exactly did the guard say?" Lotte asked Remi.

"They are gathering mages," he said, then rushed to the sobbing girl now visible on the dock.

Chapter Five

THE FIREWRAITH

Lotte followed Remi back to his father's clinic, her mind racing. How many Firewraiths were there? How did they find Twisp? Were there enough mages and town guards to defend everyone? And, more importantly, what would happen if they discovered the hatchery? Lotte wanted to question Annsley, who Remi carried in his arms, but the young girl was in shock, begging repeatedly for her mother and father to be saved.

Once they arrived, Healer Aklea beckoned Remi to place Annsley on an empty patient bed. He snatched blankets and pillows, covering her body and elevating her legs. As he examined her for injuries, Remi filled his father in on the dire situation.

"Oh, dear," Healer Aklea shook his head. "I have dreaded this day."

"What happens now?" Remi asked, wringing his webbed hands together.

Healer Aklea moved to the wall of cabinets, browsing through a collection of vials. Almost too quietly for Lotte to hear, he muttered, "I am unsure."

If this was anything like the siege of Urtica, it meant Lotte had to uproot her life for a second time and relocate. Trepidation twinged painfully in her chest.

"I must return to the hatchery," Lotte blurted.

Both Healer Aklea and Remi whipped their heads around. "No," the older helyait said sternly. "You must stay here where it is safe."

"Safe? There's no such thing as safe when Firewraiths are around," she exclaimed.

"Please remain calm, Lotte. Matriarch Ira trained our mages for this event," he said, mentioning the leader of his pod, as well as Twisp.

"Trained to fight?" Lotte raised a brow with disbelief.

Healer Aklea tucked the blanket around the young girl, before he stepped back. "Trained to protect our people."

A tremor from the ground caused Lotte to stumble, and she barely caught herself on the bed frame. The briny stench of helyait magic suffocated the room. Then, a dropping sensation proceeded — as though Lotte and the world around her were lowering. The air grew colder, and everything in the clinic vibrated, deafeningly. Annsley whimpered in her bed, tears welling in her eyes, and Healer Aklea braced the frame, pushing his weight down to stifle the shaking.

"What's happening?" Lotte crouched for balance.

"The mages are sinking the town," Remi said.

Lotte gaped at him. Had she heard the helyait's words properly? Her feet moved on instinct, carrying her outside of the clinic and away from Remi's calls to come back. She ran through the inner halls of the naval ship until she had a visual of the edge of the town.

True to Healer Aklea's words, Twisp was descending into the bay, the pillars of manacore surrounding the shipwreck illuminating with white-hot magic. Sea water did not flood into the hull but was instead held back by an invisible barrier, preventing humans and other landwalkers from drowning.

Lotte thought of the defenseless hatchery, and she took off towards where the jetty should have connected to Twisp. She could not just stand by and leave the wyverns vulnerable. The Firewraiths would undoubtedly find her home and do what they were infamous for — burning down everything with a semblance magic. Lotte was determined to keep her promise to her father and protect the hatchery. When she reached the dock, it was now eye-level with her and rising at an alarming speed.

Lotte lifted her hand to the barrier, hoping it would let her through. However, her palm met a glass-like surface that separated her from the water. "No, no, no," she muttered and pounded her fist. Growing desperate, she threw her body full force at the barrier, her shoulder popping from the impact. Lotte cursed out of frustration rather than pain, stepping back to watch the shrinking sky.

"Lotte!" Remi cried from behind. Arriving next to her, he bent over and panted. Helyaits were built to swim, not to run. "We must stick together."

"How do we get through the barrier?" Lotte demanded.

He gave her a concerned look. "To pass through the barrier, you will need someone with magic who understands this technique. Are you planning to leave?"

As he spoke, the remaining bit of sky disappeared, replaced by lapping waves. The town was now fully submerged.

"The hatchery is alone," Lotte said, spinning around and grasping Remi's hand. She brought it close to her chin. "Can you help me?"

"Help you get through the barrier?" He sounded incredulous.

"Yes!"

Remi yanked his hand away. "I cannot."

"Do you not know what technique is used for the barrier?"

He fell silent, averting his eyes.

"You do!" Lotte jabbed her finger into his chest. "Let me through!"

"No," he said. "You are protected from the Firewraiths here."

"What about the hatchery?" she demanded. "The wyverns will be slaughtered!"

"As would you if captured by the Firewraiths. The mages will return you to the surface when they deem it safe."

"Who knows when that will be! You're dooming my wyverns. What happens if they are left without their basic needs met for days?"

Sure, wyverns were naturally durable, and the ones in The Aviary could survive for weeks before succumbing to starvation. The mothers, on the other hand, would only last a few days after their water bowls emptied. Nilka and Scorn, too. Lotte would rather take her chances of being captured than let her wyverns perish.

Remi fidgeted, glancing from side to side as if they were being watched. As he debated silently, Lotte fought the increasing urge to shake him for a decision. Eventually, he dropped his head to his chest and exhaled, the gills on his neck fanning.

"What would I tell my father?" he mumbled.

"Make something up," Lotte said. "Say I escaped before the barrier was put in place."

"He would never believe that," Remi snorted.

Regardless, he wrapped an arm around Lotte's shoulder and guided her along the edge of the missing hull, past the last shop, until he found a secluded spot away from witnesses. Most helyaits had taken to the safety of the water, and only a few merchants remained to secure their goods. Lotte was not sure there were any landwalkers other than herself and Annsley on board. She imagined them fleeing town to their farms and preparing for the Firewraiths' arrival.

The town shuddered as it hit the bottom of the bay. The normally translucent waters were now inky black, a technique used by helyaits to camouflage themselves when hunting or in danger. Lotte was able to, at least, make out the dark shapes of stone buildings, archways, and other architectural structures erected on the seafloor. This was the first time she had seen the underwater half of Twisp. Too bad it was under dire circumstances.

"I will go with you to the hatchery," Remi said.

"You'd slow me down once we hit land," Lotte argued. "What if we have to hide there for a few days? How would you prevent yourself from drying out? Sit in The Aviary's pond with the wyverns? Or our bathtub? And your father — don't get me started on how upset he'll be."

"Your father would never forgive us if something happened to you," he countered.

"Nothing will!"

"And as for drying out, I have means of staying on land for long periods of time. I just have to retrieve a rune from my sleeping quarters and — "

"We don't have time!"

Remi muttered under his breath before he raised his hands and pressed them to the barrier. "Hold onto my waist," he instructed, and Lotte sprung forward, her face pressed against his rubbery back as she listened to him chant in long, drawn-out syllables.

They fell through the barrier, and icy water engulfed Lotte. Her eyes snapped shut as she felt pressure on her sockets. Letting go of Remi, she kicked and flailed her feet as her lungs screamed for air. Her clothes and boots weighed her down.

Arms enveloped her body, propelling her to the surface.

Her ears popped painfully, and she winced as the pressure behind her eyes grew almost unbearable. Squinting through the sting of saltwater, she took in the diminishing sight of Twisp. The barrier around the shipwreck made it look like a massive bubble, but soon it disappeared into the dark water.

Just as her chest seized from holding her breath too long, warm air replaced the water around her head. She coughed and sputtered, blinking droplets off her lashes. Her ears were clogged, and snot dribbled from her nose.

"Are you alright?" Remi asked.

She nodded, still gripping onto him to stay afloat. As she recovered from the swift ascent, she noticed a thick fog limiting her visual range to just a few feet. It smelled of helyait magic.

"Did the mages create the fog?" Lotte asked.

"Yes, as a means of hiding Twisp."

"Won't it give the town away? Surely the Firewraiths will know this isn't normal."

"More likely than not, the Firewraiths already know Twisp is here. Why else would they be in its proximity? And I would not put it past them to interrogate the young girl's family." Lotte's pulse quickened as Remi said these words. "This particular technique will impair their sight and protect the guards positioned in the bay. The moment a Firewraith touches the water, the guards will attack."

Lotte knew they were running out of time. The longer they stayed in one spot, the more likely a helyait guard would try and stop them, or worse . . . a Firewraith. "Can you take me closer to the stairs on the cliff?"

"Of course."

Remi glided toward the beach, his dolphin-like kicks both elegant and strong, and Lotte clung to him until the fog opened up to reveal the beach. When the bay's floor brushed against her knees, she let go of the helyait and stood up shakily, her soggy clothes feeling heavy.

Gazing over her shoulder, most of the bay was a mass of bulbous clouds. The sight churned Lotte's stomach. Thankfully, it appeared that no Firewraiths were around.

For now.

She shimmied off her cloak and scarf, ignoring the slight gasp that came from Remi as she exposed her face. Although she had revealed herself to the helyait a few times before, it had been several months — if not a year or so — since then. Remi always appeared in awe of her appearance. If Lotte was completely honest, it made her a little self-conscious.

Lotte pushed aside the uncomfortable feeling of being exposed and trudged to the beach. As Remi promised, the stairs were ahead of her on the cliff. Water and seaweed sloshed in her boots as she finally hit dry sand and took off in a run.

"Wait!" Remi emerged from the bay. "Let me come with you!"

"We've already been through this!" Lotte shouted without looking back. "Return to Twisp before you're spotted."

She never heard his response or saw him swim off to the safety of the bay's depths, already thundering up the stairs two steps at a time, her legs screaming from the exertion and heaviness of her wet boots. Yet, she refused to slow down, adrenaline at least taking the edge off.

When she passed the last step, Lotte paused to soothe her aching lungs. She dropped her head back to the sky, squinting at the sunshine, and noticed a faint haze. With it came the smell of burning wood and rubber — or rather, the scent of a building burning down. She recognized the difference between the stench and a normal chimney fire, triggering the core memory of cobblestone streets, large stucco buildings, and massive sand dunes in the horizon. The last time she smelled something like this was during the fall of Urtica.

Alarmed, Lotte observed the forest in the direction of the hatchery but found nothing. She blew out a relieved breath. Upon further inspection of around the bay, a plume of black smoke rose a few kilometers south, where Mrs. Gibbs' homestead would be. Worry rushed through Lotte for the mother and the rest of her family, who had not escaped as Annsley had done, but she forced her attention back on getting to the hatchery and defending her wyverns.

She broke into a sprint. Without her cloak, low branches and thorny shrubs nicked her skin, leaving red-glistening trails. The hatchery came into view, and soon, Lotte rounded the corner of her home, wrenching the front door open.

Nilka sprawled on the floor in front of the lit stove, lifting her head upon Lotte's abrupt arrival. Locking them inside, Lotte sagged against the door and pressed a hand against her chest. She gave herself a moment of respite.

Eventually, she pushed herself forward and strode toward the wingless wyvern. Crouching, she began stroking the top of Nilka's head. "What do we do now?" Lotte asked, as if expecting a response from Nilka. Oh, she wished the wyvern could talk. Then she would not be completely alone in this situation.

Alone.

Lotte stumbled forward and sat at the kitchen table, dropping her head into her hands. The magnitude of how truly alone she was settled in — her father traveling across the continent and the entirety of Twisp underwater. Second thoughts intruded her mind. Maybe she should have accepted Remi's help after all.

A scaly body traveled up Lotte's leg, and she grunted when half of Nilka's bulk lay on her lap. Nilka rested her head on Lotte's shoulder, her tongue flickering against her neck. The wyvern's weight was comforting, and Lotte wondered if she sensed the distress radiating from her body. It would not surprise her. Wyverns were incredibly intelligent creatures.

Protectiveness surged through Lotte.

"What would Father do in this situation?" Lotte mused. "He would . . . he would start by assessing the danger."

Nudging Nilka off of her, she hurried to her bedroom and changed into dry clothes, shoving her arms into a cloak identical to the one she had discarded at the beach. She did not have a second pair of boots, so she would have to endure their discomfort. She retrieved her blowgun and dart holder as well.

Her father kept a brass monoscope in one of the dresser drawers of his bedroom. Lotte stepped over dirty clothes, books, and items her father had collected but failed to organize. His room was only slightly bigger than Lotte's, but three bookshelves and a large bed diminished the amount of walking space. There were easily hundreds of books occupying every surface. For someone so organized with his wyverns, it was rather ironic that he was such a packrat.

Once she retrieved the monoscope, Lotte dropped to her knees and searched under her father's bed for a wooden chest where he kept some of the rarer vials of wyvern venom that they had milked for potions. It was made of polished mahogany with a metal trim, and when Lotte opened it, the inside revealed a red velvet lining with custom holders for twelve vials. Only half of them were being used.

Lotte hovered her hand over a vial with a black cork — Scorn's venom. One drop was enough to kill an adult human. If she dipped some of her darts in it and used them on the Firewraiths. . . .

Lotte shook her head. The thought of murdering another person sent goosebumps down her arms. She could never do something like that. Pocketing Scorn's venom regardless, she moved to a yellow-corked vial, a venom from a Steelhead Lancer Wyvern. The venom was a potent paralysis, and Healer Aklea often requested it for a potion given to patients before surgeries. Like Scorn's venom, only a small amount was needed. Lotte took the vial, returned the wooden chest, and left her father's room.

At the kitchen table, Lotte dipped her darts into the vial and gently waved them in the air to dry. She never thought she would use a dart against anything more than a pixie. Carefully, she returned the darts to their canister, clipped them to her belt and blowgun to its holder, and headed for the door with the monoscope in hand.

"Stay here, Nilka," she said to the wingless wyvern. "I give you permission to bite and eat any Firewraiths who enter our home." It was a joke, but Lotte secretly hoped Nilka would display some of her territorial aggression.

Lotte took a deep breath and opened the front door, poking her head just far enough to survey the compound and listen for footsteps. Everything seemed normal. She treaded lightly across the clearing and onto a short trail that led to the cliff's edge. Through the shrubs, she spotted the foggy bay. Slowing to a stop, Lotte lowered to her knees and then her belly, crawling under a leafy bush until she had a full view of the area. Fear knocked the air from her lungs when she saw a gray horse with light armor tied to a post at the beginning of the dock.

Lotte shakily brought the monoscope to her eye and adjusted the lens, hoping to find the horse's rider. The field and beach below were vacant, so Lotte surmised he was on the jetty, hidden inside the fog. Good. She prayed for the helyait guards to capture the Firewraith or create a wave strong enough to knock over and drown the. Technically, the mages could cause such a feat, of course, if their magic reserves were not depleted from sinking Twisp. Lotte may not have magic, but she understood that excessive use tired living users.

She scanned the area again for additional Firewraiths. It was quite possible that they sent one to scout the town while the rest of them waited nearby, or they could be investigating other areas. Just because she did not see them did not mean they were not there.

Movement drew Lotte's attention back to the horse. The Firewraith emerged from the fog, sword drawn. He wore the standard coal gray and blue-violet Bouldermaul colors underneath chainmail, as well as a helm that completely covered his head. Lotte fought the urge to abandon her position, and instead, she continued looking through the monoscope. The Firewraith rushed to untie his horse and elude the water.

Had the Firewraith encountered the helyait guards? What stopped them when the Firewraith was vulnerable on the jetty? Did he stave them off, or did they remain in the bay's depths, as Remi suggested, waiting for the right moment to attack? Questions swirled in Lotte's mind, physically winding her.

The Fireweraith stopped in the field, his head turning slowly as he regarded the tall grass and palm tree stumps. Eventually, his attention shifted to the cliff, and Lotte inhaled sharply, jolting back and hiding the monoscope when he seemed to lock eyes with her. Her breaths came out in short, rapid bursts, and her vision blackened. At this rate, she was going to pass out from hyperventilating.

Had the Firewraith spotted her?

Impossible. She was too far away, and she was hidden.

Lotte did not know what compelled her to risk peeking once more, but she lifted the monoscope and watched him. The Firewraith was still looking in her direction, but at something behind her.

Unfortunately, Lotte guessed what it was.

Sometimes, if a person squinted just right, the top of The Aviary could be seen from the beach. Judging by how he began searching for a way up the cliff, he found Lotte's home. Mounting his horse, he kicked his heels against its side and headed north, where he would surely discover the cliff-face stairs.

"No, no, no." She collapsed the monoscope and squirmed out of the bush, racing home in a haze of terror.

Lotte reached the compound and barreled into her kitchen. Out of pure instinct, she went through the hatchery and extinguished every manacore torch and then doused the stove's fire with a pitcher of water. Hot steam blew in her face, the discomfort clearing her mind for a moment. Lotte needed a plan.

First and foremost, the wyverns' safety was her top priority. She should release them from The Aviary so they would not be caught in the Firewraiths' infamous pyro attacks. There was a ladder on the back of the structure leading to a crank that opened the glass roof. Lotte might have enough time to accomplish that. However, there was an issue with the mothers in The Broody Room and the eggs in the basement's incubator. There was no way she could remove all of them before the Firewraiths invaded.

A ridged nose bumped her calf, and Lotte looked down at her ever-faithful Nilka. "What do we do now?" she repeated her question from earlier.

The wingless wyvern flicked her tongue.

"This was a fluke, you know." Lotte sat cross-legged on the ground and gently pulled Nilka's upper half into a hug, her face pressing against the start of the wyvern's neck. "I could have managed the hatchery for a whole month if the Firewraiths hadn't come."

Nilka slithered around Lotte's waist and jarred the canister of darts, as though she was offering a suggestion.

Lotte swallowed. A voice in her head screamed that she was only a fourteen-year-old girl. There was no way in Asoleenya that she could defeat a highly trained Firewraith.

Blue eyes met Lotte's.

"I'll try for you and the other wyverns — and Father." *And me*, she mentally added and unhooked her blowgun from her belt.

Lotte studied the kitchen for a vantage spot. Effectively hitting a target with a blow dart required camouflage, patience, and luck. When the Firewraith entered her home, Lotte wanted to hide in the last place he would look. And based on her dealings with hunting small animals for the wyverns, that was up — specifically, the rafters.

Her mouth twitched into a smile. Perfect!

Lotte wasted no time clambering on top of the table and extending her hand towards the wood beams. She hauled herself up, grunting with effort, and teetered as she balanced on her palms and knees.

Carefully, she stretched out for the next beam and crawled along the ceiling, sweat forming above her brows from the straining movement and concentration. Eventually, she pressed herself into the corner above the front door.

Lotte jerked at the sound of quiet footsteps outside. Hands trembling, she scrambled for a dart and loaded it into her blowgun. She pressed the mouthpiece to her lips but faltered at the sight in front of her.

Nilka.

The blasted wingless wyvern had followed her up into the rafters! Her bulk dominated the beams that she poised on.

"You're going to give me away!" Lotte hissed.

There was nothing she could do about Nilka, though. The doorknob rattled before it turned, and the Firewraith stepped inside.

Chapter Six
CAPTURED

Emerick blinked several times as his mind processed the black void surrounding him. He lay on stone, muscles twinging where hard bumps and pebbles jabbed into his back and aching head. It took him a moment to realize he should not be feeling anything against his upper torso. Where was his chainmail armor?

Memories of Twisp, the strange compound, the snake in the rafters, and his attacker flooded Emerick's mind. He shot into a sitting position but was jerked to the side when chained cuffs restricted his movements, indicating he was bound against a wall. It was still too dark to see anything, even with his eyes adjusting. He knew one thing for certain, though: He had been captured by the enemy.

How could I have been so dim-witted? Emerick thought. He attempted to curl his legs underneath him, only to discover that his right ankle was also bound. *This is what I get for considering magic could be the answer to my problems.*

Emerick patted the ground around him, using his sense of touch to formulate a layout of the prison in his head. His fingers bumped into something smooth, glossy, and warm. He traced the odd texture, following it up until hard ridges formed. Scales. Foreign muscles flexed under his palm, and

Emerick jerked backward with a yelp.

It was a snake!

A heavy weight settled onto his outstretched legs, and it took all of his willpower not to scream. Emerick had trained for many situations under King Bouldermaul, but waking up to a giant, man-eating snake was not one of them. What should he do? Or rather, what *could* he do? He was chained, armorless, and in a prison with no visibility. This was how he would die. This was karma for daring to go against what he had been taught about magic.

The snake crawled up his body, forcing Emerick to lay down and take short and strained breaths, before its thick, triangular head appeared inches from his eyes. Although the room was dark, he could make out its pink tongue flickering in and out, as it smelled him. It did not look like any snake he had ever seen; the sharp ridges on its brow bones gave it a more reptilian face than a serpentine one.

The snake transfixed on Emerick's face.

Worried his blinking would attract the snake, Emerick closed his eyes and vowed not to move, or even twitch, until it left. If he pretended to be dead, he could avoid triggering the snake's hunting instinct, and it would lose interest in him. Of course, he knew little about snakes except that they were disgusting and dangerous.

To Emerick's relief, the snake eventually shifted away from his head and settled its upper half on his stomach, the rest curling along his hip and legs. The weight was almost crushing.

This must be a dream. No, a nightmare!

Sweat saturated his tunic.

Emerick was not sure how much time had passed while stuck underneath the snake. The pressure in his bladder grew, and so did the anticipation of trying something risky — like pushing the offending beast off. Yet, when he brought his hands up to maneuver it off, a bone-chilling hiss sent him reeling. He cursed his stupidity, again. There really was no way out of this.

A door sounded from above, creaking opening before gently shutting. Footsteps on stairs followed, descending lightly, trying but failing to be silent. A soft glow dispersed the darkness, allowing Emerick the chance to discern his surroundings.

He was underneath a large rock arch in what appeared to be a cave. Light glinted off a glass panel, causing his stomach to sink as he realized he was trapped in an enclosure that he dreadfully speculated belonged to the snake. He lay in an empty pool built into the ground and was chained to the arch. The snake on him was as thick as a tree trunk and easily three times as long as an adult male human, its scales snowy white. Emerick almost fainted.

The moment of visibility came from a flameless torch, its magic forming light on the tip, and the person holding it was the hooded figure Emerick had glimpsed before losing consciousness. His captor stood at the height of a human adolescent. However, there was no way to make out other details underneath the cloak, other than the blasted blowgun in his captor's other hand.

So that was where the dart in his neck had come from.

"How many of you are there?" The voice under the hood was surprisingly young-sounding — and feminine. The accent was of southern Holan, vowels slightly over-pronounced and said with a drawl. Emerick was almost positive he was speaking to a kid — a teenager at most — and while he felt a sense of relief, he was also embarrassed that he was captured by such a runt.

Unless his captor was not the only person here. . . .

"Did you hear my question? How many Firewraiths are

there in the area?" his captor demanded.

Emerick sneered before firing a slew of dirty curses through gritted teeth. His captor whistled a short high tweet, and the snake on Emerick's belly snapped its head up, hissing. Its body tightened around Emerick's legs. All noises died in his throat, and he snapped his eyes shut once more.

"You can answer my questions, or I can have Nilka bite — your choice," his captor said. "Now, how many Firewraiths are with you?"

"An entire squad," Emerick lied. Revealing that he was on his own would surely sign his death. However, that lie would compel his captors into interrogating him, buying him more time to formulate a plan.

"Where are they now?"

Emerick must keep his answers vague. "On their way."

"From where? Are you the ones who have been terrorizing the aksmen settlement?"

"Yes," he said, without missing a beat.

In all honesty, he had no idea of what aksmen settlement his captor was talking about, nor if there was one nearby. King Bouldermaul typically divided his Firewraiths into squads of three members and kept their missions secretive even to each other. Occasionally, the King would pair groups up for larger missions. Emerick had yet to participate in anything more than investigations, and even then, he was more of a bag carrier. All apprentices and newly-recruited Firewraiths were.

"How did you find Twisp? And what business do you have here?" his captor asked, voice wavering.

Emerick risked shifting for more wriggle room. "Remove the blasted snake, and I'll answer all of your questions."

"Liar. That's all you Bouldermaul dogs are, murderous liars."

He snorted. This was rich coming from a magic-supporting

scum. The number of Vroaevalon citizens who perished by magic in the past three decades was in the hundreds of thousands. They were on the verge of economic collapse before King Bouldermaul erected Guldkem.

"Tell me your name."

Emerick smirked, delighted by his captor's inability to hide emotions. "My name? What does it matter?"

His captor whistled again, and the snake reared back.

"Emerick!" he cried, fighting the instinct to roll over and protect his face. "My name is Emerick."

A low tune caused the snake to calm.

"I'm Lotte."

"Like I care." Actually, he did appreciate that bit of information. Now he knew his captor was a young female. She was seriously the worst interrogator he had ever met. Emerick was getting more information from her than she was from him.

"You have one more chance to tell me how you found Twisp," she said.

"It was just a patrol of the area. We spotted the farm, and the farmer told us of Twisp," he continued to spin his story.

In actuality, Emerick's stepfather had learned of Twisp from a passing trader. It was there that they might find a cure for his mother's illness. As one of the last remaining towns in Holan, they had magical resources that trumped what Guldkem and the rest of Vroaevalon had to offer. All other settlements with medicinal magic resided in the Immorthial Forest. Absolutely no one in their right mind would venture there.

Lotte stepped forward, her torch revealing more of the room beyond the glass panel trapping Emerick. They were in a single-room basement, the floor and walls made of chunky stone blocks. Random items strewn about: large metal troughs stacked upside down; several piles of folded sheets; and a wooden table cluttered with elbow-length leather gloves, bowls, and metal sticks with smooth hooks on the end. Underneath the stairs was a massive chest-like object with manacore trim and helyait characters. The excessive use of magic alarmed Emerick.

"Will they come looking for you?" she asked.

The stupidity of her question broke Emerick from his observation. A laugh bubbled from his lips before he could stop himself. "What do you think?" he managed to say after his emotions settled.

His captor was quiet, and he smirked at the tremor in her hand.

"Whether you kill me or not, my companions will find you," Emerick grated. "And when they do, your ashes will rain down with the rest of the miserable, magical trash poisoning Asoleenya."

Chapter Seven
THE SAFEHOUSE

Lotte retreated upstairs after her efforts at questioning the Firewraith proved fruitless. She staggered to her bedroom and slid down the side of her bed to the floor, her back propped against the lumpy mattress, and dropped her head into her hands. Crickets chirped outside her window as the sky darkened to twilight.

Most of her day was spent pacing in the kitchen, waiting for the Firewraith to wake up from paralysis. That was after she had stripped him of his chainmail and created a makeshift harness around his waist that connected to one she tied on Nilka. Using the wyvern's strength to drag him downstairs, Lotte lifted him from underneath his armpits and kept their pace slow to prevent the Firewraith's head from splitting open on the steps.

Emerick's words haunted her, and Lotte struggled with deciding her next course of action. Time was slipping away, and she knew she had to alert Remi and the rest of Twisp before it was too late.

"After I transfer the wyverns to the safehouse," Lotte muttered to herself.

Twisp had yet to emerge from the bay, and although she could go to the water's edge and call out to Remi or another helyait, she was uncomfortable leaving the hatchery alone with the Firewraith. Plus, it was almost dark. Being so close to the Immorthial Forest meant a lot of strange creatures venturing into these areas. A mere human did not want to be caught in the dark alone with them.

Lotte had no choice but to wait until morning, or until Remi or Healer Aklea came looking for her. Then they would alert the helyait guards, and Emerick would no longer be her issue.

Except he would. And so would the other Firewraiths, eventually.

What would happen to Twisp? To the hatchery? They could fight, but if by the off chance the helyait guards were able to overpower the Firewraiths, Bouldermaul would just send more soldiers. The final untouched fragment of Holan — Port Labree, Twisp, and a few other establishments — would perish. No matter what happened, they would have to relocate.

The hairs on Lotte's arm rose at the thought of leaving her home. Her first thought was to head north to her mother's sanctuary. But that would take months of traveling by foot, and with the wyverns, it would take even longer. There was no way in Asoleenya she could survive such a journey.

"I gotta take it one step at a time," she said. "Safehouse first." Maybe she and the wyverns could stay hidden there until her father returned or, at least, until Healer Aklea found a boat that could transfer everyone.

Lotte exhaled, liking that plan. And although the day's events had her exhausted and her body screaming for bed, she knew sleep would not come — not with the towering amount of work needing to be done. She pushed herself to her feet and began her chores that she had neglected all day.

When she had finished cleaning water bowls, Lotte offered

the wyverns in The Broody Room an early feeding of pixies, rodents, and eggs — all stored in the kitchen ice chest. Some of the wyverns accepted the meal, but others were on an internal timer, not quite finished digesting the pixies from before her father left. Lotte wished they would indulge in at least a bite or two. Who knows how long it would be until they ate again after reaching the safehouse.

The Aviary was next on her agenda. Manacore torch in hand, Lotte scurried outside and along the compound. She jumped at every noise as she passed the sleeping chicken coop and rabbit hutch. In Lotte's mind, every twig snapping was a Firewraith approaching, and every bush rustling was someone spying on her. The jungle surrounding the compound was nothing more than an eerie abyss. She spoke the unlocking incantation quickly once at The Aviary's entrance and nearly collapsed from relief when she slipped inside and shut the door behind her.

The wyverns stirred as the torch's light alerted them to her presence. Their shadows moved sluggishly toward Lotte, no doubt investigating the disturbance of their routine. While some species were active at night, most wyverns were diurnal. Lotte set the torch onto the workbench and quickly pumped water from a spigot into buckets, and then dumped them into the pond — the wyverns' drinking reservoir. She also dropped food around The Aviary for the wyverns, planning to collect what they did not eat in the morning.

By the time she was done, Lotte had no doubt that it was midnight. An ear-popping yawn sprung tears in her eyes, and her mind buzzed uncomfortably. She shivered despite the night being relatively warm and tightened her cloak around her. This was probably the latest she had ever stayed up, but there was still one thing she must do before seeking rest.

Her father kept wooden crates for transporting wyverns in

a shed behind The Aviary. After dealing with Scorn, Lotte retrieved the crates, stacking two at a time, and hobbled back to the cabin. She left them in the kitchen before making a total of eight trips. Her lower back spasmed, and she staggered to the table. The crates took up the entire space, as well as her bedroom, with only a narrow path to The Broody Room and the basement.

Lotte was done, both physically and mentally. Eyes drooping, there was nothing more she could do that night. While she was worried for Nilka, Lotte could not face Emerick and his hatred at the moment. She was too drained. Luckily, the Firewraith appeared more than petrified of the wingless wyvern to try and escape. Lotte risked not checking on them.

With her bedroom preoccupied, Lotte trudged to her father's, shoved a desk chair under the doorknob, and climbed into bed. She barely pulled the thin blanket over her before drifting off to sleep.

The safehouse was halfway between the hatchery and the Immorthial Forest, approximately five kilometers northwest. After the rooster's fifth piercing crow, Lotte had dragged herself out of bed and began the painstaking process of transferring the wyverns, starting with the non-venomous ones, into fabric sacks that tied with drawstrings and then into the crates. She stopped after fitting a third of the mother wyverns, all of the smaller species, and fetched a pull wagon from the shed. It was small and could only carry four crates safely at a time, and Lotte almost cried at the thought of how many trips she must take. However, it was better than nothing.

Lotte followed a trail her father had made, marked by thin ropes tied to tree trunks. It was relatively flat with only a few spots where roots, overgrowth, or mud forced her to yank the wagon with all her might. The chirping of birds grew quieter the closer she came to the Immorthial Forest, replaced by shrill screeches and deep warbles from unknown creatures. Lotte caught the curiosity of a raptor glider, or perhaps she had walked close to its territory, for it followed for several minutes, soaring from tree trunk to tree trunk.

The soft mulch path gradually transformed into hard and uneven terrain, sloping up into a narrow hill. Lotte puffed and strained as she pulled the wagon up the incline, pausing frequently to wipe the sweat from her eyes and to ease the ache in her blistered palms.

As the hill rose above the tree canopy, Lotte could see that it was not a hill at all, but rather a twisting root that was interwoven with countless others, all converging towards the same destination. The network of roots spanned for miles, disappearing into a wall of trunks so colossal that their peaks could be mistaken for mountains.

The Immorthial Forest.

Home to most of Asoleenya's deadliest, yet fascinating creatures. No matter how many times she saw it, the forest always stole her breath.

The safehouse was ahead of Lotte, a crooked shack built on the peak of the root before it wound down into a valley and then inclined again. Vines and thorny fruit brambles covered the shack and gave it the appearance of a bush to anyone passing by. Thanks to her father's mock emergency evacuations, Lotte knew its location by heart.

She dragged the wagon to the front and secured the wheels from rolling backwards with wood chocks. Careful of thorns, Lotte ripped off vines from the door and wiped dirt off the handle, ignoring the pain as she irritated her blistering skin. She cursed herself for not wearing gloves. Placing a hand on the manacore lock, she whispered, "*Alsum,*" and shoved inside.

A cloud of dust met Lotte, and she hacked and waved her hand to clear the fine particles. When fresh air from outside filtered through the old, Lotte inhaled strong scents of moist dirt and rotting wood. The safehouse was a single room adorned with wall shelves, an incubator, and a small crate of extra emergency supplies, such as manacore torches, canteens, and extra wyvern handling sticks. A hatch in the center of the floor led to a cellar Orm had cut out of the root.

There were enclosures for the wyverns down below. While they were not ideal for the wyverns in the long run, cramped and without a source of water other than what Lotte and her father could lug in buckets, nor could it house all the wyverns of the hatchery; the shack provided safety from immediate danger and bought Lotte some time for deciding what to do with the wyverns. Likely, she would have to only keep the extremely endangered and the vulnerable — the rest would have to be released if she could not come up with another solution.

Lotte placed the crates on the wall shelves, planning to transfer the wyverns into the temporary enclosures below once she had the rest of the wyverns present from the hatchery. They would be okay in the crates until that night. Locking the safehouse, Lotte retrieved the wagon and began her way home. She had, at least, another ten trips to go.

Lotte returned to the hatchery by mid-morning. She glared at the crates of wyverns remaining in the kitchen. These were only half the mothers of The Broody Room. Hauling the rest of them, plus dealing with the ones residing in The Aviary would take days. She needed help, and hopefully Remi and Healer Aklea would be amenable to assisting her.

However, asking them, as well as warning them about the approaching Firewraiths, would have to wait until after she checked on her prisoner. Lotte wanted to make sure Emerick had not gotten loose and that Nilka was alright. Dragging a hand down her face, Lotte mentally prepared herself for Emerick's death threats. How could one human harbor so much hatred?

Lotte crept into the basement. There was no point in staying quiet as the stairs whined under her weight, and the manacore torch was an obvious giveaway, but she still held her breath as she approached the enclosure. Nilka remained piled on top of Emerick's motionless body. For a moment, Lotte thought perhaps the Firewraith was dead.

Until he spoke.

"I need to pee," he said through clenched teeth.

Lotte blinked. "Huh?"

"I need to take a piss!" he said. "Move your snake and get me a bucket!"

Lotte's mind floundered from the Firewraith's request. She had not considered his basic needs — such as food, water, and relieving himself — while held captive. She was not cruel enough to let a person, no matter how evil, waste away or soil their pants. However, as her thoughts drifted to little Annsley and the destruction of Mrs. Gibbs' farm, Lotte considered making an exception.

"Bucket, now!" Emerick snapped.

Huffing, Lotte fetched one of the many pails in the basement storage. She pushed the panel of the enclosure's glass aside and stepped onto the rocky platform, staying a sizable distance away from Emerick in case he tried to grab her.

"C'mon, Nilka," she said to the wingless wyvern while patting her leg.

Emerick exhaled harshly as Nilka slid off his body. He pushed himself to his feet, noticeably wincing from staying in the same position for too long, and stood as much as the chains allowed. He held out his hand. Hesitantly, Lotte threw him the bucket.

Exiting the enclosure, Lotte faced the stairs and ignored the rustling of pants and the loud trickle of fluids hitting metal. It was awkward but ended soon enough. When he finished, Lotte instructed him to lay back down, and she began whistling to Nilka to resume her earlier position. The Firewraith cut her off.

"Take the bucket away," he said.

Lotte bristled at his tone. "Why should I? I'm the one making demands."

"I don't have a lot of room to maneuver," he said, condescendingly slow. "If I bump the bucket and it spills, do you really want to be the one who cleans the mess?"

"You think I would clean it up? Ha! It's your problem, not mine," Lotte sniffed.

"It will be when this place starts to smell."

Though she did not want to admit it, Emerick had a point — a disgusting point, but valid nonetheless. Shaking her head, Lotte entered the enclosure once more and held out her hand. She waited for the Firewraith to pass the bucket. Except he did not.

His arm lashed out and caught Lotte by her elbow, squeezing so hard she thought her skin might split, and he yanked her toward his chest. Her scream was cut off as a hand smashed against her mouth and nose, cutting her off from air. She thrashed side to side, but nothing loosened his vice grip. Just when dots formed in her vision from a lack of oxygen, the Firewraith surprisingly let go of her face.

Lotte sucked in a noisy breath but was immediately stopped when an arm wound around her neck in a chokehold. She attempted to remove it, scratching his skin and pounding her fist against his forearm. The Firewraith was relentless.

"Where is the key to unlock the shackles?" The Firewraith applied more pressure.

Lotte felt like her eyes would pop out of her head. "I-In my right belt p-pouch. It's small and s-silver w-with a square h-handle."

Her vision dwindled the longer the Firewraith held her. His free hand reached for her belt, dug in the pouch, and withdrew the key. After some awkward fumbling, she heard a click and metal clattering to the ground. The arm around her neck disappeared, and Lotte was shoved down.

Coughing hard, Lotte rolled on her back and lay stunned in the enclosure. She hardly registered the Firewraith dodging Nilka's strikes and racing across the basement and up the stairs. Only out of instinct did she manage a short and high whistle, and Nilka understood her target and zipped after the Firewraith.

Staggering to her feet, Lotte rubbed her sore neck. Her coughing subsided in time to hear a yell and crates crashing against the floor above. A scuffle ensued, and Lotte broke from her daze and hurried up the stairs, afraid for Nilka and the other wyverns' safety.

In the kitchen, Lotte was met with feathered wings and scaly bodies buzzing in the air. The aggravated wyverns hissed and snapped at each other, and she ducked her head as she stepped over their fallen transport carriers. She stopped before Nilka, who was constricting around the Firewraith. Her teeth sunk into his shoulder. Emerick's eyes were closed, his lips turning blue, and he tried but failed to slip his free arm between his neck and Nilka's body.

"Serves you right," Lotte's voice was raw and scratchy. "Now you know how I feel."

Emerick moaned something incoherent, and Lotte squatted next to him. It was tempting to let Nilka strangle him into unconsciousness . . . or worse. How many innocent beings begged him and the other Firewraiths to stop when they were murdered? Yet, a whispered "please" from his lips tugged at her heart. Lotte refused to stoop to his level.

She called Nilka off.

"If you try anything else, you'll find yourself in the same position again," she warned. "These are wyverns, cousins of dragons. One command, and every wyvern in this room will attack." That was a lie, of course. Only a select few were trained by Orm. Maybe one or two, aside from Nilka, would respond, but she felt confident with her farce, especially when seeing the Firewraith's body shudder.

Blood pooled from the bite wound. No doubt he would need stitches, or at least a healing potion, to close the deep punctures. While Nilka was not venomous, her large size made her formidable. Emerick sat up slowly with his hand pressed against his shoulder. His wide blue eyes shifted back and forth as he watched the chaos of wyverns around them.

"You will stand up and return to the enclosure. You will put the chains back on yourself. Do you understand me?" Lotte stroked Nilka's head. When he did not respond, she decided to add an extra dose of fear to her fabrication. "You will want an antidote, too."

"An antidote?" he breathed.

"For the venom," she said, evenly.

The Firewraith cursed. He curled his legs under his body and stood without the use of his hands. He coughed wetly but seemed unbothered as he glared at her with pure hatred. Begrudgingly, he trudged to the basement entrance, dodging aimless wyverns. Lotte followed with Nilka as her shadow. By the time they arrived at the enclosure, tremors raked his body as his coughing progressed into an all-out fit.

Lotte studied him, concerned about his swelling cheeks and

red, puffy eyes. He was experiencing strange symptoms. Had another wyvern gotten to him? But wait, all the ones in the crate were non-venomous. This was something else. And judging by how he desperately drew in long, whiny breaths, the Firewraith was not pretending.

"Well?" Emerick said gravely. "Give me the antidote."

Lotte ensured he was chained once more before answering. "It won't help."

"You said — "

"The venom was a lie," she cut him off.

He coughed into his fist, sweat droplets bubbling on his forehead, and he swayed on his feet. "Then what is wrong with me?" he scraped out.

"By the looks of it, you're having an allergic reaction."

Lotte would have to act fast. The only reason Lotte recognized anaphylactic shock was that her father had a severe allergy to bee stings and required a potion to counter the effects. He always carried a vial or two while hunting for pixies.

Lotte ran upstairs to retrieve the spare he normally kept in the nightstand next to his bed. Sure enough, she found the tiny vial with a brownish liquid inside, next to the empty spot where he typically kept his journal. Of course, he had brought his research diary with him to deliver the basilisk egg. His other completed ones were stored on the wall-mounted shelves in the messy room.

When she returned to the Firewraith, he was lying on his side, his mouth opening and closing like a fish out of water. His eyes were swollen shut, and his lips were three times their normal size. Heart fluttering with nervousness, Lotte sat next to him on the rock platform and uncorked the vial.

"Drink this." She brought the potion to his lips. Whether he had heard her or not, Lotte tilted the vial until its contents dribbled out. She pressed her hand over his mouth to keep him from spitting it out.

The results were instant: The hives on his taupe skin lessened, the swelling of his face receded, and he cracked open his eyes. He breathed deeply. Satisfied with her prediction and quick thinking, Lotte left the enclosure and closed the panel shut. She kept Nilka by her side this time. The chains should hold the Firewraith well enough.

After several minutes, Emerick spoke. "What . . . happened . . . to me?"

"You have a severe allergy to wyverns, apparently. If I had not given you that potion, your throat would have swelled shut, and you would have died. Ironically, the medicine I gave you is made with wyvern byproducts."

Emerick froze, blinking owlishly. "Medicine made from wyverns?"

"Their feathers, skins, venom, and, in some cases, their excrement. They have many medicinal properties if you know how to brew them correctly. I'll give you something to heal the bite wound on your shoulder."

"No way," he breathed, his usually tight and nefarious expression softened with shock and something akin to hope.

Was he that surprised she helped him?

Lotte crossed her arms and lifted her chin. "Unlike you, I don't wish death upon my enemies." Then, she spun around and marched across the room. Just as browsed a storage shelf full of potions, Emerick called out for her to stop. His genuinely pleading tone confused Lotte, and she faltered.

The Firewraith's next words shook Lotte to her core.

"I'm looking for a man named Orm Skale. Do you know him?"

Chapter Eight
ELIXIR OF LIFE

C'mon, you wretched winged nuisances!" Lotte used the end of a broom to gently prod two wyverns off the kitchen rafters. Unfortunately, they curled tighter around the beam. Half the transport crates were refilled and ready for the safehouse, while the rest waited for their tenants. Catching the wyverns proved more difficult than Lotte had expected. They were already angry about being removed from their safe and perfectly tailored enclosures, and then being stuffed into bags and dark, cramped boxes for a second time. Emerick's contribution threw them into a state of fight or flight. Thank Asoleenya, these wyverns were non-venomous.

The wyvern that Lotte poked with the broom hissed and launched forward. She zipped down the broom and struck Lotte with her tail stinger. Sharp pain momentarily blocked her thoughts. Lotte gritted her teeth to keep from howling. Although she had lost track of how many times she had been stung and bitten by wyverns, it still hurt.

Eventually, she pried the wyvern off with her free hand and held her by the base of her head, body flailing and wings flapping dramatically in an attempt to escape. She stuffed the wyvern into a sack, ignoring the blood bubbling from the stinger puncture.

"Only nine more to go," Lotte muttered after counting. A deep, curdling anger formed in her belly as her thoughts shifted to the culprit of this mess. The kitchen looked like it had been raided by a group of bandits!

"I'm looking for a man named Orm Skale. Do you know him?"

The question sent shivers down Lotte's spine. After the Firewraith had mentioned her father, Lotte left the basement without a word. A mind-numbing fear settled in her. Somehow, her father had caught himself on Bouldermaul's immediate agenda, and his Firewraiths were actively looking for him.

Catching the final nine wyverns took over an hour, and when Lotte delivered the wagon with the next batch of wyverns, it was already midday. Though the temperature was hot, the gray clouds overhead added to her frustration. She cursed the Firewraith under her breath again for wasting so much of her time. She would be lucky to transport all of the non-venomous wyverns by tonight, or even tomorrow morning. For all she knew, his comrades could be an hour away!

Lotte blew a sweaty strand of hair from her face as she decided to speak to her prisoner once more before warning Twisp of his whereabouts and the impending arrival of his companions.

In the basement, light from her manacore torch revealed the slight disarray earlier's scuffle had caused: buckets that had once been stacked were now skewed across the room; a tipped-over box spilled out vials, thankfully unbroken; and a burlap sack slumped over and dumped shredded palm tree bedding. Nilka sprawled dutifully in front of the enclosure, guarding their unwanted guest. She yawned before blinking at Lotte, smacking her lips to communicate her hunger and need to hunt. Unfortunately, the wingless wyvern would have to accept frozen pixies that Lotte warmed up in boiling water.

Inside the enclosure, the Firewraith sat cross-legged, his eyes locked on Lotte. He straightened his back as she approached.

"If you have any information on Orm Skale, I will tell my comrades to stay away from Twisp." he said, surprising Lotte with the offer.

"Like I believe you." She pursed her lips and shook her head.

"I will leave this place and never return," he continued.

"More like you would take the information and stab us in the back."

"I give you my word."

Lotte scoffed, unsure whether to feel amused or offended by how little the Firewraith thought of her. "Your word holds no weight. You're a Firewraith — a murderous dog of your king — sworn enemies to magic and magical creatures. I'll never trust any promise you make."

Emerick's expression darkened. "And you remain blind to the destruction caused by magic."

"Just like all the destruction you and Bouldermaul cause without magic? If that's not hypocrisy at its finest, then I don't know what is."

His lip curled into a sneer. "Have you ever opened a history textbook? King Bouldermaul isn't banning magic for the sake of pride or hatred or whatever reasons your feeble mind has created. Hundreds of thousands of innocent lives have been stolen during the Ka'Rok Desert Strife."

"I have no idea what you're talking about, nor do I have to listen to this rubbish." Lotte turned around, about to head upstairs.

Emerick reached out his hand as if to stop her, but the

shackles halted his movement. "None of King Bouldermaul's oppositions have time to listen or consider facts. It's easy to call him evil without understanding why he chose such a difficult path."

The words struck Lotte. She stomped back to the enclosure until her forehead pressed against the panel, condensation forming where her breath hit the glass. "He takes the lives of children without blinking. He demolishes entire towns in a matter of hours. He's displaced, if not killed, hundreds of thousands of magic users and creatures. And he is actively deforesting the Immorthial Forest — the heart of Asoleenya." She started to laugh and began pacing around the basement. "So, please, tell me your king's reasoning and see how it changes my mind — even just a little — because I guarantee it won't."

Emerick narrowed his eyes, shoulders rising like a wolf backed into a corner. "Never mind. I'd be wasting energy explaining to someone like you."

"Nothing gives him the right to slaughter living beings — no matter who your king blames for your country's problems."

"Say that to the victims' families," he said, "which is everyone in Vroaevalon."

Lotte relaxed her fists, only now realizing the ache in her knuckles from clenching them so tightly. "There's no excuse. He should've figured out some other way to work with magic users. Couldn't he have developed rules for magic instead of banning it?"

The Firewraith rolled his eyes. "You don't think there have been laws before? Former Urtica had an entire council dedicated to magical laws and regulations, and they still failed to stop individuals from hurting others and destroying entire villages. And when the Blighted Horde began the Ka'Rok Desert Strife, they didn't stand a chance."

"I have no idea what you're talking about," Lotte said. "Blighted Horde? Ka'Rok Desert Strife?" What nonsense was he spewing?

Emerick continued his rant despite her confusion. "You could make the argument that magic and swords are both tools, and their lethality is based on the users' intentions. However, a sword cannot split the ground into a canyon, or set an entire town on fire, or down an entire militia in seconds. The damage a sword can cause is minuscule compared to magic."

When he finished his tirade, Emerick's chest heaved as though he had been sprinting. He ground his teeth, and his eyes became misty. His frame trembled. For a moment, Lotte thought he would either explode with rage or cry, possibly both, and she bit her lip to prevent herself from making any snide comments. She wanted to feel pleasure for causing the Firewraith to lose his composure, but all she could do was notice how young he looked underneath the scars on his face. How old was he anyway? Late teens? Early twenties? She would not ask.

"Not everyone has the choice to use magic," Lotte said slowly. "It runs through them like the blood in their veins. They are born with it. Will you punish them for simply existing?"

"They are — "

She cut him off. "You claim magic is a tool, but that isn't accurate — even for races whose magic is intertwined with their language, taught not innate. They still require an internal source that cannot be acquired and trained." Lotte bent over and hugged Nilka around the neck. The wyvern flared her nose vents at the Firewraith. "Those creatures, at the very least, should be spared."

"All magic must go," he said blankly.

Sighing, Lotte pinched the bridge of her nose. "Then why seek out Orm Skale? He is a magic user. What could you possibly need from him?"

"A potion called the Elixir of Life."

Lotte's mouth dropped open as she took a step backward.

"How do you know about that?" she whispered.

Only Healer Aklea and a few of Orm's most trusted buyers were aware of the incredibly rare and powerful potion, and they had been sworn into secrecy regarding that information. Someone exposed their secret, but who?

"My stepfather heard it from a trader, and he shared the information with me," Emerick said.

A trader? Again, it could not be this simple. He was not telling her something. She hated the tremor in her voice as she spoke. "Let me guess — Bouldermaul is sick. The Elixir of Life is made of magical ingredients. Isn't that a bit hypocritical of your beloved king?"

"It's not for him," the Firewraith mumbled, fingers curling into his palms.

The muscles in his jaw tightened as he gritted his teeth. Their conversation turned into an awkward silence, and Lotte thought he was done talking. Her curiosity demanded more explanations, like who was the trader that ratted out her and her father, and who was the Elixir of Life for, but she refrained herself.

Just as Lotte was about to leave, he whispered, "My mother is sick."

Lotte tilted her head, astonishment evident behind her scarf and cloak's hood. For once, she was speechless.

"She became sick approximately four months ago," he continued, unwilling to meet Lotte's eyes. "She was given half a year to live. No doctor in Guldkem can figure out the cure, nor can they determine the cause. She's dying of a slow, unknown illness. My stepfather grew desperate and began . . . asking around."

Lotte's own mother flashed in her thoughts, but she squashed what little sympathy she had for the Firewraith. He lost such compassion one escape attempt and a burning homestead ago.

"So you are here with your Firewraiths not only to steal the Elixir of Life but also to burn down everything in your path with the smallest ties to magic," Lotte said, unimpressed. "You do realize the potion is made with magic, correct? How did you convince the other Firewraiths to go along with your hypocritical request? Or do they know that you've taken an illegal detour?"

Emerick flinched, and Lotte raised a brow. His reaction told her that she was not far from the truth.

He shifted, chains rattling, as he spoke, "There were never other Firewraiths."

Lotte blinked, silent for a moment. "Excuse me?" she eventually exclaimed.

"I came alone," he admitted. "No other Firewraiths are with me. In fact, I would be punished severely for treason if I was discovered."

Lotte gaped at him. "You lied to me?"

"Would you tell your enemy the truth — that you're traveling alone?"

She could hardly believe her ears.

Had the last twenty-four hours of transporting the wyverns been for nothing? There was no way this could be so simple. Emerick had to be lying. Why would he travel all the way from Twisp and cause so much chaos without an entourage? It made no sense!

Lotte began to pace back and forth. "Do you know how much damage your presence has caused?"

"I planned to reveal the location of Twisp upon my return, but," he paused, seeming deep in thought, "if you help me find Orm Skale, I will leave Twisp forever. No one will ever know or touch it."

Lotte stopped directly in front of the Firewraith and stared into his wide, azure gaze. Such a promise was tempting, but obviously his words could not be trusted. She felt conflicted when the story of his sick mother cycled through her head, but then the images flashed of Annsley and the smoke from Mrs. Gibbs' homestead. Taking a deep breath, Lotte fixed the Firewraith with a glare.

"I'll never make an agreement with you. As soon as this conversation is over, I'll tell the helyait guards," she said.

Expecting her answer, Emerick smirked. "If I don't return to Guldkem, the Firewraiths will investigate my disappearance. It wouldn't take them much time to learn of my location, and then your town will be no more."

Lotte flinched.

"But if you give me the Elixir of Life and I return to Guldkem within the frame I told my mentor that I would be gone, there would be no question regarding my whereabouts. Your town and your beloved hatchery would be saved from Firewraiths invading — so long as the Elixir of Life works. It *will* cure my mother, correct?"

Blood left Lotte's cheeks at declaration, causing her mind to tingle and her stomach to churn. She said with a detached voice, "The Elixir of Life can cure any sickness or injury — it's even beaten the deadliest poisons and physical wounds."

"Then there should not be any problem. Do we have a deal?"

Lotte fidgeted, biting her lip as her heart pounded heavily in her chest. Every fiber of her being screamed for her to refuse, but there was no denying how detrimental Bouldermaul sending Firewraiths to track Emerick down would be for Twisp and the hatchery. The hardest part was knowing if he was telling the truth or not about everything he had been saying this far.

"Swear that there are no other Firewraiths — that you came on your own. Swear that you won't speak a word of Twisp or ever return. Swear on your mother's life."

"I swear," Emerick said, his voice strong with conviction.

Lotte nodded, her stomach churning. "Then I'll tell you about Orm Skale and give you the Elixir of Life."

Chapter Nine
Echoes of the Past

Just as Lotte revealed herself to be the daughter of Orm Skale, a knock on the front door interrupted her conversation with Emerick. Upstairs, she peered through the spy hole of the door, relief washing over Lotte at the sight of Healer Aklea and Remi. Tears sprang to her eyes, and she yanked the door open. She would have hugged them if it were not inappropriate for helyaits.

"Thank, Parin." Healer Aklea momentarily closed his eyes and muttered a prayer to their helyait god. Then he rounded on Lotte. "I do not know what you were thinking, but we have been beside ourselves with worry since your reckless departure!"

"Has Twisp returned to the surface?" Lotte asked.

"Not yet," he said. "We are still searching for the Firewraith who attacked the Gibbs' family. Unfortunately, we found another victim — a helyait who had been shot with an arrow and left on a beach a few kilometers south of the bay."

Lotte felt the air leave her lungs as though she had been punched in the gut. "I-Is the helyait dead?"

"She lives," Healer Aklea said gravely. "But not without serious injury to her back and sun sickness. She will recover."

Lotte nodded, the lump in her throat loosening a bit. This

was yet another tally mark on the list of Emerick's wrong-doings.

"I see you are taking the wyverns to your safehouse," Remi said, gesturing to the wagon. Only he and his father knew of their hidden shack on the edge of the Immorthial Forest.

"I was until . . . " How did she explain everything with Emerick? "You're not going to believe what happened to me."

Healer Aklea's gaze shifted behind her, and he gasped. "Under your table . . . is that armor?"

Lotte spun around, her mouth opening and closing as words escaped her. She had stripped the Firewraith of his armor while he had been unconscious, and she had been too preoccupied to do anything with it. She at least hid the sword behind the incubator downstairs. Healer Aklea stepped through the doorway, gently pushing Lotte aside, and crouched under the table. He inspected the chainmail armor.

"Where did you find these?" he asked, and then scanned the kitchen. "Is the Firewraith here?"

Lotte did not understand her hesitation. She should have told Healer Aklea right away that she had captured Emerick and locked him in the basement enclosure. She should have told him about his threat of more Firewraiths, despite his admission of coming alone. And she should have told him about the trader that blabbed their location when the hatchery was meant to be a secret. All of her problems would be resolved if she just turned Emerick over to the helyait guards.

Except, they would not be. . . .

"If I don't return to Guldkem, the Firewraiths will invest-igate my disappearance. It wouldn't take them much time to learn of my location, and then your town will be no more."

The warning reverberated in Lotte's mind. The last thing she wanted was to initiate a raid on their town. But she also did not want to fall for a farce.

"Lotte!" Healer Aklea snapped her from her thoughts.

She really should tell him.

"He's not here," Lotte barely whispered.

"How did you come across this, then?" His webbed fingers tapped the armor.

She licked her lips, her brain scrambling for ideas. "I found the armor."

"Where?" he demanded.

"In the woods not far from here." Lotte swallowed, air grinding painfully down her dry throat.

"The Firewraith was not there?"

"I think he ran into a swarm of pixies." Lotte's hands felt abnormally clammy, but she resisted wiping them on her pants. "There were bones in the armor, and they looked fresh."

Healer Aklea hummed, dropped the chainmail for the helmet. "We must tell Matriarch Ira at once. Lotte, you will come with us."

"I can't," she said, "at least not right away. I've been transferring wyverns to our safehouse, but with the threat out of the way . . . " she trailed off. Was it out of the way?

To her surprise, Healer Aklea nodded in agreement.

"What are your plans for them?" he asked.

Lotte rubbed her chin thoughtfully. "I suppose I should return them to the hatchery."

"Remi will help you."

"I don't need — "

"You have been on your own for too long. Imagine what your father would say if I willingly let you continue without a companion. There is safety in pods."

Lotte ground her teeth. She resisted looking toward the basement door, not wanting to alert the helyaits of her farce. Having Remi around would only increase those odds, but both the father and son were stubborn. Arguing would only raise suspicions.

"You brought your amulet, I'm guessing?" Lotte raised an eyebrow at Remi.

He tapped the rune on his belt buckle, a symbol etched into the polished manacore that protected him from long exposures to the sun and dry air. "I would not be here without it," he said.

Healer Aklea gathered the armor and stood up. He headed out of the hatchery with Lotte and Remi following close behind. He stopped next to the wagon. "I will take this to the matriarch. Return to Twisp no later than dusk. Otherwise, I will send a search team for you."

"We shall be swift," Remi said when Lotte grumbled with displeasure.

As Healer Aklea staggered away with the armor, Remi began unloading the crates from the wagon. Instead of The Broody Room, Lotte directed Remi to The Aviary, not wanting him to hear any noises Emerick might make. The wyverns hissed and snapped at Lotte as she slid them out of their sacks and onto the saturated ground, spraying saliva on her boots and pants. Luckily, after stretching their wings, they seemed more interested in fleeing than attacking and zipped toward the foliage or took off toward the roof.

Releasing the mother wyverns in The Aviary meant catching them later and having to walk through the enclosure for clutches of eggs, but it was not safe for wyverns to remain in transport carriers for long periods of time. She was already pushing her luck with the ones at the safehouse.

Lotte was aware of how many mistakes she had made while trying to handle the situation, the biggest one residing in her basement. Now more than ever, she wished for her father's presence.

Remi flexed his hands and winced, and Lotte knew this was

the most work he had done on land in a while. As a silent thank you, she grabbed a clean bucket from The Aviary's workstation and filled it with water she pumped from the well. Handing it to him, Remi took several loud gulps before he dumped the rest of the water over his head.

"Are you sure you'll be okay traveling to the safehouse? It's quite far." Lotte watched as the droplet rejuvenated his rubbery skin, causing them to reflect light.

Remi chuckled. "There is a reason why I am an *Idateori* and not a warrior."

"I thought you were chosen to be an *Idateori* because of your love for knowledge and exploration, not because you lack the physical strength. I'm sure the strongest helyait warriors struggle on land."

Remi gave her a toothy smile. "Humans are lucky — they can run, climb, swim, and survive in most climates."

"Maybe . . . but we can't breathe underwater or handle the pressure of the deep sea like you can. Oh, and we don't have magic," Lotte said. "You haven't answered my question."

"I will be fine," he said. "Shall we go, now?"

After locking The Aviary door, Lotte took one of the wagon's handles while Remi gripped the other, and they steered it onto the path Lotte had used before. Traveling to the safehouse took longer due to the constant breaks for Remi; however, it was not as taxing, and for that, Lotte was grateful. The extra time allowed for Lotte to mull the conversation she had with Emerick. There were a few pieces of information she wanted to verify, and Remi was a perfect person to ask.

She waited until after Remi stopped for a drink at the creek, which led to a waterfall over the cliff, before inquiring, "You know the history of Asoleenya, correct?"

"I know general information, the kind everyone knows." He

wiped water on his forehead and shoulders before they proceeded with their journey. "Most of my knowledge is of the Slokyl Ocean, not so much landwalker affairs."

"What of the Ka'Rok Desert Strife? Have you ever heard of that?"

"Yes, of course," he said automatically. "We had a different name for it, though — The Red Culling."

"Why do they have different names?" Lotte asked.

Remi shrugged. "Every region has its own terminology for events, but both refer to an era of mass genocide. While Urtica and settlements in the Ka'Rok Desert faced the brunt of the deaths, everyone was affected — land, sky, and sea."

"I've never heard of either," she confessed.

Her friend blinked at her with surprise. "Has Orm not taught you the history of your land?"

"Only geography and of Bouldermaul's reign," she said. "He was more adamant about me learning the care and types of wyverns."

"I should not be surprised. Why do you have sudden interest?"

Lotte chose her words carefully. "I recently heard about it, and I never thought of hardships before Bouldermaul."

"Before Bouldermaul, there was the Red Culling. And before the Red Culling, there were the Northern Wars of Endlor. Wars and tribulation cycle through history, as do times of peace."

Lotte gazed at the forest canopy, a wave of disbelief hitting her. Why did her father never teach her any of this? "Tell me more about the Red Culling."

"Well — " Remi paused to push a branch away from his face, wincing as it trailed along his skin " — it was the targeted destruction of over fifty settlements, including a major port city on the Akeltic Sea coast. No motives were ever discovered, just senseless killings."

"And Vroaevalon lost half its population?" Lotte asked.

Remi nodded. "As I said, most of the attacks focused on the towns surrounding Urtica."

So Emerick was telling the truth, after all.

"When did it start? How long did it last? And what ended the Red Culling?" The questions spilled from her mouth.

"It started with the sudden disappearance of gruiks — all of them — gone like a flash of lightning. Not just in Gruik Territory, but also across the seas."

"What happened to them?"

"No one knows. There has not been enough time or resources to investigate. But, immediately preceding their disappearance, strange and inflicted creatures emerged and began hunting anything with a beating heart, feasting on them. At first, it was believed they were mindless, but it was later determined they were being controlled."

"The Blighted Horde?" Lotte remembered Emerick's words.

Remi nodded.

"Who were the people controlling them?"

"That's another mystery."

"How long did it last?"

"Approximately six months," Remi said.

Lotte gasped. "That's it? Half a population gone in half a year."

"Yes, sadly."

The wheel on the wagon sank into a patch of mud, interrupting their conversation. She yanked the handle, leaning forward with all her weight, and popped it free. Sweat cascaded down her face and seeped into her parted lips. She spat out the salty taste, wiping a gritty hand across her face. The sun seemed hotter than normal — bigger and brighter —

teasing Lotte as it sunk from the center of the sky. They stopped in the shade for another break.

"How did the Red Culling end? I heard . . . I heard Bouldermaul stopped it. Is that true?" Lotte did not like thinking that the tyrannical king was, in fact, a hero for stopping the violence. Replacing one form of violence with another form was just as bad.

"He was the one who defeated the Blighted Horde, ending the Red Culling." Remi paused, giving Lotte a pensive look.

"What is it?" she urged.

"The abrupt end to the Red Culling and the start of Bouldermaul's reign was rather unnatural — no resistance from those controlling the Blighted Horde. Some of my people suspect that Bouldermaul may have ties to the Blighted Horde and, perhaps, is a part of their plans."

"But he hates magic!" she said. "He wants to rid Asoleenya of magic! Emerick said — " Her words died in her throat at her slip-up. How could she be so careless and mention the blasted Firewraith's name!

"Who is Emerick?" Of course, Remi would ask this.

"A client of my father." Lotte looked ahead, noting wheel tracks from her earlier transportation. "He stopped by right before my father left."

"And he mentioned the history of Asoleenya during his visit?"

They started moving again, and not long after, the ground began to ascend. Lotte evened her breathing as much as she could while pulling the heavy wagon uphill. He was remarkably receptive, one of the reasons why he was chosen to be an *Idateori*, and the slightest hitch would alert him.

"Bits and pieces," she said. "He mostly discussed the reason why Vroaevalons support Bouldermaul and hate magic."

"I doubt we will ever discover the truth," Remi said.

Blowing out a frustrated breath, Lotte decided pondering the subject any longer would result in a headache. She confirmed Emerick's story, at least. The new information regarding Bouldermaul and his possible attachments with the Blighted Horde was incomprehensible.

Yet, she indulged the notion: Could the king be the real cause of death for half of Vroaevalon's population? Could he have done so to obtain his current role as king? Could the banning of magic be his way of making sure no one stood up to him? And even more unbelievable, if the king was affiliated with the Blighted Horde, does that mean he — despite his propaganda of hatred — utilizes magic? Lotte was curious how Emerick would respond to her thoughts if she brought it up with him later.

But for now, she focused on her current task.

Finally at the safehouse, they stopped for a moment to gaze at the sprawling Immorthial Forest. Remi's eyes roamed the rolling roots. "Do you know of Fern Lake?" he asked, to which Lotte said no. "It's the largest lake in Asoleenya. There is a helyait pod that lives there."

"Have you ever been there?" Lotte asked.

"No, only squads issued by Matriarch Ira ever venture up the river, near Port Labree. Doing so is foolish as the creatures of the water are just as dangerous as the ones on land. There is no reason for the matriarch to send me to Fern Lake, so I doubt I will ever see it — and for that, I am grateful. Nonetheless, I cannot help my curiosity. I heard the pod is quite different from ours in Twisp — more rustic and with their own language." His voice rang with mirth, and Lotte bit her lip to refrain from chuckling, finding his spew of knowledge enduring.

Lotte had to admit that exploring the Immorthial Forest, the most mysterious wonder of Asoleenya, tugged at her temptation. If she could enter the forest without being a creature's next meal, she would.

They loaded the wagon before making the painstakingly slow process back to the hatchery — taking two trips back and forth. It was already dusk when they finished, and both Lotte and Remi were too tired for conversation. They released the wyverns in The Aviary and returned the wagon and crates to the storage shed. Lotte eyed the cabin, the windows darker than outside, and an intrusive thought caused the hairs on her neck to rise: What if he had escaped the chains and slipped past Nilka's watchful eyes? What if he was waiting for her inside? Despite recalling the story about his mother and the desperation in his voice, she knew better than to lower her guard, and she mentally prepared to ward off the Firewraith.

"Do you need to retrieve anything before we see to my father?" Remi asked.

Lotte wanted to smack her head, remembering she was told to meet Healer Aklea for dinner and, probably, be questioned about the armor. Again, she realized how terrible her lie was and how it placed everyone in town in danger. If interrogated or asked to show them the fabricated pixie swarm's location, Lotte would not be able to hide the truth.

"I'm too tired to travel anymore today," Lotte said, not exactly lying.

"My father is adamant about you joining us tonight." Remi rubbed the back of his head self-consciously. "He was far from pleased with my decision to help you leave Twisp's protection. He plans to uphold his promise of keeping you safe, and so do I."

"Obviously, you two can confirm I'm alive and well." Her voice sounded hollow even to her.

"Your father has requested your physical presence at our

clinic each evening while he is away. Already, we have broken that promise on numerous occasions," he argued.

Lotte rolled her eyes. "C'mon, Remi! We've been traveling all day!"

He hummed thoughtfully for a moment. "I could see if my father will meet us here for dinner."

Lotte jolted. That was an awful idea. They would surely discover Emerick. There was no getting out of this.

"No, that won't be necessary. I'll go with you to Twisp," she said.

"Good." Remi sounded pleased. "I still need to give you my gift."

"Your gift?" She raised an eyebrow.

"The relic I mentioned before — I planned on giving it to you before the Firewraith's arrival."

"That's right!" Lotte snapped her fingers. "I'd forgotten about that."

"I am not surprised." Remi adjusted his belt, fingers dragging along the rune that kept him from drying out. He was obviously eager to submerge in water. "Shall we go?"

Lotte nodded.

Leaving the hatchery behind was grueling without knowing the status of Emerick, Nilka, and the other wyverns. Her stomach churned with anxiety. She snuck glances over her shoulder until the trees obscured her view and they were descending the cliff stairs.

Twisp remained underwater and, according to Remi, would stay that way until the investigation was completed and Matriarch Ira deemed the surface safe. Remi led her to the end of the jetty, no longer shrouded by fog. The bay's water, however, was still inky black compared to its normal pristine clarity. Remi offered his hand to Lotte. The skin of his palm was rough, like coarse sea coral, but the webbing between his fingers was smooth and slightly sticky. Together they jumped into the bay.

Water enveloped her body, but it stopped at her neck, a bubble of air forming around her head. Remi's eyes flashed with bright blue light as he muttered an incantation in his native language. The briny smell of magic intensified inside the bubble. Remi slipped an arm under Lotte's armpit and around her back, tightening his grip as he began to swim. While Lotte felt a current of water rush past her body as they went deeper into the bay, the air bubble protected her from the pressure.

Unfortunately, the magic used to darken the water prevented her from seeing beyond her nose, and only the chilling temperature told her they were approaching Twisp. Soon, Remi's swimming slowed. The bubble around Lotte's head opened up as they passed through the barrier of the shipwreck's hull. She stumbled when her feet clopped against the ground, and Remi balanced her. Another incantation dried her clothes.

Lotte blinked several times, eyes adjusting to the artificial light of manacore torches. Twisp was barren — all the stores and helyaits vacant other than their flimsy sheet-metal walls. Even the town guards were missing from their patrol. The lack of chatter and notes from pearl flutes was eerie. Lotte shivered.

"My people have returned to their homes." Remi said, reading her expression. "Only my father has remained to care for the family whose farm was burnt down. Although, now that they are mended, I believe my father returned the oldest members of the family to the surface, so they can salvage what is left of their property. Once this whole mess is over, we will help build what they have lost."

Lotte's chest constricted painfully. A flush spread across her cheeks, and she averted her gaze to the side of a nearby building. *Tell Remi the truth. Tell him now!* Her mind screamed. The Firewraith should face punishment for his crimes, not walk away with the Elixir of Life. There was no guarantee that he would not send his comrades to Twisp, nor was it her decision to pose such a risk on everyone's lives.

"Remi . . . " she began, ignoring the fear of disclosing the truth. Maybe she could blame Emerick and say he was holding the hatchery hostage, thus preventing her from revealing his presence. "I need to tell you — "

"Lotte!" Healer Aklea's voice echoed through Twisp, cutting her off. The helyait healer rounded the corner and jogged toward them, a massive grin stretched across his face. A heavy lump formed in Lotte's belly, and she snapped her mouth shut.

"I am relieved that you and my son have arrived. Are you well?"

Words died in Lotte's throat, but Healer Aklea was too excited to notice her hesitation. He beckoned for them to follow, rattling on and on about his meeting with the matriarch and the next steps for the mages to return Twisp to the surface. First on the agenda was making sure there were no more of Bouldermaul's followers. A lone Firewraith was rare, but not unheard of, and Healer Aklea was feeling optimistic. The helyait trackers had no evidence of more Firewraiths other than Emerick, both the Gibbs' family and the injured helyait confirmed their encounter with only one assailant. The more he spoke, the more Lotte ducked her head, wishing the world would swallow her.

When they reached the clinic, Healer Aklea ushered them inside. Lotte froze in the doorway. Two of the examination beds had been pushed together, and Mrs. Gibbs and her three youngest children occupied them. The mother combed Annsley's hair with her fingers, while the other two children, Korey and Balin, worked together to solve a helyait puzzle putting together carved stones to form a miniature whale statue. Mrs. Gibbs looked up and gasped at Lotte. She gently pushed her daughter to the side and stood, tears springing to her eyes.

"Is it true?" she asked, lip quivering. "The Firewraith who hurt my family is gone?"

The heavy feeling in Lotte's stomach turned sour at the sight of Mrs. Gibbs' hope and anguish. For a moment, Lotte thought she might throw up. She was grateful that her hood and scarf hid most of her face: They could not see her pained expression. Her earlier courage to tell Remi the truth dissipated. All Lotte could do was a sharp nod.

The woman sagged, letting out a relieved cry. "Thank Asoleenya!" she murmured and staggered back to the bed. She lay down with the back of her hand pressed against her forehead.

"Come inside, Lotte." Healer Aklea pulled her from the doorway. "I do not want the warm air escaping."

Lotte jerked her legs to step further into the clinic. Her joints ground like rusty gears, tight from tension. She sat on the ground by the room's manacore pillar, which glowed with lazy warmth. It was strange having it activated when southern Holan's summers were so hot. However, the air inside the town's barrier was stagnant and cold from the bay's depth.

Carved into the manacore, alongside helyait language, was an oven opening. Inside, an iron pot simmered with seafood stew. A loaf-shaped seaberry cake baked in a rectangular pan next to it. There was enough food for everyone if they rationed fairly, though Lotte was not the least bit hungry despite the strenuous labor she had endured that day.

"I will retrieve the relic for you." It took Lotte a moment to register that Remi was speaking. He crouched in front of her and whispered so no one could hear. "I must hide it on land so my father does not find out."

Lotte could only nod, not trusting her voice.

Tell them! Her mind shrilled over and over again.

After Remi left, Healer Aklea gathered bowls and spoons and passed them around. Lotte scooted back as the children bumbled over to the stove and formed a line, while their helyait host ladled them soup. Mrs. Gibbs filed in last, eyes wet as she thanked Healer Aklea for the meal and everything else he had done for her family.

The helyait's black eyes fell on Lotte and then her empty bowl.

"I'll eat at home," she whispered.

He tilted his head, ignoring her mild rudeness. "Nonsense! You must be hungry!"

"Well, I'm not." Lotte pushed herself to stand, handing the bowl and spoon back to him. "Now that I've checked in, I want to go home."

"That was hardly a check-in," he argued, "and the danger has yet to fully pass."

"The Firewraith is dead, right?" Her tongue was uncomfortably heavy. "No more danger."

"That does not mean there are no more Firewraiths in the area. Even though reports from the Gibbs family and our injured pod member indicate that the Firewraith traveled this far alone, we must continue obtaining concrete evidence that this is, in fact, the case," he said. "Until the investigation reaches a conclusion, we must stay alert and take necessary safety precautions. Surely, other Firewraiths will notice he is missing and search for him."

"All the more reason to return home. The hatchery needs protection."

Healer Aklea pinched his thin lips together and shook his head. Under his breath, he muttered, "Stubborn like your father." With a sigh, he cut a slice of seaberry cake and loaded it into the bowl. "At least take this with you."

Lotte stared down at the greenish-brown, generous slice of one of her favorite helyait staples. Seaberries were a bulbous seaweed that tasted like pickled dates. They were an acquired taste, one that travelers often spat out at first bite. But they made the thickest, most delicious cakes that were equally sweet, salty, and sour. Unfortunately, the combination unsettled her stomach in the wake of her guilt.

When Remi returned, his father announced her plans. "Leaving already!" he exclaimed half-heartedly, but he made no complaints. In fact, he smiled and bobbed on the balls of his feet eagerly. What kind of relic had he found that made him so antsy?

Saying their goodbyes, Lotte and Remi headed to the edge of town. She wrapped her arms around his waist, and they passed through the barrier and into the water. When they hit the surface, it dawned on her that the seaberry cake was uncovered and now a mushy soup in the bowl. She dumped it on the beach, causing Remi to *tsk*.

"Seaberry cake is just as tasty in the water as on land," he said. At that, Lotte gagged.

Remi had thought ahead and brought them to where the cliff stairs met the beach. He led Lotte to a cluster of ferns at the base, sand clinging to his ankles. "I hid the relic over here," he told her. Reaching into the feathery leaves, he withdrew what appeared to be a six-foot-long pole wrapped in wide locks of kelp.

Remi held it out to her.

Curiosity briefly negating her remorse, Lotte took the gift and noted a sturdy firmness under the kelp.

"Do not open it yet," Remi instructed, "or else someone might see."

"And you would get in trouble," she reiterated his earlier

worries. "Will I have to hide it forever?"

"No, you can say you bought it from a trader. I just cannot be seen giving it to you."

"Won't it be obvious that I'm carrying a helyait relic?"

"Remember what I said? It is a human relic. I believe it originated from Kullusk," he said.

Lotte's mouth fell open. Kullusk was an island country in the Slokyl Ocean, northeast of Holan. It was strange to think of lands beyond Asoleenya. Lotte clutched the gift to her chest and thanked Remi.

"Thank me when you open it," he said, returning to the water.

Chapter Ten

DANGERS OF THE NIGHT

As eager as Lotte was to open Remi's gift, the moment she crossed onto the hatchery, all she could think about was what lurked inside her home. Not wanting to enter unarmed, Lotte leaned the kelp-wrapped gift against the exterior wall and withdrew her blowgun from its holder, loading the chamber with a dart. She unlocked the front door, brought the blowgun to her lips, and stepped inside.

The late-evening's soft purple light was too faint to brighten the darkness of the room. Lotte listened for creaks from the floorboards, rustling of clothing fabric, or shifts from the rafters above. So far, nothing.

Inching toward the table where a manacore torch rested, she whispered the incantation. A bluish glow cast across the kitchen. Everything was how Lotte had left it before retrieving the wyverns from the safehouse. Good. Lotte swept her eyes across the room one final time, deeming it clear of threats, and headed to the basement.

She half expected Emerick to be waiting for her as she peeked through the crack of the basement door, but thankfully, he was not, and her body relaxed. Lotte descended the stairs and saw Nilka lounging in front of the enclosure. The wingless wyvern's head whipped up when Lotte's boots hit the final step, flicking her tongue to smell any food. Lotte mentally apologized, vowing to let Nilka outside to hunt tonight.

Lotte exhaled the tension that she had felt over the last several hours. Her knees would have buckled had she not grabbed the railing. Emerick was still captive. As she approached the enclosure with her torch outstretched, Emerick blinked several times and squinted into the light.

"Water," he croaked.

Lotte scrunched her face. Water for what?

"I need water." He turned his head, revealing his sunken eyes and chapped lips. "Unless your plan was to withhold food and drink." His eyes narrowed, and he frowned.

Lotte pinched her lips. She had not considered the basic necessities for her prisoner since his earlier escape attempt, nor had she thought about his other bodily needs. Despite his identity as a Firewraith and the harm he had inflicted upon Mrs. Gibbs' family — not to mention his deceptive assault with the urine bucket — Lotte could not bring herself to let him perish under her watch due to neglect.

What if this led to another trick?

Lotte planned to take precautions this time.

Retrieving a pitcher of water from the kitchen, Lotte slid the glass panel of the enclosure and stepped inside. She whistled for Nilka, who followed dutifully. Lotte crinkled her nose at the stench of sweat and something sour emitting from Emerick's body. He had been unmoving most of the day, as well as yesterday, so it made sense that he smelled. Another whistle caused Nilka to coil her body in an offensive stance, and Lotte watched Emerick blanch and close his eyes. She placed the pitcher by his fingertips, eyes tracking him for movements. Slowly, she retreated outside of the enclosure, the wingless wyvern acting as her shadow.

Emerick shook as he sat up. He groaned, stretching out his

arms and rotating his shoulder. Then, eyes landing on the pitcher, he snatched it up, brought it to his lips, and drank greedily. Water dribbled down his jaw. He emptied the pitcher without a break for air and slammed it down when he finished.

"Food," he demanded.

Lotte nodded, even though Emerick was staring at the ground and not at her. "Come on, Nilka," she said, and together they left the Firewraith.

In the kitchen, she gathered ingredients for soup. With everything going on, there was no way for her to purchase fresh fish for roasting, so she rummaged through their pantry for a jar of fermented rockfish and pickled leafy greens. Lotte filled a cooking pot with water and placed it onto the stove. Then she hesitated. The fire her father had started, which she had kept alive for days, was out, thus there was no heat. Lotte cursed. She hated using flint and stone, never quite striking the right way to produce a strong spark. At least, not for a good fifteen minutes or so. Then there was the whole bit of getting the wood hot enough so it would hold a flame. This is why her father warned her not to let the fire go out.

When Lotte opened the stove's door, a plume of soot spilled onto her boots before bursting into the air and expanding throughout the kitchen. Lotte hacked and covered her nose and mouth with her arm. A hiss from Nilka had her looking down. The wyvern snapped its head side to side and then launched toward the front door. Lotte fumbled over, waving the soot from her face.

"This is ridiculous!" Lotte spat between coughs, throwing the front door open.

Nilka rushed outside, her milky body a faint glow as she glided across the yard and into the forest. Meanwhile, Lotte hurried to each window, expertly unlatching the shutters and throwing them wide open. She snatched an oven mitt and vigorously waved it through the air, attempting to create a flow of circulation and guide the stifling dust towards the outdoors. Gradually, the particles began to settle, relieving Lotte of the suffocating sensation. With a sigh of relief, she ceased her frantic motions, finally breathing again without expelling a lung.

Well, Lotte and her father certainly did not account for cleaning the stove while he was away. Given the stove's small size, Lotte should have been emptying the ash box every evening. Now, it overflowed onto the floor! Huffing, she swept the mess as best as she could with a broom, scooped the debris from inside the firebox, and loaded kindling and wood inside of it. Lighting another fire took as long as she expected, and when the wood glowed red hot and flames reached past the flue collar, she was covered in a thick, powdery layer of ash and soot.

Cooking Emerick's food was not supposed to take this long! Lotte was eager to discuss their plan of getting him the Elixir of Life without being caught so he could fulfill his promise and leave Twisp forever. And hopefully, he would keep his word and not tell Bouldermaul of their location.

With newly rekindled determination, Lotte boiled the water in the pot, ignoring the bits of ash on the surface, and threw in the ingredients. The fish cooked fast, and the leafy greens wilted into slimy strings. She seasoned the water with salt and juice left over from the rockfish jar. The soup was simple and most likely one of the worst things Lotte had ever made, but she was tired, and Emerick hardly deserved anything more. Once a layer of fish fat coagulated along the edge of the pot, Lotte filled a bowl and carried it on a tray with a spoon and an overly ripe nightfruit.

Lotte realized that returning to the basement without Nilka was incredibly risky, but the wingless wyvern needed to hunt. Lotte at least left the front door open, hoping Nilka would hear her whistles and screams from wherever she hunted. Approaching the enclosure, Emerick's eyes locked onto the food, and he visibly shook with hunger. Ignoring the twinge in her chest, Lotte unlocked the enclosure and slid the tray to him.

As she closed the panel, Lotte expected the Firewraith to attack the food like a starving dog. Yet, he picked up the spoon with trembling hands and dipped it into the soup, stirring the contents around while inspecting its contents. He smelled the broth and went as far as picking out a chunk of fish and peeling it apart.

"What are you doing?" Lotte asked.

He fished out some of the leafy greens. "What are these?"

"Mustard leaves," she said dully. Then his strange actions dawned on Lotte. "Are you looking for poison?"

He glanced at her briefly with an empty expression before he observed the fruit.

Lotte barked a laugh. "I'm not that kind of person. I'm not like you or the other dogs of Bouldermaul."

Emerick was silent despite the barb. He forwent the spoon and brought the bowl straight to his mouth. His face crinkled as his body jolted, no doubt finding the food revolting. Yet, he did not complain. The soup was gone in several large gulps, and he moved to the fruit, rubbing the smooth, dark purple skin. Lotte reluctantly explained he would need to peel the fruit, first.

"You don't need to keep me chained anymore," he said, sounding as exhausted as Lotte felt. "I swore on my mother's life that I would not harm you or your home."

Lotte snorted. "Nice try."

Dropping the fruit's skin to the stone ground, Emerick bit into one of the fleshy bulbs on the inside. Juice rained down his chin and neck. This time he froze, turned his head, and spit the palm fruit out. He hacked several times and wiped an arm across his mouth.

"That tastes like a plum mixed with old onion," he said.

"It's nightfruit," Lotte said, "common in southern Holan."

"Is it supposed to taste that awful?"

"I think it's delicious."

Emerick scrunched his face. He set the nightfruit back onto the tray before he stared at Lotte for a long, uncomfortable moment.

"What?" Lotte narrowed her eyes.

"I cannot believe you are the daughter of Orm Skale," he said.

"Why is that so hard to believe?" She raised a challenging brow.

He was silent.

"I lied for you." Lotte uttered the words so softly that if Emerick had not shifted, lips thinning, she would have thought he had not heard. "Everyone in Twisp thinks you are dead. They have stopped looking for you."

"Am I supposed to thank you?"

She bristled but kept her tone even. "You owe me a debt."

"A debt!" he guffawed. "Explain to me why you think so."

"They won't try and capture you now."

"I highly doubt that. Please, by all means, tell me how you convinced them I died," he smirked.

"I gave them your armor." Lotte took pleasure in seeing his face fall.

"You what!" he shouted, and she tensed.

"They came to the hatchery and found your armor. I told them you walked into a swarm of pixies and were eaten."

The Firewraith hauled himself to his feet and leaned forward until the chains strained. His hands grayed as the cuffs dug into his skin. "Do you know what you've done? That armor nullifies magic! It was my only defense, you fool!"

Lotte disregarded the insult and addressed the glaring issue in Emerick's logic. "You do realize the only thing that nullifies magic is magic, right? Bouldermaul must have used an enchantment."

"The armor is not enchanted," he scoffed. "It is made from a special material that stops magic upon contact."

"Oh, yeah? What's the material called?"

Emerick lips pinched together, eyes narrowing. His fists clenched and unclenched with frustration. His silence told Lotte that he did not know.

"Ha!" Lotte snapped her fingers at the Firewraith. "Maybe you aren't a hypocrite, after all. You're just brainwashed." She could not believe Emerick lacked the ability to recognize manacore and the knowledge of enchantments.

"Excuse me?"

"You know a lot about a lot of things, but nothing about magic."

"I assure you I know more about — "

"This — " she tapped the warm, glowing end of her torch " — is manacore. It's been combined with a helyait rune to produce light."

Emerick opened his mouth to speak, but Lotte barreled on.

"Manacore contains minerals that are the essence of non-organic magic. Users mold it into runes for whatever magic they desire. In your case, Bouldermaul must have enchanted your armor with magic in the same way that helyaits enchanted my torch to produce light." She pointed to the shackles binding Emerick. "These cuffs cancel magic. My father bought it from a trader years ago. Can you guess what he discovered? It's made of manacore. The cuffs are the same material as your armor."

"That's absurd!" He shook his head. "You're telling me

that Bouldermaul lied to all of his followers and is, in actuality, using magic to end magic?"

"If you don't believe me, then you can — "

A crash from upstairs cut off Lotte. Both she and Emerick tensed, heads turning toward the stairs. It had sounded like ceramic breaking. Lotte remembered leaving the front door open, and she wondered if something sneaked in. It was still too soon for Nilka to return from a hunt.

"What was that?" Emerick said, pressing his forehead and hands against the glass.

The hairs rose on Lotte's arms, and she pulled out her blowgun. Giving Emerick a grim look, Lotte crept toward the stairs and stepped lightly as she ascended the steps. At the top, she grasped the doorknob to the kitchen — but stopped. A scraping sound, like a straw broom dragging along the floor, from the other side of the wall caused her to hesitate. The movements were larger than those of a raccoon or mink that might be scavenging for food.

A breeze hit Lotte's face when she peeked into the kitchen, wheezing through the open front door from the darkness of night. While the soot had cleared, the smell of charcoal lingered. Only the stove casted a faint glow, reflecting off broken ceramic shards of what caused the shattering noise she and Emerick had heard: The leftover fermented rockfish from the soup had fallen off the kitchen counter.

But how?

Skrrrt.

Lotte whipped her head toward the ice chest. The scraping sound!

Skrrrt. Skrrrt.

Holding her torch up, an abnormally tall woman appeared across the kitchen. Lotte yelped, startled by their visitor, but calmed now that she knew some wild animal had not invaded her home — or worse, another Firewraith. She chuckled nervously, studying the woman's chalky white face, shrouded by the wormy strands of black hair that cascaded down her unclothed body and hid her private regions. That rang alarm bells in Lotte's mind.

"Can I help you?" Lotte found it within her to ask, grip tightening on her blowgun.

The woman said nothing, and Lotte felt even more uneasy. Was the woman hurt? Why was she naked? Was she a customer of her father's? She doubted it.

The sound of clicking drew Lotte's attention below the woman's abdomen where her skin morphed into thick brown fur of what appeared to be a giant spider's abdomen. Two arm-sized fangs tapped together — *clicking* — under a ring of eight beady eyes.

Lotte screamed and jerked backward, losing her footing on the stairs. She shot her hand out, catching the rail, but her sweaty fingers slipped and she fell. White light flashed across her vision as her head smacked against a step. Lotte barely registered herself sliding the rest of the way down into the basement, or Emerick calling out her name.

Lotte lay in shock, blinking rapidly as her senses dulled and thoughts dwindled away until all she could process was the rasping of her breath. She was oblivious of how much time passed — for all she knew, she could have fallen asleep — but when awareness returned to her, so did the pain and reason for her urgency.

An arachnea had entered her house.

Click. Click.

Gaze flickering to the top of the stairs, Lotte found the arachnea staring directly at her and realized the "woman" partially slumped on its back was actually a lure. Based on what she had read in her father's field journals, the lure replicated the prey that the arachnea's prey consumed. It lacked eyes or a mouth — just indents on an awry face.

Lotte sucked in a breath. She kicked her legs and propelled herself across the basement floor, until her back hit the enclosure. The panel vibrated from Emerick slapping the glass, demanding to know what was going on.

Where was her blowgun? If she was forced to fight the arachnea, she would need the dart dipped in wyvern venom. Yet, when she felt around her body, lifting her cloak so she could see underneath, her blowgun was nowhere. She must have dropped it when she fell down the stairs.

A creak from the upper landing sent Lotte's heart racing. She scrambled to her feet, hollered out *"alsum"* as she pressed her hand against the manacore lock, and slid the panel open with a grunt, before she joined a shocked Emerick in the mock habitat. Shutting them inside, Lotte grabbed the Firewraith's wrists and unlocked him from his chains before freeing his ankles. She beckoned him into the empty stone pool. They climbed inside, and Lotte forced them onto their bellies. She prayed the slanted wall of the pool was enough to hide them. Lotte dared to peer over.

Skrrrt. Skrrrt.

The creaking and scraping grew louder, and the arachnea slowly came into view. It crept to the torch Lotte had left in the center of the floor. Shadows casting across the human-like lure's face gave it a hollow appearance.

With each step of the arachnea's segmented legs, Lotte's breath seized. She clamped her hand over her mouth to muffle a rising cry. Maybe if she was completely still and silent, the arachnea would think she was a rock or miss her presence entirely. However, Lotte knew that was wishful thinking.

The arachnea could smell the sweat on her skin — feel the

vibration of blood flowing through her veins.

The terrifying creature approached the glass, the *skrrrt*-ing noise coming from the hooks of its legs dragging on the floor, and it stopped only when it bumped the panel.

Time seemed to freeze as Lotte stared into the ring of black eyes. She had never seen an arachnea, only ever reading about them, as they lived in the Immorthial Forest. Of course, the arachnea was more horrifying than what he had written. Lotte jumped when Emerick placed a hand on her back, leaning toward her to whisper.

"What do we — "

The arachnea pounced.

Fangs pierced the enclosure's panel. The glass cracked into jagged webs, somehow still standing. Lotte shrieked as oily liquid dripped onto the rocks. If being impaled did not kill them, then its venom would.

Arms wrapped around her waist and lifted her to her feet. Emerick guided her to the back of the enclosure.

"Where is my sword!" he demanded.

Lotte opened her mouth but the arachnea retracted its fangs and lunged again. The cracks in the glass stretched across the entirety of the panel. One more hit and there would be nothing between them and death.

"My sword! Where is it?" Emerick shouted.

The arachnea removed its fangs.

"Behind the incubator." Her voice quaked, gesturing to the giant chest made of manacore across the basement room.

The arachnea crouched, readying for a third attempt.

"Dodge the side and get to my sword. I'll distract it."

Lotte wondered how the Firewraith planned to hold off the bear-sized creature, but she never got a chance to ask.

The panel exploded. They threw arms over their faces as glass sprayed them, the noise deafening. Lotte had not realized she screamed until it died in her throat.

She expected the arachnea to catch her right away, but as she lowered her arm, blinking rapidly through all the dust kicked into the air, she found the creature shaking off jagged shards like a wet dog. Some larger pieces lodged into the top of its body.

Emerick pushed her toward the opening. "Go!"

Lotte lowered herself out of the enclosure, the debris crunching under her boots, and she darted along the wall and toward the incubator. The movement attracted the arachnea, though, and it scrambled after her, no longer dazed by its injuries.

Fangs struck the ground mere centimeters from Lotte's feet. She felt the hairs of the arachnea catch on her cloak, and she threw herself forward, landing on her knees. Hook-clawed legs stamped on both sides of her face, and bile rose in her throat. Her arms gave, and she collapsed to the ground. Rolling over, Lotte faced the arachnea looming over her. Its chelicerates lifted up, fangs extending to their full length, before —

Emerick slammed his body into the arachnea, shoving it away from Lotte.

"Run!" he shouted.

Wasting no time, Lotte struggled to her feet, legs quaking, and she headed towards the stairs. The sword was out of question now, so retreating was the only other option. Yet, Emerick was still grappling with the arachnea, his arms encompassing the dip where the head and the abdomen connected. If he let go, he would surely be bitten.

Despite Emerick being a Firewraith, Lotte could not just leave him. Such cowardice would make her no better than him and his comrades, especially since he risked his life to save hers. Plus, if he perished, then Bouldermaul would investigate his disappearance. Lotte searched around for something to help. Her eyes landed on her missing blowgun, partially hidden under knocked-over boxes.

Gasping, Lotte retrieved the pouch of darts from her inner cloak pockets. With a steady hand, she pulled out a metal dart from her canister and the vial of Scorn's venom she had taken from her father's chest two days ago. Uncorking the vial, she carefully dipped the dart into the oily substance, ensuring the lethal venom coated the tip thoroughly. She lifted the dart out, holding it just above the glass flange as a drop fell back into the vial. The last thing she wanted was to get any excess venom on her fingers or hand. Holding it away from her body, she blew on the dart until it was dry. Then, with precision, Lotte retrieved the blowgun and loaded the tube, brought the mouthpiece to her lips, and aimed for the arachnea's abdomen. She blew.

The dart hit just above its spinnerets.

The arachnea continued to struggle in Emerick's hold, chelicercea shifting its fangs until they were inches from his leg, and Lotte wondered if it was immune to Scorn's venom. That was impossible, though! According to her father, the wyvern was the most venomous creature in Asoleenya. Nothing survived its bite. Maybe Lotte needed a larger dose?

As she loaded her blowgun with another dart laced with venom, the arachnea froze.

An ear-splitting hiss filled the air, and the arachnea began thrashing violently, hind legs scratching at where the dart entered its body. Emerick sensed the arachnea was no longer attacking him, and he let go and rushed towards the stairs, stopping beside Lotte briefly to watch the venom take hold, melting the arachnea's exoskeleton around the dart.

The venom worked!

"Let's leave," Emerick said.

Upstairs, they slammed the door shut, breathing heavily

against the frame, before they stepped away. Lotte cringed as the arachnea's pained screeches seeped through the floorboards.

"We should barricade the door," Emerick said. "Just in case."

Lotte nodded.

Together, they pushed the kitchen table against the door and stacked everything they could find on top and underneath: chairs, storage chests, and even sacks of potatoes.

"That should do it, right?" Emerick looked at Lotte.

"I-I don't know," she said.

"Aren't you a magical creature expert?" he demanded.

"That's my father's role," she said, snappishly. "I know what I've read from his journals, and none of them explained what to do if an arachnea invaded your home!"

Watching Emerick drag a hand down his sweaty face, another realization dawned on Lotte as her adrenaline tapered. Emerick was out of the enclosure. There was nothing preventing him from attacking her and destroying the hatchery. Her grip tightened on her blowgun, and she inched toward her darts. Their eyes met. Something flickered across his face, probably noticing his freedom as well. As Emerick took a step toward her, Lotte raised her blowgun to her mouth.

Chapter Eleven
Trials of Cooperation

Emerick shot his hand out and slapped the blowgun from Lotte's fingers. It clattered to the floor as the girl stumbled backward, fear evident in her eyes. She tripped over something on the ground and fell on her rump. Scrambling to put distance between them, she searched around the kitchen, no doubt, for her gargantuan snake.

Wyvern, Emerick corrected himself.

"We already made a truce," he said. "I stand by my word."

Without waiting for a response, Emerick took a seat at the table. His muscles were sore from lying in one position for most of the two days he spent chained in the basement. Lack of sleep and the battle with the arachnea resulted in a bone-deep ache. Emerick wanted nothing more than to sleep for a month . . . or, realistically, until dawn. Of course, he needed to make sure Lotte would not stick him with another dart and feed him to her wyverns — or worse, the monster shrieking from below their feet.

"I cannot believe we are alive." Emerick propped his elbows on the table and dropped his head into his hands.

He heard Lotte push herself to her feet. A drag of wood told Emerick that she retrieved her blowgun, and he cracked an eyelid and turned to watch her. Lotte stood awkwardly, hood off and scarf missing, form visibly shaking. Small splatters of blood dotted her dirty face, and a lump the size of small apple visibly swelled underneath her hair, on the side of her head. She most likely had a concussion from her tumble down the stairs and was incredibly lucky not to have worse injuries. No doubt, adrenalin was keeping her on her feet.

Emerick shifted, wincing when his crusty clothes grated against his skin. "If you can tell me how I can have a bath, that would be appreciated."

"What?" Lotte sounded confused.

"A bath? Ever heard of one? Judging by the mud on your face, that's a no."

"Mud!" She patted her flushing cheeks. "These are birthmarks, you mutt!" She then yanked her hood back on.

Emrick sniffed at the nickname. At least the girl snapped out of her stupor.

"I'll need some blankets for sleep, something I haven't done much thanks to your wonderful hospitality." All of his camping supplies were, unfortunately, with Bones. Emerick's heart weighed heavily as he thought of his horse.

Firewraiths were sworn against relationships beyond absolute devotion to His Highness and his hierarchy of chivalry, as friends and even family were a liability. Although Emerick understood that, he would be lying if he denied the deep loneliness that came with the honor of his position. Bones was the closest thing that could settle that ache. The thought that the horse had been unattended for two days sickened Emerick. He hoped tying Bones near a water source was enough to sustain him until he could retrieve him in the morning.

"Well?" Emerick forced his mind back to the present.

Lotte's grip tightened on her blowgun, and her face contorted with contempt. "First, you must agree that you owe me a debt."

Was she seriously still on that topic? Lying to the helyaits was on her, not him. Plus, she did not exactly spare him when she trapped him under her wyvern, as well as denied him food and water. However, if complying meant he could bathe and wash his soiled clothes, then he would. For now.

"Fine." He raised his hand to mock-swear. "I owe you my deepest gratitude."

Lotte scoffed at his sarcastic tone.

"Can I wash up now?" he asked.

Glaring at him for a moment, Lotte jerked a thumb toward the pump sink. A metal wash tub was shoved underneath. "You will need to warm the water on the stove. Soap is in a bucket next to the tub."

"How about a towel and fresh clothes?" Emerick knew he was testing his luck, but the girl nodded, left the kitchen down a short hallway, and disappeared into what he assumed was a bedroom. Alone, Emerick crouched in front of the stove to add more wood. As the fire roared, the light it produced allowed Emerick enough visibility to move around comfortably.

Dragging the metal tub close to the stove, Emerick used the bucket holding the soap to fill with water at the sink and pour into the tub. He mentally cursed this primitive method, missing the plumbing of his quarters in Guldkem. Although a warm bath was tempting, cleaning all the grime off his body trumped such luxury. Plus, the night's air was warm, and he would have the stove's heat against his back.

Lotte returned with not only a towel and clothes but also two thick blankets and a pillow. She dumped them on the table and left in silence, slamming the door as she retreated into another room. Too bad, Emerick almost thanked her.

When the tub was full, Emerick dipped his fingers in the cool water. It was considerably warmer than the streams and lakes he had bathed in while on missions with his squad. He stripped himself of his clothes and slowly stepped in, goosebumps forming on his arms and legs. He waited until his body acclimated to the temperature change before washing himself. The process took only a few minutes, and when he was finished and dressed again, he proceeded to wash his dirty clothes in the tub. Emerick dragged a chair closer to the stove and draped the wet clothes over the back so they would dry.

Feeling cleaner and fresher since starting his two-month journey, the soft scent of flowers lingering on his skin from the soap, Emerick folded the blankets in half and laid them on the ground. He exhaled, eyes dropping as he lay down. The straw-stuffed pillow was rustic compared to the goose-feather ones he had in his quarters, but it certainly was better than using his arm or a rock on the outside ground. Exhaustion fizzled his thoughts, and within seconds, he was asleep.

Emerick crept out of the cabin just as the morning light filled the kitchen, rays slipping through the cracks on the window shutters and awakening his internal clock. When the sun is up, so should he — one of the many things Firewraith training taught him. He explored Orm Skale's property, cataloging the layout, noting the six raised vegetable beds, the stone path that led to the surrounding forest, and the chicken coop and rabbit hutch next to a crooked shed. What intrigued him the most was the glass dome. While condensation on the window panes obscured his view, he could make out the silhouettes of tall tropical trees and vegetation.

Something told him that it was not a normal greenhouse. Despite the hairs on his neck rising, curiosity won the better of his judgment, and he gripped the door handle.

"What are you doing?"

Emerick jumped, fingers slipping, and spun around to find Lotte dressed in her cloak and scarf, blowgun in one hand while the other rested on the raised head of her wyvern. Although only a small section of her face was visible, Emerick could tell it was scrunched with distrust. He expected nothing less, but he still pinched his lips and crossed his arms.

"Relax, I was just looking around," he said.

"We're to make your elixir, and then you're leaving. Nothing else." Lotte pushed past him and checked The Aviary's door, jiggling the knob to show it was locked.

"Fine," he relented. "What's the first step of making the Elixir of Life?"

"Gathering ingredients," she said, as though it was the most obvious thing in the world, and Emerick wanted to sneer. He composed himself, though, not giving her the satisfaction.

"And what ingredients must we gather?" he asked.

Lotte ignored his question, crouching down in front of Nilka, whose scales blinded like as snow in the sunlight. "Stay here, girl. You'll be safer," Lotte cooed and rubbed a hand down the wyvern's back.

Emerick gaped as the girl treated the monstrous creature like a dog. And it acted like one, too! Listening to Lotte's words, the wyvern slithered to a soft patch of grass next to the chicken coop, watching the hens peck at grain that Lotte must have put out for them earlier. Oddly, he had not heard her wake up that morning. He would have roused to someone exiting and entering the cabin's front door. Perhaps there was another entrance?

"You seem lively who fought off an arachnea with a head injury," he snarked. "Let me guess — you have a potion for bruises and stuff."

Her eyes narrowed, and Emerick assumed he was right.

"Let's go." Lotte said coldly. She marched toward the jungle.

"Are you going to tell me where we're going? Or what we're getting?" he asked, rooted to his spot.

Lotte called over her shoulder. "You can follow me or stay here. I don't care. No more talking."

Emerick bristled. He should at least be told how long they would be away so he could determine what survival supplies to bring. Even a short hike required food, water, and first aid. Better to prepare for the worst than be caught off guard. Obviously, Lotte disregarded this philosophy — or never thought of it in the first place — for she entered the jungle without an ounce of caution.

Left behind in front of the hatchery, Emerick's attention fell onto Nilka. The size of her head, easily larger than his two fists combined, made his stomach queasy. She flicked her tongue and flared the vents of her upper lip. Emerick cringed, a shiver running through his body. He rejected the thought of staying with the wyvern until Lotte returned, and he quickly bolted after her.

Lotte led him on a worn path until they reached a mossy creek, scented heavily of rotting fruit from a nearby date tree, before she stepped off trail, unsheathing a medium scimitar sword from inside her cloak. Alarmed, Emerick purposely stood out of range. He would have to be careful of what else the girl had hidden on her person. Lotte began hacking vines and thick shrubbery out of their way. She was slow and obviously untrained, chopping the sections of foliage multiple times when it should only take one swift swipe. Emerick considered offering to cut a path for them . . . but he knew her response would not be welcoming.

Instead, he compared the lush, tropical foliage to the rugged pines of his home, where hardly any shrubs grew and he could see between their trunks for miles. The climate in the outskirts of Guldkem was cold and crisp, not as severe as the snowy tundra of Ceris, but there were more days of winter than summer with only three or four days a year as hot as this region of southern Holan. The shirt he had borrowed was already drenched in sweat, and his throat constricted from thirst. Though he had guzzled water down throughout the night and early morning, he knew he was still dehydrated after two days of no liquids. He eyed Lotte's cloak, wondering if she had a canteen, but he was too proud to ask.

After an hour of clearing and taking short breaks for Lotte to rest her arms, they reached a break in the dense jungle, the peak of a hill overlooking a glade of tall palm grass. A hot breeze wafted floral scents from clouds of rust-red flowers that grew in large patches, giving the clearing a quilt-like appearance. Emerick licked a bead of salty sweat from his upper lip as he stared up at the pellucid sky. It, too, was vastly different from the constant overcast of his home.

What weather was Guldkem experiencing at this exact moment? It had been spring when he had left two months ago. That meant summer was now drying the sopping, dreary days. Emerick pictured his mother sitting with pillows propped behind her back, window open, and her umber eyes closed as she inhaled fresh air. How stifling must it be for her to require assistance just to walk across the room. The simple act of brushing her silky hair had become too tiring, resulting in mangled mats before she decided to simply chop it all off. Progress and setbacks with her health occurred hourly. Emerick tried not to think of her deterioration over the past two months. And he still had to travel back to Guldkem!

Was she still alive?

Enough! Emerick almost shouted aloud. Now was not the time to have such thoughts. He pinched the skin of the top of his hand until the pain stole his focus. Then, he exhaled and let go.

As Emerick returned to his senses, he realized they had been standing on the edge of the clearing for a while. Lotte was abnormally still, her eyes shaded by her hood, and after more time passed, Emerick could no longer abide by her earlier request of no talking.

"Why have we stopped?" he asked.

Lotte shushed him immediately. Emerick felt his patience waning, but before he could complain, a deafening squeal pierced the glade's peaceful atmosphere. Emerick jumped back, raising his fists and crouching in a defensive stance. The eerie sound was accompanied by primal grunts emanating from the depths of the tall palm grass. Lotte crept forward, waving for Emerick to follow, and they silently descended the hill and crossed the clearing. The stench of feces hit Emerick, and he covered his mouth as he gagged. Slowing to a stop, Lotte lowered to her hands and knees, and then to her belly. Emerick copied her actions. Peering through the swaying blades, he caught sight of the massive, hairy backs of several behemoth creatures, resembling boars the size of bull moose.

"What are those?" Emerick whispered.

"Entelodonts," Lotte said. "They are cousins of pigs."

"More like wolves." He tracked the fang-like tusks protruding from their upper lips. "Do they eat meat? Humans?"

"Without hesitation."

"Lovely." Emerick's mouth became dry, and he fought a shiver. "What ingredient do we need from here?"

Lotte leered at him from underneath her furrowed brows. An unsettling feeling filled his belly. Her silence spoke louder than words.

"*They* are the ingredients?" he said, voice squeaking.

His hand twitched to where he normally kept his sword. He

was without any gear that would help him in this situation, and he doubted hand-to-hand combat would do much against a beast larger than a draft horse.

Lotte smirked. "One of their byproducts."

"Like what? Hair? Pee? Please don't tell me you use their feces."

Emerick's stomach churned when she raised an eyebrow. Reaching into her cloak, Lotte pulled out an empty cork bottle. She gave it to him.

"Fresh urine is ideal. Try not to upset them. They will eat you."

"This is absurd! You cannot be serious!"

"I'll be collecting herbs over there." She pointed back to the edge of the clearing.

Emerick balked. "Why can't you collect the pee? You obviously have experience with these beasts."

"Can you tell the difference between flowering wild carrots and Weeping Queen's Yarrow? One neutralizes the wyvern venom used in the Elixir of Life, the other does nothing. So if you don't want to accidentally kill your mother, I suggest you leave the harvesting to me. There are ten different plants I need to collect."

Sighing with resignation, Emerick turned back to the entelodonts as they rutted their massive jaws along the ground, teasing him with how easily they could split his body in half with just one bite. The ground vibrated every time one slammed a hoof down. This was a terrible, terrible, idea, but he had no choice. He needed that elixir.

"I'll do it," he said.

"Good luck," Lotte said, and she crawled back the way they came.

Emerick maneuvered forward until only a thin layer of grass blades separated him from the herd of entelodonts. He counted ten of them, six adults and four young — all enjoying the half-rotten remains of a deer. Their hot breaths ghosted his cheeks.

He did not have to wait long for one to relieve itself. A trickling sound came from the largest entelodont, and Emerick fumbled with the bottle, popping off the cork. His excitement was fleeting, though, as he realized he had no way of reaching the puddle pooling on the ground. He could not exactly walk into a herd of omnivorous beasts with hooves larger than his head. He would need to move the herd without upsetting them.

Actually . . . the thought of angering the entelodonts gave Emerick an idea. He doubted he could scare them away from the deer carcass long enough for him to fill the bottle. Perhaps getting them riled up enough to charge was a solution. The only question was whether or not he could outrun them.

Slowly rising to his feet, Emerick dragged a rock along with him and chucked it at the herd, hand trembling as it dropped back to his side. A grunt followed a faint *thrawp*, and Emerick held his breath.

Nothing.

He reached down again and felt around the mud for more rocks, hucking them one, two, three more times — all with no results. He aimed as best he could without giving away his position, but the rock bounced off the entelodonts' thick hide.

Emerick froze when a high-pitched whine sounded from next to him. One of the young entelodonts poked its head through the grass and roamed its soppy snout along his leg. Its back reached Emerick's hips when standing, and tiny tusks were just beginning to emerge.

The young entelodont opened its mouth to bite Emerick, but he jumped back just in time. He was afraid that the sudden movement would cause alarm, yet the young entelodont huffed the ground where Emerick once stood before moving forward, searching for the fresh meat of his leg. Slowly retracing his earlier steps, Emerick tried to place distance between them, but the young entelodont was persistent. Before he knew it, Emerick had led it astray from the herd and halfway to the jungle's edge.

Emerick's lips tugged into a small smile, as he realized the opportunity the young entelodont presented. If he could capture and keep it preoccupied until it urinated, then he could collect the ingredient without alerting the herd. Continuing to walk backward, Emerick stretched out his hand and let the young entelodont sniff his flesh, coaxing it near the tree line. He jerked his hand back every time the hot spray of breath came too close. With his other hand, he awkwardly undid the belt Lotte had provided last night. Emerick risked looking away to fix a loop large enough to go over the young entelodont's head, and then he reached out one last time to draw the beast closer. Belt ready, Emerick's body tensed, heart thudding as the young entelodont ignorantly took another step forward.

Now!

Emerick lunged. He trapped the young entelodont and tightened the belt.

AHWEEEEEEE!

The squeal's velocity shocked Emerick, and he was swept off his feet as the young entelodont bucked and snapped its head back. It took all of Emerick's training not to let go of the belt. He landed heavily on his back, blinking through a flash of white light in his vision, before he was ripped side to side, his shoulder stretching further than it should, threatening dislocation. Emerick knew he must gain control.

Digging his boots into the ground, Emerick leaned all of his weight backward and caused the young entelodont to stumble. He shot around to its side and threw one arm over its neck and formed a headlock. The young entelodont's movements became frantic as Emerick applied pressure, its squeals forever scarring his ears.

Emerick barely noticed the hoof vibrations in the ground growing with magnitude. He screamed when the massive head of an adult entelodont, most likely the mother, burst into view with a strident roar.

Saliva dripped from her gaping maw, reeking of rot. When she spotted Emerick restraining her young, she howled and barreled toward him. Releasing his hold, Emerick spun around and leaped away. A tusk grazed his back, catching his shirt and tearing the fabric.

Out of instinct, Emerick sprinted toward the jungle. Hooves thundered after him. He saw Lotte sitting at the top of the hill, next to a basket of all sorts of freshly picked flowers and plant stems. Her wide, startled eyes met his, and without any logic whatsoever, Emerick changed course, narrowly avoiding being impaled, and headed straight toward Lotte. Perhaps together they could intimidate the entelodont.

A look of horror crossed Lotte's face. She stood, not bothering with the basket, and sprinted to the nearest tree, quickly starting to climb. There was no time for Emerick to follow. He darted behind another trunk just as the entelodont charged again, narrowly avoiding a deadly collision. Instead, the beast slammed into the tree, causing the leaves to rustle violently. While the entelodont paused to shake her head, Emerick scrambled to another tree, gripping the rough bark as he pulled himself up to the first branch. Another ear-splitting roar spurred him on, climbing until he was clinging to the highest branch that could support his weight.

The entelodont paced through the foliage, rutting the dirt for Emerick's scent. Eventually, she looked up, searching unsuccessfully as the leaves and vines shrouded him. However, her eyes locked on something nearby. Lotte. The foolish girl was on a branch only a meter above the entelodont. A cloud of snot sprayed from the raging beast's nose, and she rushed forward. Her temple slammed against the tree with such force that the wood groaned and splintered.

Lotte screamed, holding on for her life. The entelodont continued to push the trunk, stabbing tusks into the barks until the roots lifted out of the ground with a loud *RIIIIIIP*, raining dirt and other debris. Emerick thought the tree would fall, yet the entelodont tired and relented, leaving the tree at a dangerous angle. She stepped backward and readied to attack again.

This was not good. If Lotte fell, then it would be over for her. Emerick's entire mission would be for nothing.

And his mother. . . .

"Over here!" Emerick hollered, descending the branches. "Come get me!"

But he was too late.

The moment his boots hit the ground, the entelodont threw her mass and uprooted the tree completely. The thud drowned out Lotte's shriek as she was thrown backward into the leafy branches. The entelodont began searching the debris.

In an effort to save Lotte, or at least buy her time to run, Emerick shouted taunts and grabbed a large stick and threw it at the entelodont's head. She rounded on him, her dark eyes reflecting as he hesitated, arm frozen mid throw. Chest heaving and foam forming on the corners of her mouth, she was showing signs of tiring.

At the same time, Lotte's head poked out of the fallen tree, her hood no longer covering her face.

"Do you have your blowgun?" Emerick called, as the entelodont circled him.

"Y-Yes!" she stammered.

"Do you have a dart similar to what you used with the arachnea?"

"I do."

"Throw me your scimitar," he said, "and get ready to shoot."

Just as Lotte scrambled for the blade and hurled it through the air, the entelodont stomped her foot and bolted toward Emerick. He waited until the last second to jump out of the way, landing hard on his chest and rolling to where the scimitar had dropped. He hastened to his feet as the entelodont pounded her hoof where his head had once been.

"When a beast towers over you, go for its eyes," his mentor's crude voice rang through his mind.

The entelodont growled, opening her mouth to bite Emerick, but he lashed out with the scimitar and sliced her nose. Blood spurted. She jerked back and wailed. With the entelodont distracted, Emerick pivoted to her side and lunged the blade into her eye, ignoring the sickening squelch. A piercing scream tore from her throat, and she waved her head side to side, bucking and kicking her feet with pain and rage. Her body slammed into Emerick, and he fought to stay upright. Unfortunately, the force knocked the scimitar out of his hands. He had no time to look for it.

Then, the entelodont froze, breathing heavily as a shiver overcame her body. In the fallen tree beside them, Emerick saw Lotte lower her blowgun. Her face was grim.

The entelodont's body began jerking even more violently than before. A howl of pure agony caused the hair on Emerick's arms to rise. He dodged for cover, joining Lotte in the shroud of firm branches and leaves. Together, they ducked and crawled down until they met where the trunk sunk into the ground. Lotte covered her ears to drown out the horrendous noise.

Closing his eyes, Emerick tried to focus on something else. *Anything* else. It was then he felt Lotte's shoulder brush against his, the touch almost electrifying, reminding him that she was his enemy. Yet, as she quaked, her already small frame making her appear younger, Emerick could not help but compare her to the image His Highness had painted of magic users and their supporters. She was the opposite, in fact. Lotte had helped him win against the beast when she could have easily let him perish. So far, she was more trustworthy than a majority of his comrades.

The entelodont lasted for what seemed like an eternity, before a reverberating thud marked the end, and the cries dwindled to wheezy moans. Lowering her hands, Lotte looked to Emerick for direction. Emerick nodded to the opening above them, and he clambered out first.

He found the entelodont on her side, legs twitching and mouth opening and closing. A dart stuck out of its ribs. The skin around it had melted and revealed the inner flesh oozing blood and, to Emerick's horror, bone.

A chill ran through Emerick. What kind of poison had Lotte used that had such terrifying effects?

They approached the entelodont cautiously, watching as the fearsome creature took one last rattling breath and stilled. The forest around them was silent.

"What did you do?" Lotte asked shakily.

"I was getting the urine like you told me to!" Emerick's self-control slipped.

"Entelodonts are aggressive by nature, but my father has made peace with this particular herd," she said.

"Made peace? What does that mean? He tamed them?"

"Taming implies that he has some level of control over them, which he does not. They have a relationship, one that allows us to approach them without being trampled."

"You couldn't have given me this information? Why all the theatrics before? You didn't act like you could stroll up to them when we first entered the glade!"

"I hadn't expected you to abduct their young!"

Emerick pinched the bridge of his nose. "We could have avoided all of this had you just spoken up. The way the creature died . . . words can't even describe." Sure, he hunted boars and deer at home, but it was out of necessity. His family needed to eat! This . . . this was purely negligence.

"As if you care."

A growl rumbled in Emerick's chest, and he admitted begrudgingly, "Not all of King Bouldermaul's Firewraiths are killers."

"Just like how not all magic and magical creatures are evil?" Lotte fired back. "You're a hypocrite. What is one entelodont compared to the hundreds of people you've murdered for your wretched king!"

Emerick brought his hands up to the tuft of hair on top of his head, gripping them painfully by their roots, and he roared with frustration. Lotte startled and lifted her blowgun in a defensive stance. Forcing himself to take several deep breaths, Emerick relaxed his body and mentally grasped the little control he had left of his emotions.

"Unfortunately, other than livestock and game animals, I haven't had the opportunity to kill magic-supporting scum," Emerick mumbled.

It was a bitter truth that shamed him to his core. No matter how much he wanted to, no matter how many times he had been flogged when he could not, Emerick wanted to execute His Highness' order of exterminating magic. Yet, when it came down to actually killing an intelligent life — a human being — he wavered. His thoughts would drift to their mothers, and sometimes his own. Could he stand the guilt of being the one who ended their offsprings' lives? Emerick had threatened, destroyed property, and beaten people unconscious — but he had never killed. It was that reason he had never progressed past his apprenticeship.

Killing the entelodont was not the same as offing a sentient being, but he still ended a life and orphaned the young entelodont from earlier. The fact that a small piece of information could have prevented the entire situation made him even madder.

"I'm sorry." Lotte crouched down beside the entelodont and placed a hand on her tough skin. "My father and I have a rule — all life must be treated delicately and with compassion. If death must occur, we have the responsibility to ensure it happens humanely — no suffering."

Emerick exhaled, shoulders sagging. He rubbed his forehead where a headache bloomed behind his eye. All the anger flooded out of him, and he was left a deep emptiness. He wondered, for a moment, if this was all a nightmare — that his mother was not sick, and he had simply fallen asleep with Bones in the stables after a day of grueling training.

"I purposely didn't tell you," Lotte said, face flush and tears forming in her eyes. "I was wrong."

They stood in silence as Emerick processed her apology. Her decision being "wrong" was an understatement, but he could not exactly blame her. He was her enemy, after all. She should be doing everything in her power to get rid of him. Not sabotaging him in some way was, well, impossible. Yet, an illogical part of him felt a thread of betrayal. Here he had told her all about his mother and made a promise to withhold information about Orm Skale and Twisp from His Highness, which was considered treason, and Lotte pulled a stunt like this!

Emerick was exhausted. It had not even been a day since their fight with the arachnea!

"We can extract the bladder for urine," Lotte remarked. Normally, entelodonts are edible, but I don't recommend eating this one since the venom is in its bloodstream."

"You dip your darts into venom?" Emerick tilted his head.

"Yes, I milk the wyverns."

"Wait a moment," he grew alarmed, "was the wyvern you left with me venomous?"

Lotte smirked but shook her head. "Each breed of wyvern has a unique set of properties, some magical and some not. Nilka is non-venomous, remember? But her size makes her deadly. She is the largest wyvern my father has ever rescued."

Emerick accepted the response, changing the subject to a more pressing matter. "What ingredient do we obtain next?"

"Other than the urine and plants that I may need to re-harvest, we have everything else at the hatchery." Lotte said, patting her cloak. Her eyebrows scrunched together as she frowned. Opening her cloak, she checked the various pockets inside, and then the small pouches on her belt. Her face paled behind all her freckles. "Oh, no," she whispered and searched the ground for whatever she had lost.

The girl circled the entelodont and even crawled back into the fallen tree. After a few minutes, Emerick caught a muffled curse. Lotte resurfaced and sat on the trunk, dropping her head into her hands.

"What's wrong?" he asked, concerned. "Tell me!"

"The final ingredient was in my pocket. It fell out, and the tree crushed it," she said.

His heart picked up pace. "Can we get more?"

Lotte exhaled, finally looking up and gazing into the jungle.

"Lotte!" Emerick needed answers!

"We can." Her voice was full of dread. "Are you ready to meet the most venomous wyvern in all of Asoleenya?"

Chapter Twelve
SCORN

Water sloshed over the edge of a cooking pot as Lotte slammed it onto the hot kitchen stove. She added another log to the fire before heading to the table where all the ingredients lay in bowls — all except one. Behind them was the alembic still. Brewing the Elixir of Life would take twelve hours of intensive care: timed stirring between each ingredient, different temperatures depending on the stage, and monitoring a consistent simmer in the alembic. It was a tedious but doable process.

The difficult part was milking Scorn's venom. No, "difficult" was an understatement. It was more like a death sentence.

The air in the kitchen became stuffy suddenly, and Lotte staggered to the front door, stepping outside for the fresh breeze. She spotted Nilka still sunbathing since finding a comfy spot this morning, the middle portion of her body descended from whatever she caught last night for food. Approaching her, Lotte sat down and smiled when the wyvern moved her head onto Lotte's lap. Reaching up to trace the crests above Nilka's eyes, Lotte surveyed the rest of the compound.

Where was Emerick?

Shame washed over her as she recalled the incident with the entelodont. The Firewraith was turning out nothing like the bloodthirsty murderer she had expected him to be. His dedication to his mother and reaction to the entelodont proved he had a fragment of heart. Yet, he could not be forgiven for what he had done to Mrs. Gibbs and, according to Healer Aklea, the injured helyait left to die in the sun.

Emerick confused her.

Nilka yawned, rotating her massive jaws and showing off her impressive rows of curved teeth. Her fangs were longer than Lotte's middle finger.

"Of course, you're tired!" Lotte said, massaging down the wingless wyvern until she reached the first mound of scars where her wing had once been. The area was still sensitive after all these years. "It looks like you found yourself a fawn or perhaps a howler monkey."

"Lotte," Emerick said from behind.

Lotte yelped and jumped to her feet, Nilka slipping off her legs. She adjusted her cloak, double-checking that her hood and scarf were in place. Her face was no longer a secret with him, but habit was habit. Where had he come from?

"I made noise so you would know I was approaching." Emerick crossed his arms.

"Where have you been?" she demanded.

"To the cliff stairs." Sweat glistened on his forehead.

"What! Why? Did anyone see you?" The last thing she needed was for Remi or Healer Aklea to discover the truth about the Firewraith.

"I was looking for my horse," he said, his tone rigid. "He's gone. Do you have any idea what happened to him?"

Humming, Lotte raked her mind for the conversation she had with Healer Aklea the other day. He had mentioned the town's guards discovering the Firewraith's horse, but he never delved into what they did with it. This was a concern, as Emerick would need a horse to return home.

An animalistic growl from the Firewraith startled Lotte, and she tensed as his body shook with barely contained ire.

"I will kill the person who harms a hair on Bones' body," he whispered.

"No one will harm your horse," she promised. "The helyaits of this pod are gentle. Despite your crimes, they would never fault your horse. Likely, they brought him somewhere and are currently taking care of him."

Emerick stared at her in utter disbelief.

"I'll ask about your horse the next time I'm in town," Lotte said, though she would have to come up with some sort of excuse as to why she was interested in the first place.

He exhaled loudly, fists unclenching. "Are we ready to start making the Elixir of Life?"

"First, we need to feed all the wyverns, including the one we will be milking," Lotte said, a little unnerved by his drastic switch in emotions. "Otherwise, he will be too aggressive to handle."

"Shall we get started, then?" Emerick sounded eager.

Lotte clicked her tongue. "We? You plan on helping me?"

"If it means starting the potion sooner, then yes."

"Hmmm." She rubbed her chin thoughtfully. "You must listen to my instructions without argument. Wyverns are not just snakes with wings. They're cunning and far more dangerous." While she spoke, she had déjà vu of her father giving her this same speech.

"As long as you promise not to repeat what happened this morning and deny important information, I'll follow your direction."

Lotte swallowed, guilt intensifying. The entelodont's screams were still fresh in her mind. "I promise."

This morning had been a serious relapse of her judgment. She shuddered to imagine what her father would say about her blatant disregard for a living creature. Hopefully, she had not ruined the relationship between Orm and the herd.

Beckoning Emerick inside the hatchery, they headed to The Broody Room. She retrieved a chart from the workbench that listed all of the wyverns in this area of care. The list was divided into three sections — The Broody Room, The Aviary, and incubator — and she would need to account for every wyvern and document their meal.

As Lotte explained this to Emerick, gathering the gloves and rods, she turned to find Emerick no longer next to her. Instead, he wandered down one of the halls, peering into each enclosure at the mother wyverns, some coiled around their clutches of eggs. He stopped when one wyvern fluttered her wings and left her post, gliding along the glass. Emerick pressed his fingers where her head was and shivered. Snapping his hand back, he spun around and breathed harshly. His normally light brown cheeks were ashen. He looked ready to puke.

"We have one hundred and fifty wyverns to feed," Lotte announced. "Are you sure you can handle it, especially with your allergy to wyverns? You could always go for another run."

Do you keep them all locked up in here?" Emerick asked.

"Only the mothers who need a quiet and dark place to hatch their young. We also have a quarantine enclosure for the sick."

"It's not cruel confining them like this?"

It was almost funny, the concern Emerick showed for the creatures he claimed to hate. Once more, he was turning out to be a perplexing individual.

"Most wyverns seek small crevices and spaces to brood. They will remain in one spot for the entire three-month gestational period. By providing enclosures for the mothers, we eliminate predators and competition with other wyverns. Plus, we are able to monitor what they eat and drink, both of which they often go without for long periods of time in the wild. Once the eggs hatch, we move the mothers back into The Aviary and let the babies grow for a few weeks in the enclosures."

Lotte figured her long-winded explanation was more than Emerick had expected, but he seemed interested enough.

"These are the venomous wyverns. We keep the non-venomous ones in the other hallway, but they are not there right now." She refrained from glaring at the Firewraith.

"Where are they?" he asked as he returned to the work-bench. He studied all the various tools Orm kept there.

"For obvious reasons, they'd been evacuated and then returned to the hatchery, specifically The Aviary, after our agreement. You met them yesterday."

"And their eggs?"

"In an incubator in the basement . . ." Lotte trailed off. Were the eggs okay? Had the arachnea succumbed to Scorn's venom like the entelodont? Did the chaos cause the incubator to fail?

"We can check on them after we get done milking venom." Emerick surprised her with his promise.

Once again, he caught her off guard with his kindness.

"Come, I'll show you where we store their food. But first, you need to drink another allergy potion."

He nodded with agreement.

For the next hour, Lotte guided Emerick in warming frozen pixie bodies and rabbit meat. They also collected eggs from the chicken coop, before they returned with everything to The Broody Room. She showed him how to use prongs so the wyverns would not accidentally bite his hand. While he refused to participate in the actual feeding, backing up with panic in his eyes when she held out a pixie to him, he instead watched intently. Lotte did her best to answer all of Emerick's questions.

"How did Orm Skale acquire wyverns?"

"He's always been fascinated with wyverns. What started as a childhood hobby of catching and documenting wyverns turned out to be a major job for developing an understanding of what magical beasts live in Asoleenya. If you didn't already know, he is incredibly knowledgeable with most known magical creatures. He was the advisor for the king — *err*, the former king of Vroaevalon."

He ignored her slip of the tongue. "What does he do with the babies when they are grown?"

"They go to a special sanctuary." She was careful not to give away too much information in case Emerick decided to relay everything to Bouldermaul.

"And he uses them to make potions?"

"Their byproduct," She corrected, "mostly used for medicinal purposes."

"Mostly," Emerick repeated. "What else can you make besides medicinal potions?"

"It depends on the wyvern's properties and the ingredients used to make the potions. One made from Patera Swift Wyverns allows the person who drinks it to become fire repellent. Another helps with resisting fatally cold temperatures. One even enhances your senses, allowing you to hear a pin drop in a noisy room."

"Do you just keep the potions stored for personal use? Or do you sell them?"

"We mostly sell them to a helyait healer in Twisp, but occasionally, we'll exchange them for goods from nomadic traders. Honestly, the potions keep the hatchery running."

"Do the people know what you use for ingredients?" His face scrunched with disgust, eyeing the wyvern feathers Lotte had collected while she fed the mothers. "Are the potions even sanitary?"

Lotte chuckled. "We filter and boil the bacteria dead. They are perfectly safe."

They finished offering food and cleaning the final wyvern's enclosure. The process took longer than normal, the opposite of what she had intended. Yet, Lotte forced her lips into a neutral position, even though they wanted to lift into a smile. She would never admit how much fun it was sharing her world with an outsider — her enemy, even!

"Time for The Aviary," she announced.

In the kitchen, Lotte rinsed and restocked the food bucket. She and Emerick then headed outside. Instead of taking him straight to The Aviary, however, she walked past the door and around the back of the dome-shaped building to Scorn's private enclosure. Her breaths turned short and fast, goosebumps forming on her arms, and her vision darkened as she approached. Tonight's dangerous task flashed through her mind. She slowed to a stop.

Was she willing to risk death for her enemy?

"Are you okay?" Emerick asked.

She gulped. "I'm fine."

The Firewraith raised a brow, obviously catching her lie. Resuming her pace, she brought them to the peep door next to the main entrance. Lotte spoke the incantation, causing the markings to glow. Through the glass and layer of condensation, Lotte spotted a black, scaly body sprawling on the feeding platform, waiting for his weekly meal.

"This is the most venomous wyvern — and possibly the most venomous known creature — in all of Asoleenya," Lotte said, and she slid the latch open.

Emerick reached out as if to stop her, mouthing the word "wait." He jumped back as Scorn's head appeared at the opening, yellow-brown eyes peering through. His slitted pupil darted between him and Lotte.

Lotte grabbed a pixie with the prongs and slipped it through the opening. There was a pause, both Lotte and Emerick holding their breath, and then the prongs jerked, and she retracted them empty. Quickly, Lotte slid the latch shut.

Emerick asked, his voice a higher pitch than normal. "How are we supposed to catch him without getting bit or stung?"

"His stinger was removed by black market traders. We won't have to worry about his wings."

Emerick frowned. "His wings, too? Is that also what happened with Nilka?"

"Yes."

"Why? To make them easier to handle?"

"Yes, and to make crude versions of the potions we make." Lotte led him toward The Aviary.

He turned down going inside, but he stood in the doorway and watched the wyverns of the tropical section flock to Lotte, swooping down and snagging food whenever she held up the prongs. Some slithered up to her like snakes. She counted each wyvern under her breath. When she came across the mothers that she had released into The Aviary yesterday, she caught the ones that she could and brought them back to The Broody Room. It was already late afternoon by the time Lotte fed everyone.

Emerick had gone from standing in the doorway to sitting cross-legged on the ground. None of the wyverns approached him, as they all settled down to digest their food. Standing in front of him, Lotte peeled off her gloves and tossed them into the empty bucket.

"Are we done, then?" Emerick asked.

Lotte exhaled shakily. "Yes, we're done. Let's have something to eat — I'm hungry." She tried not to think of what loomed ahead of her. . . .

The suit her father used when dealing with Scorn was too big, so Lotte improvised. She layered herself with three shirts and her leather rainy-season jacket, as well as two of the thickest pairs of pants she owned. What she did take from her father was his overalls, rolling up the bottoms and tightening the straps. Lotte looked and felt like a bloated puffer fish.

The trick was making sure no part of her body was exposed. Just the touch of Scorn's scales would be excruciating. The layers would prevent her from the wyvern's bite. All she needed was her gloves and her father's metal helmet.

As she shoved her feet into her boots, there was a knock on her bedroom door.

"Someone arrived calling your name," Emerick said.

Lotte's breath caught in her throat. Remi. "Did he see you?"

"No, I hid out of sight," Emerick said.

"Good."

"Are you almost done?" he asked. "It's getting dark, and I don't want to know what other creatures lurk here at night."

Lotte waddled to the door and opened it, meeting Emerick's amused look. "One word about my outfit from you, and we'll be switching places, got it?"

He raised his hands in mock surrender.

On the kitchen table was the rest of her body gear, a net, and a jar with a rubber lid. Nilka waited under the table, still sleepy from her nearly-digested meal. The bigger the wyvern, the faster their food digested. Lotte shakily placed the helm over her head and gripped the net and jar tightly. Emerick carried her torch.

The walk to Scorn's enclosure felt like a dream. The darkness of the late evening made her tunnel vision worse, and not even the drops of cool rain broke her from a daze. Before she knew it, she activated the torch installed over Scorn's entrance. Light filtered through the glass, nowhere near enough to fill the entire inside.

Lotte gulped. She should have waited until morning. In fact, there were a lot of things she should have done differently, starting with telling Healer Aklea and Remi about the Firewraith. There was no going back, though, and while she had never handled Scorn before, she had seen her father do it enough to anticipate the wyvern's aggressive behavior.

Breathing deeply, Lotte held the jar to Emerick. "When I say so, hand this to me."

"Got it," he said, a determined look in his eyes.

"If Scorn escapes, run."

Emerick deadpanned.

Gripping the net, Lotte whispered the unlocking incantation, and the runes around the door illuminated a bright blue light. Lotte entered the wyvern's habitat. All sound around her dwindled as her foot sunk into the red sand. Large stones and a variety of cacti littered the inside. The rock Scorn normally sunbathed on was vacant, and so was his feeding perch. He was nowhere to be found. This could only mean one thing: Scorn had buried himself in the sand.

Clicking her tongue, Lotte nudged the sand around her with the long handle of the net. *C'mon, you grumpy old demon!* Lotte thought, tapping around a cluster of stout, furry cacti.

The only warning Lotte received was a deep hiss, almost like a dog's growl. Black scales materialized out of the sand, and Scorn lunged. Thankfully, his target was the long handle. It took all of Lotte's willpower not to scream and drop the net. Her heart felt like it would explode from her chest.

Fangs digging into the wood, Scorn realized his mistake and rotated his jaws free. He coiled back, eyes now on Lotte, and readied for another strike.

It was now or never.

Scorn moved, and Lotte swung the net. Out of pure luck, she pinned him on the ground. He hissed and spat and began wiggling himself into the sand. Bile rose in Lotte's throat. If he got deep enough, he could burrow himself out of the net. She quickly dragged the net with Scorn inside to his bathing rock, scooped him up, and pressed the net's opening to the stone's surface. He was trapped.

Unfortunately, there was nothing else she could do at this point. The angle of the rock and the surprising strength of the small wyvern put Lotte in an awkward position. If she released any of the pressure she had on the net, Scorn would escape. She needed help.

"Emerick!"

The Firewraith rushed forward with the jar, staying a sizable distance away from the wyvern.

"Take the handle," Lotte said.

Emerick flinched. "You want me to come near that?" He gestured to Scorn. "Without gear, too?"

"Do you want to save your mother or not!"

Emerick snapped his mouth shut. Without any more hesitation, he placed his hands above Lotte's on the net. She counted to three, let go, and sprung forward to the wyvern. She waited until Scorn was in the right position, before she snatched his head, pinching his jaw shut with thumb and index finger. No matter how hard he thrashed, Lotte maintained control of his head.

"You can let go, now," Lotte said, grabbing Scorn's flailing body with her other hand. "I have him."

Emerick slowly released the net. He stared at the wyvern with bulging eyes. For a moment, Lotte thought he would faint.

"Jar. Now." Lotte gritted her teeth.

He complied.

Lotte recalled all the times her father milked wyvern venom, and she brought the jar to Scorn's lips. She nudged him, releasing some of the pressure she had on his head, and he instinctively revealed his fangs, an oily substance covering them. Lotte pushed them down against the rubber lid. She mentally cheered when she felt a pop, and she began exfoliating his venom glands. Yellow liquid trickled down the jar's walls.

She did it! She actually did it! If she was not holding Scorn at the moment, she imagined herself laughing maniacally. Oh, she wished her father was here to see her — and, more importantly, her mother. If she could successfully capture and milk the deadliest wyvern in Asoleenya, then she could handle other magical creatures living at the reserve.

"Almost done!" she announced excitingly, turning with Scorn so she faced Emerick. A large grin plastered her face, though her scarf hid it.

"How much venom does the Elixir of Life need?" Emerick watched her with wide eyes.

"As much as his glands have to offer," she said. "If we're lucky, we will have some left over. Just one drop is lethal."

Emerick placed a hand on his chest and made a sound of disgust as his entire body shivered. "I have a new greatest fear," he muttered.

Lotte chuckled. "Do you find Scorn scarier than the arachnea?"

"Easily."

An electrifying burning sensation ignited the skin of Lotte's wrist. Her hand seized, and she nearly lost her grip on Scorn. Gritting her teeth, she searched for the source.

"What's wrong?" Emerick asked, alarmed.

Lotte gasped, her heart sinking at the sight of Scorn's tail wrapping around her wrist. The tip dipped inside her glove.

"No, no, no," she whispered.

The pain magnified. Lotte screamed, ripping Scorn off the jar and throwing him across the enclosure. She staggered to the door, where Emerick joined her side and placed a hand on her back.

"Were you bit?" he asked. Guiding her outside, Emerick slammed the door to Scorn's enclosure shut.

Lotte did not answer. She *could* not. The only thing her mind could process was her hand feeling like someone was sawing it off. As the cool night air engulfed her body, she collapsed to her knees and ripped off her glove. Just from the few seconds the wyvern's scales brushed against her skin, a piping-hot rash extended from her hand and into the sleeve of her arm. Her muscles visibly spasmed underneath her skin.

Her last meal rose from her belly, and she vomited into the grass.

"Lotte!" Emerick's sharp voice cut through the ringing in her ears. "What should I do? What medicine would help?"

Dizziness flooded her head, and the world tilted. Arms caught her before she fell onto her side. Squinting up, Lotte saw Emerick forming words with his mouth, but she could not hear him. In fact, the entire world seemed to have gone silent. Her vision swam, and she could no longer tell if her eyes were open or closed. Soon there was nothing but the throb of her wrist.

Then, darkness.

Chapter Thirteen
EXPOSED

Lotte awoke to her body jerking from side to side, her head dangling over the ground. It took her foggy brain a moment to realize that she was draped over a shoulder. Emerick The grass below morphed into wood floorboards, fresh air into dust and smoke. When she blinked, she found herself slumped on the kitchen table with her arm outstretched. Emerick was sitting beside her, dipping cloth in a bowl of water. He pressed the cloth against her rashy skin, and she moaned.

"What happened to the venom?" Lotte asked in a whisper, and the cloth froze its movement.

"You're awake," Emerick sounded slightly relieved.

She lolled her head to the side, squinting from the glow of a manacore torch on the table. "Why wouldn't I be?"

"You're kidding, right?"

"Where is the venom?" Her vision focused on Emerick's face.

The kitchen was dark, other than the orb of torchlight surrounding them. Rain pelted the closed shutters of the window. Thunder rumbled in the distance, and an occasional flash of lightning beamed from the bottom crack of the door. Wind creaked the house and rustled leaves loudly, sounding like rushing water. Southern Holan was notorious for its tropical storms.

"I left the jar on the counter," he said.

"And Scorn?" Her heart clenched at the thought of the Desert Deathbite Wyvern loose in this region.

"In his enclosure."

"Thank Asoleenya," she exhaled with relief. "Now we can make the potion."

Emerick continued caring for the rash raging from her wrist to her elbow — red, lumpy, and hot. "We should wait until you're better."

"You've come all this way for your mother, haven't you? Why stop now for an enemy that you hate?"

Emerick was silent, his mouth twitching.

"If it were my mother, I'd want to return back with the elixir as soon as possible."

Silence fell upon the two. Eventually, Emerick sighed and leaned back in his seat, throwing the rag across the kitchen, landing it in the sink. He rubbed his chin as he studied Lotte.

"I didn't realize you have a mother," Emerick said.

"All things have a mother."

He rolled his eyes. "I meant a living one. I assumed since you lived only with your dad . . ." he tapered off, looking away and scowling.

"Assumed what?" Lotte raised a brow.

"Everyone has lost someone over the past two decades. For me, it's my father — my blood father, I should say."

Lotte blinked, perturbed that the Firewraith was opening up to her.

"It was so long ago that I barely remember the pain of his absence. My mother remarried to a man named Brok who is willing to break his devotion to His Highness for her. I wish I had gotten to know him better. After I was chosen for the Firewraith program, I only got to see them once a month or so."

Lotte's heart fluttered. In a way, Emerick was like her, longing for family connection. At least, he got to see his mother on a monthly basis.

"How old are you?" she asked, abruptly.

"Fifteen summers."

"Fifteen!" she exclaimed. "There's no way!"

"What do you mean?"

"You're only a year older than me. I thought you were an adult," she admitted. "When did you become a Firewraith?"

"I'm an apprentice, still, not a fully knighted Firewraith."

That was news to Lotte. "How does that all work, anyways? What's the process of becoming a Firewraith?"

Emerick smirked. "Why? Interested in becoming one?"

It was Lotte's turn to roll her eyes. "The day I become a Firewraith is the day you become a mage."

He barked a laugh. "You're too old, anyways. Potential Firewraiths are selected once they turn five years old."

"That young!" Lotte gaped.

Emerick shrugged.

"Then what happens?" she inquired.

He brought up a finger and waggled it side to side, like a parent saying "no" to an unruly child. "I think you've had enough questions answered for now. It's only fair that, in return, I get to ask some things."

She tensed. "What kinds of things?"

"Where is your mother?" he asked, crossing his arms.

"Why do you want to know about her?" She squinted suspiciously.

"I shared about my family," he said. "You always speak of your father, but this is the first time I have heard you mention your mother. I'm curious."

"You're curious? About my mother? Somehow I find that hard to believe."

"Your choice if you want to know more about Fire-wraiths."

Lotte huffed. She mentally cursed his cunning, exploiting her interest. Unfortunately, the desire to understand how Emerick and the other Firewraiths became the pyro-assailants won over the need to keep a distance between her enemy. She would just be careful not to give out locations or names.

"My mother lives with my four half-brothers on a sanctuary dedicated to healing and restoring endangered magical creatures," she said.

Emerick looked surprised. "A sanctuary? Is it nearby?"

"No," she said, ducking her head. "And I won't be telling where it is. But I can assure you, it's not anywhere near here."

"Got it, got it," he surrendered. "So she lives there with your brothers. Why not you? Why are you and your father not with them?"

"It's . . . complicated. My parents aren't exactly together." She struggled to explain what even she did not fully comprehend. "When Urtica fell, my father fled to Holan with his best friend and colleague — a helyait healer — picking up human and helyait stragglers along the way. As they searched for a place to temporarily live, they found a helyait pod living in the bay and soon Twisp was born."

"What turned temporary living into permanent?" he asked, looking around. "Why not go with your mother to the sanctuary?"

"She built the sanctuary long before Bouldermaul. It's incredibly far away, and we had neither the resources nor transportation to its location. Plus, Bouldermaul was invading Holan and Endlor at the time. Traveling north — *err* — anywhere was not safe. By the time things calmed down, we had already settled in Twisp."

"I see. So, you visit her every now and then?"

"Every few years. I've seen her four times in my life, not counting my birth. Like I said, it's incredibly far, and I'm not even allowed — " she cut herself off, a familiar frustration surfacing.

"Not allowed to do what?" he pressed.

Lotte took a deep breath. "My mother refuses to let me into the sanctuary. I have to stay at a camp nearby."

"Why is that?"

"They think I'm inexperienced — that I lack the skills to handle creatures of magic."

Emerick snorted and shook his head. "You're joking, right? You seem to hold your own pretty well with the wyverns."

"Thank you!" Lotte was amazed that a Firewraith could see her skills, but not her own parents.

"What separates you from your brothers?" he asked.

"Nothing really," Lotte said, frowning. "At least, I don't think anything does. They're not much older than I am. I've met them once."

"Only once?"

Cheeks heating up, Lotte was embarrassed by how pitiful she sounded. "The sanctuary keeps them busy." She did not want to reveal that she only met three of her four brothers, the fourth unable to leave his duties to meet her at the camp. Lotte did not want Emerick's sympathy.

"What does your father think of the situation?" Emerick reminded Lotte of a kid trying to solve a helyait puzzle for the first time.

"Oh, he doesn't really have a say. My mother is the head of the sanctuary," she said. "But that's why I insisted I could manage the hatchery on my own. It was finally time to prove myself to them — that I'm ready to learn of my mother's world."

Tears welled in her eyes, but she sniffed and shook her

head, blinking rapidly to force the moisture back. When her composure returned, she said softly, "My plan was foolproof, until you showed up."

Emerick's throat bobbed as he swallowed, and he took a moment to reply. "I'll be gone soon enough, and I'll keep your hatchery a secret."

Lotte laughed hollowly, "Can I trust the word of a Firewraith?"

"You can trust that I wouldn't willingly swear on the life of someone I would break King Bouldermaul's laws for unless I had no other options."

"I think it's only because of your love for your mother that I believe you," Lotte said, shifting back in her chair and scanning the table of all their equipment and ingredients. "I will instruct you on how to set everything up and make the Elixir of Life. Then when it's done, you can leave."

Emerick flinched. "I can't make it. I'll mess up."

"Not if you follow my directions. If I do it, with my injury, then the elixir will surely fail."

"Can't we wait until you're healed?" he asked. "Don't you have a potion or something to heal your arm?"

"I used the last upstairs bottle on me after the arachnea. The rest are in the basement."

"What about asking me more questions about Firewraiths? I owe you now." He was stalling.

"I'll save them for another time."

Emerick stood and began pacing, running his fingers through his hair before placing his hands on his waist, defeated. "Shall we begin?"

Brewing the Elixir of Life began with adding various wyvern skins to the ceramic alembic's pot and setting it onto the stove, fanning the flames to boil the byproducts. Placing the top on so the gooseneck dripped hydrosol into a bowl on the ground, Emerick moved onto the herbs, mincing the ones Lotte told him to and grinding others into a paste with a mortar and pestle. At one point, he had to measure the entelodont urine they had extracted from the dead beast's bladder and reduce it in a cooking pan next to the ceramic alembic.

Emerick lost count of the amount of ingredients and steps, listening carefully to Lotte's droning instructions. He added five petals from a twilight calendula and, much to his consternation, ground manacore from the smallest spoon he had ever seen in his life, measuring five milligrams when leveled.

"Whoa!" He stepped back when the reduction fizzled and a plume of steam nearly seared his eyebrows. The combination of ingredients neutralized the enteodont's stench, and Emerick found himself relaxing as the normal smell of burning wood wafted from the stove.

"We are almost at a breakpoint. Now, add the crushed larkist scales." Lotte rested her head on the back of her chair, eyes closed, her injured arm still outstretched on the table. She would crack a lid when prompted by Emerick, asking for the next step or a repeat of the current instructions. If it were not for her groggy replies, she appeared asleep. Emerick hoped she was not too far gone, or in a delusional state where she thought she was giving the right directions but she was not.

Emerick did as he was told, though, and poured the shimmering dust, wondering briefly what kind of creature a larkist was. The reduction turned from yellow to a silvery white, reminding him of a pearl.

"Stir it gently for the next ten minutes, and then we can let it simmer for a half-hour. My father keeps a pocket watch on a workbench in The Broody Room. Find it, will you?"

When Emerick returned with the pocket watch, he had

a guarded look. He slapped it onto the table next to Lotte, yanking his hand back as though he had been burned. His sudden shift from cooperative to tense and standoffish confused Lotte, that is until she picked up the pocket watch and rubbed her thumb over the insignia etched into its metal. The crest of Urtica. The coat of arms for the monarch of Vroaevalon before Bouldermaul. The pocket watch had been given to Orm and all the other advisors of the former king. This was yet another reminder that she and Emerick were on opposing fronts.

Luckily, the Firewraith refrained from saying anything, and Lotte timed him as he stirred. The pocket watch did not have the exact time, as Orm hardly ever remembered to wind it, but she could at least tell when the minute hand had moved ten ticks. That was good enough for her. When the time came, Emerick placed a lid over the cooking pot and wiped the sweat from his forehead.

"That was not too bad," he said, eyeing the slow drip from the alembic.

"Good." Lotte sagged heavily against the table, breathing shakily. "We have many more hours of this."

"Will you be up for that?" Emerick noted her deteriorating state.

She swallowed thickly, wincing as the rash stabbed needles into her skin, and whispered, "Y-Yeah."

Raising a brow, Emerick was not convinced. However, his stomach rumbled uncomfortably, reminding him that he missed dinner, and he dropped the subject. He asked, "Do you have any food to cook with?"

"There's not enough room for us to add another pan to the top of the stove without disrupting the potion. There are some dried fruit and smoked fish in the pantry. You can also open one of the small pots of fermented kelp."

"Fermented kelp?" He scrunched his face with disgust. "I'll stick with fruit and fish. Do you want some?"

She shook her head. "I'm not hungry."

Lotte dozed as Emerick rummaged through the kitchen. She jerked when the air shifted next to her, a chair sliding across the floor, but relaxed when she heard crunching and the occasional sip of water. The smokey smell of fish made her queasy, and she turned her head away. After a while, and nearly nodding off into a deeper sleep, a wet rag pressed gently against her injured arm. She yelped from both pain and the coldness of the moisture.

"The rash is getting worse," Emerick said. "Some of the blisters opened up."

Lotte hummed. That was to be expected of Scorn's scales.

"Is there anything I can give you to prevent infection?"

There probably was, but right now, she couldn't think of it.

"Lotte?"

"How much time do we have left on the reduction?" she asked.

There was a pause as he checked the pocket watch.

"About six more minutes."

"Good."

The next couple of hours bordered on delirium, and Lotte barely stuttered out instructions as more and more of her energy diminished. Despite her earlier insistence, she internally admitted that Emerick was right: She should have waited. Yet, finishing the potion as soon as possible meant Emerick could return home and this entire situation would be resolved. She just needed to picture the recipe in her head, which was another difficult task she had taught herself in order to change her parents' conditions regarding the sanctuary, and then drown the rest of the world out, mainly the pain of her arm.

When the alembic had finished, Emerick bottled the hydrosol and then washed all the instruments before setting it up for another round. This time, though, he filled the pot with herbs that he had minced and placed another clean bowl under the gooseneck. Lotte told him of a cauldron in the pantry, black and made of iron, tiny enough to only hold a liter of liquid. They had thrice that amount between the various hydrosols, reductions, and solutions, plus they still had not added the wyvern's venom. He replaced the cooking pot with the cauldron, and he began adding assorted measurements of each solution, stirring in between each pour for different amounts of time. Soon, the cauldron was bubbling mere centimeters from the lip.

A hand fell on Lotte's shoulders, rousing her. "What's next?"

Lotte opened her mouth, but her lips cracked and split, and the words died on her heavy tongue. She shook her head to regain her composure, but it was useless. A cup appeared in her line of sight, water splashing over the edge. She watched droplets drip down the side, her throat feeling more parched than ever before, but she was too lethargic to lift her good arm and take it. To her astonishment, the cup moved to her lips and tilted gently, cool water awakening her tongue, and she gulped greedily. Her brain could hardly process that Emerick — a Firewraith — was caring for her.

"What do I add next?" he asked, again.

Lotte finished the cup and smacked her refreshed mouth. "Nothing," she said.

"But we haven't added the venom yet."

"We will tomorrow," she said. "The cauldron needs to simmer until at least the morning. Then we'll add a few more things, let it sit for half an hour, and then we can add the venom."

"So, I just monitor it until the morning?"

"Stirring occasionally," she nodded. "Oh, and find the lid for the cauldron — don't want all the potion to evaporate."

"Where's the lid?" Emerick asked.

"In the pantry, next to where the cauldron was on the shelf."

There. That was it. She was done and could let go now.

A tingling sensation filled Lotte's head, as Emerick walked away from her, and a wave of dizziness hit her so hard that she nearly threw up. She lowered her head to the table, wincing at the temperature contrast between the wood surface and her boiling forehead. She never noticed Emerick returning to her side and patting her arm. Her eyes closed, and she drifted off into oblivion.

"Lotte?" She heard her name called several times, rousing her. When she came to her senses, she was lying down in bed. A scaly body compressed her into the mattress. Her arm was now bandaged and propped up with a pillow. A chair creaked beside her, and she felt the bed dip.

The person continued to speak with her. Then another voice joined in. A flash of worry crossed Lotte. Who was here? Where was Emerick? The thoughts left her as quickly as they came, though, and she fell back to sleep.

Intense sunlight filtered through the window shutters and warmed Lotte's cheeks. She scrunched her face, blinking rapidly, and shifted to get more comfortable until Nilka's eyes appeared in her line of vision. The wyvern was curled around her body, trapping her under the blanket. Lotte tried to lift her hand and pet Nilka, but she cried out when white-hot fire lit her nerves.

That's right. Scorn touched her skin. No doubt the bubbling blisters burst into shallow craters. Much to her shock and confusion, white gauze casted her arm. Had Emerick treated her injury?

Where was the Firewraith? Lotte scanned the room. A kitchen chair had been dragged next to her bed, but it was empty. Only she and Nilka occupied the room.

Careful of her arm, Lotte wriggled out from underneath the wingless wyvern and swung her feet over the mattress' side. She stood slowly, holding onto the bed frame as blood rushed to her head, vision darkening momentarily. When the sensation subsided, Lotte padded across the room to the partially cracked door and peeked into the kitchen. Low tones of a conversation hung in the air. She gasped when she saw Emerick sitting at the table with Remi.

"Pardon me, but I must inquire where you are from again?" Remi sounded overly polite, with an edge in his voice that told Lotte he was suspicious.

"I travel from place to place, never staying anywhere for too long," Emerick lied coolly. "But I grew up in a town north of here."

Yet, your accent is clearly Vroaevalon," the helyait mused, clasping his hands together.

Lotte winced. Had Emerick lied to anyone else, his calm yet confident demeanor would have fooled them. However, this was Remi — the most inquisitive person Lotte had ever met. Not only that, but he was also an *Idateori*, and *Idateori* questioned everything.

Without Lotte realizing, Nilka had slunk off the bed and made her way over to the door, pushing it open even more with her nose. A whiny creak gave Lotte's presence away.

Both Remi and Emerick jumped to their feet, and the helyait rushed toward her. He hugged her, much to Lotte's surprise as helyaits typically avoided physical contact. As they parted, his hands remained on her shoulders and his eyes stared imploringly into hers. Over his shoulder, Emerick shifted nervously.

"How are you feeling?" Remi asked quietly.

Lotte opened and closed her mouth, unable to articulate an explanation for Emerick. They could not know he was a Firewraith, correct? He did not have any markings that distinguished him as a follower of Bouldermaul, at least not that she knew of. She should just play his presence off as a client of her father's — which she had already told Remi when he had helped her transfer wyverns.

"My father will return soon," he promised. "He will take care of everything."

What did that mean?

"How long have I been asleep?" Lotte asked. "How long have you been here?"

"I came early this morning to retrieve you as you had missed your nightly check-in," Remi said. "That is when I found your father's client treating your wounds, " he emphasized his disbelief.

"Oh, yes. We were, *er,* gathering ingredients for, *um . . .*" Her stammers trailed off.

"Explanations can come later." Remi gently turned her around and pushed her back to her room. "You should rest until my father returns."

"I'm fine," Lotte said, despite her injured arm quivering.

"I insist," the helyait said.

Lotte dug her heels down underneath the door frame. "I can sit at the table."

"I insist!" he repeated sharply.

Lotte swallowed, looking over her shoulder at Emerick. The

Firewraith's face was devoid of expression, yet his body tensed as if readying to flee. Their eyes met, and Lotte could feel the dread radiating off of Emerick.

The front door flew open with such force that the top hinge broke off. A stream of water sailed through the air and collided into Emerick, forming a cocoon around his body before hardening into ice. Only his head remained uncovered. Four helyait mages filed into the kitchen, each pointing a spear at the Firewraith. Healer Aklea followed their flank. He gasped when he saw Lotte and rushed to her side.

"Come with me." He ushered her into her bedroom, shutting the door behind Remi.

Lotte wobbly staggered to her bed, sitting down with her head in her hands. The weight of her actions bore down on her, and she struggled to justify why she decided to hide Emerick. Each second of silence stretched into eternity of regret. While Healer Aklea seemed to be listening to the commotion beyond the walls, Remi watched her with a piercing gaze. As she grappled with the consequences of her need to prove herself, harboring the perpetrator everyone had been searching for for days, Lotte uttered a mere, "I'm sorry."

"You should have told us," Healer Aklea said softly.

"I-I — " she struggled to form words.

"He forced you not to speak, am I right?"

Tears sprang to her eyes, and Lotte wanted more than anything for that to be the case.

"No."

Healer Aklea whipped his head toward her, a growl bubbling deep in his chest. "You willingly kept him a secret? Why?"

Lotte flinched. The helyait had never spoken to her with such anger before — such disappointment. Unable to hide her intentions any longer, she told them about hiding in the rafters and using her darts to neutralize the Firewraith, and about locking him in the enclosure in the basement with Nilka while she transported wyverns to the safe house. She detailed his first escape attempt, followed by his knowledge of her father.

Both Healer Aklea and Remi were visibly shaken when she explained the deal she made with the Firewraith to brew the Elixir of Life. Though she disclosed their battle with the arachnea, Lotte left out her blunder with the entelodont. By the time Lotte mentioned Scorn and his scales rubbing against her wrist, Healer Aklea raised a hand to stop her.

"Enough," he said. "I know what happened next."

Lotte wiped the tears from her cheek. "I'm sorry."

A murmur of voices from the kitchen quieted their conversation. Heavy footsteps dwindled, moving outside of her home. Remi stood and looked into the kitchen. "They're gone," he said, and Lotte's stomach sank at the unknown fate Emerick faced with the helyaits. She should be glad that everything was over — that she no longer had to work with her enemy. Yet, Lotte felt even worse about all that had transpired. Her thoughts went to his mother.

Now she would never receive the Elixir of Life.

"You are not entirely to blame, as you are still a child. However, you can no longer be trusted to make mature decisions. Not only have you nearly gotten yourself killed a litany of times since agreeing to work with the Firewraith, but also you have risked the lives of everyone in town. Until your father returns, you shall stay at the clinic with me," Healer Aklea chided.

"What about the wyverns!" Lotte exclaimed. "I must — "

He cut her off. "I have taken care of the wyverns on a few occasions. Remi shall help, too."

"But — "

"You may continue the tasks your father has laid out for you once you have recovered from your ordeal with the Desert Deathbite Wyvern. Until then, you will be under my strict supervision. Wherever you go, I shall be with you. Normally, I would have Remi keep an eye on you, but my son bows to peer pressure and also cannot be trusted with ensuring you make good decisions."

Remi frowned at the jibe, but otherwise he stayed quiet. Lotte's guilt swelled even more. Her actions had gotten Remi in trouble.

Healer Aklea continued, "You shall instruct Remi with what you need for staying overnight at the clinic. In the meantime, I tend to the wyverns."

"They'll need — "

"Fresh water and clean bedding," he finished for her. "Have they been fed?"

Lotte nodded. "Yesterday."

"Good." Healer Aklea pushed himself to his feet. Again, he fixed Lotte with a stern look. "Do not leave this bed. Your arm injury is quite serious. While I have healed most of it, your body is still recovering from shock. You will feel foggy and unbalanced for the next few days."

As he passed Remi, Healer Aklea spoke too low for Lotte to hear. Remi nodded in agreement to whatever was said, and then he took his father's spot in the chair next to the bed. Lotte could not meet his eye, and instead watched as he wrung his webbed hands. They sat awkwardly once Healer Aklea left, with only the sound of birds chattering outside filling the silence.

Eventually, Remi spoke, "I have never seen my father so angry."

Lotte slumped even more, flushing with shame.

"He is more upset about the situation, not you," he explained quickly, realizing his words' effects on Lotte. "Although, he is astounded that you did not speak up about the Firewraith. As am I."

Licking her lips, Lotte said, "Emerick said if I made him the Elixir of Life, he would leave and never cause us trouble again."

"And you believed him — or rather, you still believe him," Remi noted.

"I — *well* — his argument . . . " She paused to gather her thoughts. How did she explain, without sounding like a fool, that she had a gut feeling the Firewraith was telling the truth. "He was so honest."

"Have you considered that he was trained to deceive his enemies?"

"If that was the case, why did he save me from the arachnea? Why did he treat my wound from Scorn?"

"First of all, he got you into those situations," Remi argued. "And secondly, you know how to brew the one thing he traveled from Guldkem for. Of course, he planned to keep you alive."

"I know all that!" Lotte shook her head, closing her eyes. Her thoughts went to the conversation they had after defeating the entelodont, specifically when he had admitted to never being able to kill a person. "He told me other Firewraiths would investigate his disappearance if I turned him into the town guards. However, if he returned, he would keep Twisp a secret."

"The Firewraith manipulated you. Lotte, you must understand that." Remi sounded desperate.

Nausea forced her to lay back on her pillow. She rested her uninjured arm over her eyes, not knowing what to believe anymore.

Lotte heard Remi sigh.

"Even if what you say is true and the Firewraith upheld his promise, he still must atone for the damage and injuries he has caused for the Gibbs family and the helyait found injured on the beach. Do you not agree? " he inquired.

"What about the other Firewraiths?"

"It is not your decision how they are handled. Matriarch Ira holds that responsibility."

She bit her lip. As much as she hated to admit it, Emerick must face the consequences of his actions. Where did this sense of camaraderie come from? Lotte certainly had not thought this way when she first met Emerick, nor should she be feeling it right now. Remi was right: the Firewraith caused the events that forced her to work and, dare she admit, bond with him. Reluctantly, Lotte nodded.

"How did you and your father know that Emerick was a Firewraith?" she asked.

"Matriarch Ira had her suspicions when the investigation of the Firewraith's gruesome demise failed to commemorate your story. She had spoken to us about the matter before we came to retrieve you," he said.

This could not get any worse. Lotte wanted to pull the covers over her head and hide from the world forever. She feared what punishment the matriarch might bestow upon her for her naive thinking. Hopefully, she had not broken the trust the helyait pod had with her and her father.

"Everything will be sorted out," Remi promised. "Shall you instruct me on what belongings you wish to bring to the clinic?"

Nodding, Lotte told the helyait where he could find a bag and then listed off what she would need, which was hardly anything — just an extra pair of clothes and a few books to keep her busy while she recovered. She would retrieve her undergarments personally while on her way out, too uncomfortable letting someone else do so. While the helyait was busy packing the bag, Lotte spotted the kelp-wrapped gift he had given her partially hidden in her closet. Remi must have moved it from where she had left it outside to avoid drawing attention. When this whole disaster was resolved, she would open the gift.

The remainder of the time passed in silence as they waited for Healer Aklea to water the wyverns. While Remi returned to the chair and stared out the window, Lotte fought dozing off. Her body was incredibly sore from the past few days: her arm zinged with pain from Scorn; her hip ached from where she landed after the entelodont toppled over the tree; and a bone-deep weariness jarred her every movement, making her sluggish and unsteady. Now that she no longer had to worry about Emerick, her body decided to rebel. Lotte lost the fight to stay awake once more.

"Healing your arm is slow going due to the nature of Scorn's toxicity." Healer Aklea hovered his hands over the unwrapped welts running up and down Lotte's forearm, a soft glow cooling her skin as the helyait used magic to repair the damage.

"Okay," Lotte mumbled, staring at her lap.

"I shall heal you enough so you can travel to the clinic without needing a stretcher. Although, if you feel any sort of dizziness, please speak up," he said. "When we found you this morning, you were suffering severe shock. The effects can likely last between a week and a month."

"Yes, sir."

Healer Aklea sighed. The magic around his hands died, and he drew them away. "I should let you know now that Matriarch Ira wishes to speak with you personally. She wants to hear your perspective on the events that transpired."

Lotte sniffed, chest tightening. She had only met the leader of the pod a few times in passing, but from how Remi had described her, she was a wise, yet harsh helyait with magical abilities beyond any of their imagination.

"Will I . . . will I be arrested?" she asked.

"I doubt it." Healer Aklea leaned forward. "However, do not be too surprised if her words are sharp, and she issues a punishment."

Lips curling down, Lotte struggled against the tears in her eyes.

"Father," Remi piped in from behind the healer, "perhaps this can be discussed when she has had more time to heal. I imagine her arm is still quite painful, and causing her distress is counterproductive."

Healer Aklea swiveled his head and shot Remi a warning glare. At least her friend was still willing to stand up for her despite all the trouble she had caused.

"As a healer, I would agree with you," Healer Aklea said, "but as a father, I have every right to chastise her. She may not be my offspring, but Orm Skale entrusted her well-being to me. Until he returns, I shall fill that role."

Shame scorched Lotte's heart at the sincerity of his words. Although she was grateful he was still willing to support her, she knew she did not deserve his devotion. If she could go back in time, she would have told them the moment she caught Emerick.

"My mother is sick."

Lotte shook Emerick from her thoughts. He did not deserve her sympathy.

"Did you get everything you need?" the older helyait asked Lotte.

She nodded.

"Then, we shall make our way to the clinic."

Healer Aklea rewrapped Lotte's arm with fresh bandages,

discarding the old ones in a bucket he had placed next to where he worked. He helped Lotte to sit up and then made a sling from cloth, fastening it behind her neck. With her arm snug against her chest, the pain dulled considerably.

Lotte swung her legs over the bed. To her dismay, she still wore her filthy outfit from yesterday, smelling heavily of sweat and entelodont urine. More than anything, she wanted a bath and a change of clothes. Yet, Healer Aklea already threw her cloak over her shoulders, helping her good arm through the sleeve, and then grabbed her scarf.

In the kitchen, Lotte searched for her beloved companion. The wingless wyvern was nowhere around.

"Where is Nilka?" she asked.

"Outside now that it is no longer raining," Healer Aklea said. "I will return in the evening and let her in for the night."

"Just don't let her in the basement," Lotte said.

"Ah, yes. Where the arachnea is locked inside. I already had a less-than-appealing encounter with her."

Stopping mid-step, Lotte gawked at the helyait. "The arachnea is alive? How is that even possible! Nothing can survive Scorn's venom."

"That is peculiar." He hummed in thought. "Are you sure you dipped your dart into the correct venom?"

"Yes, I'm sure."

"Arachnea's have exoskeletons," Remi offered. "Perhaps it managed to discard its exoskeleton before the venom reached its innards."

"Though unlikely, that is a possibility," his father agreed.

Lotte smacked her hand against her head. "Our incubator is downstairs, full of eggs. What am I supposed to do?"

"You mean what we shall do," Healer Aklea corrected. "My son and I should be able to draw the creature out."

"Uhhh," Remi sounded dismayed.

"And we will fix the front door tonight before dark."

Once outside, Lotte scrunched her face as the sun blazed from the center of the sky, evaporating last night's rain until the humidity was so thick that she could lick it. The scent of wet wood overpowered the chimney smoke from her house. True to Healer Aklea's words, Nilka stretched in her favorite spot by the coop. Lotte's eyes scanned The Aviary before they fell onto Scorn's enclosure. She shivered.

"Come along, Lotte," the helyait healer called, already crossing the edge of the compound to the path in the trees. "No point in dawdling."

Taking a shaky breath, Lotte left the hatchery behind. Each step chiseled her core, whispering taunting words that echoed through her mind. She could not escape the haunting feeling that he failed to live up to the expectations of her father. And of her mother. Her handing over the reins of the hatchery to Healer Aklea seemed to reinforce her fear that she was destined for mediocrity.

The dream she once held so tightly of earning a place at her mother's side was now a distant mirage. Her half-brothers were good enough to stay at the sanctuary, Why not she? Jealousy flared, but the burden of her actions bore down on her shoulders, leaving her feeling utterly defeated.

"What's the matter?" Remi asked, walking beside her on the path.

They were halfway to the stairs on the side of the cliff. Footprints stamped the muddy path from the helyait mages. Lotte could make out Emerick's boot tracks in the mounds.

"I was supposed to protect the hatchery, yet I failed," she admitted under her breath so Healer Aklea could not overhear from his pace ahead.

Remi shook his head. "You have done a remarkable job taking care of the wyverns. The only reason why you struck a deal with the Firewraith was to protect the hatchery."

"And now I'm in trouble for it," she said. "It was a stupid idea. I don't know why I let myself be swayed by him."

"She was given six months to a year to live. No doctor in Guldkem can figure out the cure, nor can they determine the cause. She is dying of a slow, unknown illness."

Reaching the cliff stairs, Healer Aklea seemed to have stopped for Lotte and Remi to catch up. At least, he looked like he was waiting. As they approached him, Lotte took in his stunned expression and frozen body. She followed his gaze to the ground below.

Dozens of helyaits littered the beach, all withering on their sides and hacking violently. Even from on top of the cliff, their cries of agony reached Lotte's ears. More helyaits emerged from the water and struggled ashore.

What in Asoleenya was going on?

Chapter Fourteen
BATTLE ON THE BEACH

Lotte flew down the stairs of the cliff faster than she had ever done in her life. Injured arm forgotten, her feet barely touched a step before launching to the next one, sometimes skipping a few. Only the jutting rocks of the cliff's face acted as a railing. She was surprised by how fast Healer Aklea moved ahead of her, being a helyait whose body was hindered on land. Remi was a few paces behind.

When their feet hit sand, they rushed toward the nearest fallen helyait. She hacked wetly, gills straining, and remained limp when Healer Aklea kneeled down next to her. He propped her head in his lap. Lotte scanned the beach, eyes wide with shock, at all the helyaits suffering from an unknown force.

A scream tore her attention to the waters. Swimming erratically, a helyait carried an unconscious infant in their direction, wailing in their language meant for underwater. Lotte did not need to understand the language to know the helyait was begging for help.

"I will assist her," Remi said, and he raced to the water.

"What should I do?" Lotte turned to Healer Aklea. "How can I help?"

"We need to figure out what ails them." He shifted the helyait in his lap and patted her cheek gently. "Come on, wake up."

She moaned, head lolling side to side. After some more encouragement, her black eyes cracked open. Her scales appeared paler than they should, and she lacked the rune necessary to preserve her body in air. The helyait needed water, but there was nothing for Lotte to carry some in. An idea struck her, and she shook off her cloak. Jogging to where the waves lapped the sand, Lotte dunked her cloak until it was heavy and soaked. She brought it to the helyait, carefully slipped her injured arm out of the sling, and wrung her cloak over the helyait's legs.

The helyait screamed and snatched her foot back from the water, thrashing in Healer Aklea's arms to get away from Lotte. "*PHYRA!*" she barked over and over again. Lotte felt her blood run cold. *Phyra.* Poison. Her eyes darted to the bay. Had the water been poisoned?

Lotte's heart dropped when she saw Remi with an arm around the helyait mother and infant. He too had begun to cough, scratching his gills. His pace slowed to a stop a few meters from shore. He would likely not make it.

"They need to get out of the water!" Healer Aklea cried. "Swim, Remi!"

But it was no use.

Dropping her cloak and kicking off her boots, Lotte sprinted to the water. She ignored when Healer Aklea called her name and waded toward Remi until she was neck deep, and then she began to swim. Afraid the poison might get into her eyes and mouth, she kept her head out of the water and paddled awkwardly. Her injured arm stung excruciatingly as the saline attacked it, but Lotte gritted her teeth and pushed forward.

When she finally reached his side, the helyait grated, "Something is in the water."

"I know." Lotte gripped his forearm. "Can you still swim?"

He wheezed but nodded. "I can, but they cannot."

Both helyaits in his other arm were now unresponsive. Eyes closed and mouths foaming on their corners, Lotte prayed the mother and infant were still alive.

"Let's work together," she said, kicking her legs.

Remi's weakness in water attested to the poison's strength. They inched forward for what felt like an eternity, until Lotte's legs struck the sea floor. By then, Remi's energy gave out, and he flopped over onto his back. Thankfully, he was still afloat, and Lotte pulled him and the other two helyaits to where Healer Aklea ran into the water to help them.

No longer carrying dead weight, Lotte crawled on her hands and knees until she was on the hot, dry sand. She lay on her side, closed her eyes, and breathed the fresh oceanic air, tiredness washing over her. More had happened to her in the past week than the eleven years she lived in Twisp.

Frantic muttering drew her attention, and she looked to Healer Aklea who was digging through the pouches of his belt. He pulled out vials of potions that Lotte recognized as those she and her father brewed, setting aside three of them. They were antidotes for common poisons and venom. One in particular vial contained a highly potent antidote that Healer Aklea had helped enchant during the brewing process. If that did not work, then nothing would. Other than the Elixir of Life, of course.

The first vial had no effect, as it was more for mild jellyfish and bee stings, and Remi shook his head and gripped at his throat like he was choking. Lotte held her breath while her friend sipped the second potion. As Healer Aklea pulled away, the tension in Remi's body melted away. He dropped his arms to his side and spent the next moment breathing. Relief flooded Lotte so strongly that she almost broke into tears.

"That . . . was awful," he said between pants.

"What were your symptoms?" Healer Aklea demanded.

"I will tell you . . . after you heal . . . them," he pointed to the mother and infant helyaits laying on their sides.

Crouching next to Remi, Lotte watched Healer Aklea dip his finger into the potion before rubbing the antidote on the inside of the infant's mouth. He repeated the action twice, until her arm twitched and eyes fluttered. While she continued to rouse, Healer Aklea moved onto the mother, pouring the rest of the vial into her slack-jawed mouth. He pinched her lips together and massaged her throat. By the time the mother showed signs of waking, her infant was wailing with fear and discomfort. Lotte let out a thankful sigh, glad they were no longer in death's sight.

"Unfortunately, that was my only bottle of that particular antidote that I have with me. The rest are in my clinic." Healer Aklea eyed the rest of the helyaits. "Lotte, do you have more at the hatchery?"

"Yes, we keep some in stock. I don't think we have enough for everyone, but I can brew some more. It takes about an hour."

"We may not have an hour," Remi said grimly. "It felt as though someone put a metal clamp around my airways and slowly wound it tight. I thought I would suffocate."

"Go with Lotte and bring back what you can. Lotte, can you start the . . . " he tapered off.

"The brewing process?" Lotte finished for him, but he failed to respond. Instead, he stared at something behind her with impossibly wide eyes. Remi, too.

Stomach squirming, Lotte turned her head. As the sun cast its golden hues upon the sandy beach, her gaze swept across the helyait bodies on the shoreline, drawn to a group of individuals wearing chainmail, helmets, and an infamous coat of arms on their blue-violet tabards that sent a chill down her spine. There, amidst the gentle waves and swaying palm trees on the south side of the bay, stood Firewraiths. There were three of them, but only one held a gold staff with a massive blue crystal ball at the end. Manacore. Lotte recognized it instantly.

The Firewraith pointed the staff at Lotte, and her pulse quickened. An earthy smell filled the air, like rotting leaves, and Lotte felt something slither around her ankles. Peering down, she found thick, spiked vines growing out of the ground and winding up her calves. They tightened sharply. Lotte screamed as dozens of thorns dug into her flesh, blood mixing with sea water and trickling onto the sand. Collapsing to her knees, Lotte yanked and scratched the vines. She tried shoving her fingers between them and her skin, but they were as tough as boat lines.

With an animalistic roar, Remi wielded his spear and placed himself in front of Lotte. He muttered an incantation, and a jet of water rose from the bay next to him and shot toward his hand. The water coagulated into a hovering ball, before it expanded and formed a barrier between them and the Firewraiths. Then, it cooled rapidly into a thick sheet of ice.

Healer Aklea dropped next to Lotte and revealed a scalpel from his bag. He began cutting into the vines. It took several slices, but he managed to untangle one ankle, careful to pull the thorns from her skin. Lotte scrunched her eyes shut and cringed. The helyait healer moved to her other ankle.

"When I say so, head for the stairs," he said.

"What will you do?" Lotte asked.

He was quiet as his hands glowed, healing the dozens of bleeding cuts. The way his fingers trembled told Lotte that Healer Aklea was reaching his magic's limit. He had been healing her earlier that morning, after all.

Something hit the ice shield, causing a web of cracks. Remi drew upon more water, reinforcing the barrier, but another blast caused it to spray tiny ice flakes from its weathering edges. The attacks were relentless, and it was only a matter of time before the barrier failed.

"They're using magic," Lotte whispered with disbelief. "Bouldermaul banned magic."

"Now, is not the time to analyze Bouldermaul's hypocrisy," Healer Aklea said.

Lotte opened her mouth to say something, but a small *thawp* on the other side of the shield stole her attention. A sharp, pointed object embedded deep into the ice. It took Lotte a moment to realize she was looking at an arrow. Remi called forth another jet of water, but as soon as it touched the shield, he cried out as the water dropped unexpectedly, splashing onto the sand. He tried the incantation again, but every time it got near the shield, it failed.

"Something is wrong!" Remi said, peering over his shoulder. "My magic — it's like something is forcing me to end it."

Lotte raked her mind for possibilities, and she remembered what Emerick had said about his armor — how it canceled magic. Perhaps the arrow in the ice was enchanted in the same way. "I think we should — "

Swoosh.

An arrow hit Remi in the side of his abdomen. The force caused him to stumble backward, and Healer Aklea shouted, catching Remi as he began to fall. Lotte's stomach churned at the sight of a shaft sticking out of the helyait, blood seeping through his father's fingers as he applied pressure around the wound. Her knees quaked, and muscles threatened to give out as fear gripped her senses more than it had ever done in her life. She felt lightheaded, all hope she had for escaping vanished.

Through the numbness of shock in her mind, Lotte wondered how an arrow shot Remi from such an angle, bypassing the shield he had erected. Her eyes flicked toward the long stretch of dock, and sure enough, one of the Firewraiths was knocking an arrow into a menacing crossbow. He pointed it in their direction, tilting his head as he gauged their distance.

Lotte suspected this was how she would die.

The next arrow whizzed past her cheek, and Lotte yelped and rolled over until she hit the barrier — which continued cracking from blast after blast while the archer hunted them like wild boars. Her ears rang and pulse raced, and she almost missed a pained grunt from beside her. She spared a glance and gasped. An arrow completely impaled Healer Aklea's thigh, protruding out the other side. Somehow, he kept a firm hold on his son.

"Lotte," he rasped.

She shakily squeaked, "Y-Yes."

The Firewraith on the dock withdrew another arrow from a canister on his side.

"Take Remi and leave," he said.

"What about you?" she asked, and then nodded to Remi. "How will I transfer him?"

Despite his eyes being closed, Remi gritted out, "I can walk."

"You're awake!" Lotte exclaimed.

"Take him." Healer Aklea placed Remi's arm around her shoulder, and she hunched under her friend's partial weight. Then he handed her a rune she recognized immediately. "Don't hesitate — run now!"

Lotte guessed the helyait had a plan to ensure they escaped. Without sparing a glance at the Firewraiths, she led Remi through the air. Remi groaned, his body flinching, but Lotte dragged him forward. No doubt the movement was doing more damage. Yet, she pushed the worry aside and recalled her father's lesson about magic. Reaching the cliff face, she stared at the word on the rune.

"*Sfavatt*," she whispered, and she felt it — magic.

The pulsing warmth, the briny smell, and the feeling of being weightless. Lotte rose faster than when she learned the incantation from her father, purposely leaving out *galm*, the command for a slower pace. And when an arrow swooshed mere centimeters from her head, flakes of rocks crumbling where it struck the cliff, she shouted, "*Bans*!" They shot up faster than a wyvern could strike. Lotte's eyes seared as she squinted through the wind. She mentally willed the magic to slow and hover, floating far higher than the top of the cliff. The Firewraiths and fallen helyaits were specks below.

Remi lolled his head against her, panting wetly while pressing his hand against his side. Blood oozed through his fingers as he pressed them around where the arrow shaft was lodged.

"Hang on, Remi!" Lotte said the incantation to move forward until they were over trees, and then she lowered them.

Leaves and branches scraped them as they descended into the jungle. A glider raptor hissed as they interrupted its bug hunt. Breaking through the tree canopy, Lotte spotted the path leading to the hatchery. When Lotte's feet touched the ground, Remi pitched to the side, tearing her down with him. Her hip hit a hard root, and she inhaled sharply as her muscles in that area spasmed. The pain vanished at the sight of Remi laying on his back, though, and Lotte crawled toward him.

"Oh, Remi." She wanted to gag at the overwhelming stench of copper.

"My father," he moaned. "Where is my father?"

"He had us run, remember?"

"Ch-Check on him," he said.

"We don't have time," she argued.

"Check on him!" His body shivered as he raised his voice, and Lotte felt her heart break. She nodded before wiggling off her tunic. All modesty about her exposed undergarments was lost due to the situation. She balled it up and held it out to Remi. "Press this around your wound. Do not pull the arrow out. I'll be back."

She waited for Remi to follow her directions, before heading to the cliff's edge where she could overlook the entire beach. It was only a few meters away from Remi, yet anywhere but his side made Lotte antsy. Every other step, she looked behind at her friend as though he would disappear. Eventually, she crouched down on her hands and knees, wincing as her injured arm zinged, and crawled into a bush. Lotte slowly scooted forward until the gaps in the leaves threatened to give away her spot.

The beach was a heart-wrenching sight with the collapsed helyaits. The Firewraiths were advancing toward the north side of the crescent. Wailing drew her attention to where Healer Aklea and the helyait mother and infant would be. A cry escaped Lotte's lips as she found the helyait healer lying face-first in the sand, his arms folded at awkward angles. Two additional arrows protruded from his back and side, looking like toothpicks from Lotte's distance. A jolt of horror punched Lotte's stomach, knocking the air from her lungs. The acidic taste of bile filled her mouth, and she turned her head and vomited.

There was no way he could recover from three arrows, two of which hit vital areas of his body. And with the arrows made of manacore and enchanted to nullify magic, Lotte could not fathom what the effects would be for someone whose magic runs through their veins like blood.

Healer Aklea was dead.

Lotte bit her lower lip to stifle a sob. How would she tell Remi? His state was so severe that the news of his father would cause him more distress than his body could handle at the moment. She was not ready to lose two friends in one day. No, Lotte would keep the image of Healer Aklea's fallen form to herself until Remi was well on his way to recovery. That is, if they survived long enough. . . .

The Firewraiths neared the helyait mother and infant. Lotte wanted to scream for them to run. Yet, that would surely ruin her cover. If they stayed still, they would die; if they fled, they would die. There was nothing anyone could do. The helyaits, the wyverns, and her home — no matter where they went, they could not escape Bouldermaul. First, the hatchery in Urtica, and now the hatchery Orm had spent the last eleven years building — the tyrant king would not stop until they took their final breaths.

The water of the bay pulsed, cutting Lotte from her despair. Birds in the trees around her shrieked and exploded from the leaves. A tremor caused the waves to grow violent and slosh onto the teetering dock. The Firewraiths stopped and turned to watch as the water bubbled at the center of the bay, and Lotte too wondered what was going on. She gasped when stone pillars breached.

Twisp was resurfacing.

Chapter Fifteen
Destined to Fail

Emerick wiggled his thumb under the tight shackles of his wrists, trying to encourage circulation to his numb fingers. He lay on a thin floor mat in a dark room, where the only source of light seeped through the cracks of the door.

So far, he had spent more time than not imprisoned in southern Holan. At least here he had somewhat of a bed, though. After two months of sleeping on the ground or the rocky enclosure at Orm Skale's hatchery, the scratchy fabric and uneven hay stuffing were a luxury.

A sharp voice pierced the silence that had enveloped him since his transport through the water by the helyaits. They had placed a bubble-like barrier around his head for air and confined him in a cell within an underwater shipwreck, deep inside its converted hull. *This must be Twisp,* he had thought, recalling how he had been led past rows of empty, scrap-metal shops and into the ship's inner depths. They had traveled down several hallways to reach his current holding room. He wondered what the place had looked like above water, bustling with townsfolk.

The lock clicked, and the door slammed open. Emerick quickly sat up. Two helyait guards filled the room. Behind them appeared a visibly older female helyait with a hunched frame, numerous scars all over her red body, and several layers of necklaces made of pearls, shells, and whale bones. She wore a spiked headpiece made of manacore, veins glowing with magic.

Stopping halfway into the room, the elder helyait raised her hand, and water swelled on her palm, growing to the size of a pumpkin. Wordlessly, she divided the water into a dozen floating spheres, before they started to grow and elongate. Once each was as long as Emerick's arm, they hardened into ice, the ends forming sharp points.

Emerick swallowed as the spears glided through the air and positioned themselves around him.

The room grew cold, and Emerick's shaky breaths formed white clouds. Another mass of water formed behind the elder helyait, morphing into a chair and hardening. She sat down and crossed one leg over the other. Her expression was vacant.

"Do you require anything before we start this interrogation?" the elder helyait asked.

Huh? Emerick knitted his eyebrows together, confused. What did she mean by that?

"Food, drink, or extra clothes," she said, as though reading his mind. "Do you require anything before we get started?"

Oh.

Emerick clamped his mouth shut, knowing that this was some sort of tactic. Either it was her way of gaining his trust or the sustenance would be laced with something — poison or, if it existed, a truth-bearing potion. His eyes flickered to the ice spears.

Had they moved closer? Or was it his mind playing tricks on him?

"Very well." She lifted her chin, yellow eyes narrowing on him. "I am Matriarch Ira, leader of this pod and the town of Twisp."

Emerick would have offered some sort of acknowledge

ment, but he was too focused on the ice spears. They *were* moving. Slowly and threateningly, they loomed closer millimeter by millimeter. Only Emerick's trained eye noticed. He sprung to his feet to escape the ice spears' trajectory, but a jet of water traveled up his legs and froze him from his waist down. He was immobilized.

Growling, Emerick pounded the ice. He wiggled his body, but the pressure was relentless. There was no way of escaping. He whipped his head up, finding that the guards had shifted in front of Matriarch Ira.

She spoke in their language, and the guards returned to their original positions. With Emerick's attention on her, Matriarch Ira gestured to the ice spears. "They will stop when I feel satisfied with the information I receive from our discussion."

Emerick glared at her, gritting his teeth to keep back the slew of curses he would have spit in any other situation. He felt stupid by letting Lotte's talks of hypocrisy sway his opinion on magic. All users were the same — they deserved His Highness' wrath.

"Show me behind your left ear," Matriarch Ira demanded.

Emerick flinched. Balling his fists, he made no movement to follow her instructions. The elder helyait raised two fingers and flicked them twice. The guards strode forward, catching Emerick's hands as he tried to defend himself, and yanked them behind his back. One guard punched him in the stomach, forcing him to bend over as his muscles tightened painfully from the impact. The other guard pressed down on his back, keeping him bowed, and he folded down Emerick's ear.

Tattooed onto his skin was King Bouldermaul's insignia surrounded by a ring of markings in a language unknown even to his Firewraiths. Emerick had received a tattoo at the age of five when he was recruited for chivalry training. It was touched up at the start of every year, keeping the markings a dark black. The tattoo featured a crimson circle above an image that people debated was either a pair of eyes or reaching hands.

All Firewraiths had this tattoo behind their left ear.

"How many of you are there?" Matriarch Ira asked.

The guards released Emerick, and he straightened his posture despite how taut his stomach felt after receiving such a harsh blow. He held her gaze as he refused to answer, lips pinching together. No matter if he spoke or not, his fate would be the same. He would rather die by the hands of his enemy than a rat who had betrayed His Highness.

"Silence will only waste more time. Remember, I must be satisfied with your answers to stop the spears," she warned.

Somehow, Emerick doubted he could satisfy the elder helyait. He kept his mouth shut.

Matriarch *tsked*. If she was annoyed, she hid it well. She leaned back in her chair, head tilting to the side as she relaxed. She acted as though this was an afternoon exchange of tea and gossip, not an interrogation.

"They may seem slow and far away right now," she said, "but you will regret holding your tongue when they slowly pierce your flesh and then your inner organs."

He fought a shiver.

"Our pod's primary healer discovered peculiar ingredients inside Orm Skale's hatchery — ones used for an elixir that only a scarce few individuals know about." Matriarch Ira paused before asking, "Who told you about the Elixir of Life?"

Again, he said nothing. They sat in silence, Matriarch Ira staring him down, until Emerick was sure the spears were a few centimeters closer. Judging by their positions, they would miss any major organs that would cause instant fatality. The helyaits planned to make him suffer for as long as possible.

Emerick tried not to panic. He was conditioned for this, as all Firewraith apprentices were beaten and tortured to desensitize their bodies and minds to pain. For six months, he endured taunts and various methods of breaking his body — and he made it out without losing his sanity. The helyaits' plan of torture was nothing in comparison. He could take it.

Yet, as he told himself this, his body shook until his teeth chattered. Why was he such a coward!

Eventually, Matriarch Ira sighed and broke their staring match. "Bring me Lotte Skale," she told the guard. "She ought to be interrogated as well, for harboring a Firewraith."

A surge of protectiveness washed over Emerick, catching him off guard. He could not deny his and Lotte's short and antagonistic history, full of clashing views on magic, lies and misunderstandings, and violence. Yet, despite their past animosity, Emerick had witnessed a side of Lotte that did not fit the picture His Highness and other Firewraiths had painted of their enemies — her stubbornness, her naivety, and her compassion for wyverns. In that moment, Emerick found himself defending her, speaking up against her offenses.

"It was not her fault!"

Matriarch halted the guards by raising her hand. She leaned forward, a predatory glint in her eyes. "Explain."

"I blackmailed her." He shocked himself by admitting. "She was not a willing party."

"Yet, she kept you a secret when she had plenty of opportunities to tell her guardian."

"The hatchery — I was holding it hostage."

"You confess your crimes when it comes to Lotte, but not your others," Matriarch Ira noted. "Why?"

Why, indeed. He should keep his mouth shut. He should embrace his fate. He should not care about his enemy. There was no reason to spare Lotte now that he could no longer pursue the Elixir of Life for his mother. He had failed his mission. His mother would die, if she had not already.

Emerick had no reason to defend Lotte.

Except that his stomach squirmed at the thought of not.

"It is suspicious that your first words are on her behalf," Matriarch Ira said. "If you wish to spare her, then tell me what does your king need with the Elixir of Life."

"It's not for him," Emerick muttered.

"Then who? You burnt down someone's home, you critically injured one of my scouts, and terrorized our community — all for who?"

Emerick felt like a wagon wheel spinning around and around with the same old story, so he decided not to discuss his mother. That information was useless. Let the helyaits spin scenarios until their heads burst. Instead, he addressed something that Matriarch Ira mentioned which had confused him.

"You mentioned a scout?" Emerick asked.

"The one you embedded an arrow in her lower back," she said with barely contained anger. "She may be able to swim with her upper body, but it will take time for her to propel with her legs again."

"That was not me."

"We are past determining your innocence."

"I'm serious. I have not met a helyait until last night — the ones who tended to Lotte while she was hurt."

"The arrow was made of manacore and marked with the language of gruiks — the language Bouldermaul uses to enchant his armor and weaponry. You are telling me that you are not the wielder of the bow and arrow that injured my scout?"

"You're mistaken. King Bouldermaul has forbidden magic," Emerick said, forcing what little confidence into his words as he had left. "Offenders are burnt on the pyre. Neither he nor I would use such cowardice and evil tactics."

"You believe your king does not use magic?"

Emerick fell silent. An uneasy feeling washed over him.

"You are a child and — "

"I'm not — "

" — a victim of Bouldermaul. However, your actions deserve capital punishment, and I will not be lenient despite your ignorance."

Although he had been called ignorant before, the way Matriarch Ira's words were laced with pity stung Emerick. Being a Firewraith for King Bouldermaul was an honor! It weeded out the weak from the strong — the normal from the talented! After ten years of his life dedicated to His Highness, he earned his apprenticeship. He was not a victim.

A frantic voice interrupted the interrogation from outside of the room, and a helyait guard barged in, spewing a string of garbled words in their language. Matriarch Ira stood swiftly from her chair, replying sharply. They conversed back and forth for less than a minute, before Matriarch Ira whipped her head toward Emerick, snarling with more anger than he had ever seen emit from a person. For a moment, he thought she would change her mind and impale him right then and there.

She barked an order at the guard, and then her chair made of ice and even the spears around Emerick melted and splashed onto the ground. To his amazement, Matriarch Ira left the room along with the other helyaits. Only when the door shut, lock clicking, did the ice encompassing half his body turn to water, joining the pool around his feet and seeping into the mattress. Soaking wet, Emerick stood gobsmacked at the sudden shift in events. What could have caused Matriarch Ira to abandon the interrogation?

With the mattress too soiled, Emerick retreated to the only

dry corner of the room and sat down, slumping his back against the wall. He shivered as his clothes clung to his goosebumped skin. Exhausted, he closed his eyes and leaned his head back. He dodged a harrowing death for now. How long would his luck last?

The metal floor shuddered below him, walls creaking and the door vibrating. Then came a rising sensation, one Emerick could only compare to the time he traveled up and down the Vroaevalon coast, shadowing His Highness' water patrol as a prospective Firewraith duty. Storm-generated waves, taller than buildings, violently pushed the boat up and down until the stench of vomit mixed with seawater and fish. Emerick felt like the boat rising from the wave — yet in this case, it never went back down.

He hoped whatever kept the underwater shipwreck from flooding had not failed. Locked in the room, he would surely drown as the water slowly seeped through the cracks in the walls and door. The sensation continued for quite some time before it stopped and was replaced with the faint sound of waves and seabirds. Twisp had been abnormally silent, abandoned of all life and noise, so what changed?

The answer hit him: The town had emerged from the water.

The relief was instant. At the bottom of the bay, he had nowhere to go if he escaped. There was no telling the depth of the waters. Even if he managed to hold his breath until the surface, the helyaits had the upper hand. He would be chum in a shiver of sharks. Now that Twisp was floating, however, he had a chance.

Emerick felt along the door for weak spots, noting cracks and any bolts that looked worn. He slammed his upper body against areas that looked questionable, then kicking when his shoulders jarred with pain, but nothing caved.

After a while, Emerick ceased his fruitless attempt and flopped onto the mattress. His chest heaved from the exertion, muscles tingling under his skin. It was of no use. The shabby room was built better than he had thought. His only option was to somehow create a diversion and flee when Matriarch Ira returned. He would have to make it work, or die trying. Death in battle was better than death from torture.

A glow flashed out of the corner of his eyes. A blue-violet mist materialized through the door, surrounding a tether made of light, both leading to Emerick and encircling his body. He yelped, sprung to his feet, and dodged around the room — but it followed him like a leash on a dog. Reaching for the tether, Emerick's fingers fell through as he tried grabbing it. There was nothing he could do to stop the magic!

Chest heaving, Emerick had no choice but to wait and see what or who was to come. He heard voices again from the other side of the door. The accents were from northern Vroaevalon, and one voice, in particular, sounded much too familiar. Emerick's stomach fluttered with both hope and dread.

His comrades had arrived, potentially sparing him from the helyaits' deplorable interrogation tactics, but this also meant they knew his whereabouts. Emerick could only imagine how they acquired that information and how much trouble he would be in now that they undoubtedly knew he had lied to His Highness about his location and intentions over the past couple of months.

Had they created the mist-shrouded string of light? That would be impossible, though. Magic was the ultimate sin. They had punished hundreds with death for breaking the law. They had been sworn to never even think of using magic, let alone use it. Doing so was an act of treason. No Firewraith he had ever met knew how to conjure magic, nor the words and origin of magic that correlated with manacore.

"You believe your king does not use magic?"

Emerick flinched, the elder helyait's words penetrating his thoughts. He brought his hands up to his ears to block out the voice that was not there.

His turmoil was interrupted by a reverberating bang against the door, followed by another and another. The metal groaned before emitting a loud pop, and something hard clattered to the floor, echoing throughout the shipwreck. The hatch on the door turned, and a foot kicked it open. The gnarled face of Emerick's mentor appeared in view. Patchy red stubble, oily skin with large, black pores, and a grin as yellow as a lemon — Emerick always wondered why His Highness chose such an ugly, unclean man to mentor future Fire-wraiths.

After learning from him for the past ten years, Emerick knew Reginald "Reg" Cassius' only skill was his undying loyalty to His Highness. Everything else about his personality was as lacking as the bald spot on the top of his head, crowned thinly with scraggly strands of gray hair. His mentor sauntered in with his hands out to his side.

"Ta da!" he smirked. "Thought we'd never find you? I'd say I'm surprised to see you here, but I knew one day you would keel under the pressure of serving King Bouldermaul. What a pity that he wants you alive."

Emerick's stomach dropped.

"I was following a lead," he tried, but Reg spat, "Save it!"

Emerick's mind was blank, unsure how to respond. His gaze lowered to the tether of light, shocked and confused. His mentor had all but confirmed that he and whoever else was with him had used magic. Yet, his entire existence screamed that it simply could not be true.

"What a naughty boy you've been, lying to our dear king,"

Reg said. "You say you were aiding your ill mother, but in reality, you were traversing enemy territory with fishheads."

"I was aiding my mother," he tried. "Then I heard a rumor about a settlement in southern Holan that our naval fleets missed, so I decided to see for myself."

"That's an awful long journey sparked by a rumor. Could it be that the rumor had some sort of *reward* that you didn't want His Highness to know about?"

Blood drained from Emerick's face, and it took all his power not to swoon. Through his clouded head, he heard Reg laugh.

"You lie as far as a rabbit can spit," Reg said, and Emerick's eyebrow twitched. His mentor often compared him to a rabbit — shy and cowardly. *Always skittish, always ready to bolt at the first sign of trouble. Just like when you failed to light that pyre, you froze up instead of taking action. You've got to toughen up, Emerick. A Firewraith can't afford to be a scared rabbit.*

"Let's go — time for a little reunion." Reg beckoned him out of the room.

Emerick's body moved to complete the order despite his gut telling him to resist and flee. He trudged in Reg's shadow through a long, curved hallway of holding rooms, lit by manacore torches, and into a circular room aligned with rows of benches that surrounded a stone chair adorned with shackles and helyait runes. *A trial room,* Emerick concluded.

They travelled the hallway through the ship to the open hull and shops. Emerick squinted as sunlight fell over his eyes. He breathed the sea air deeply, noting a faint smell of rotting eggs — sulfur.

The only time he had smelled such pungent sulfur was when a criminal he had helped catch used elemental fire magic.

Heavy hacking drew his attention to the boardwalk forming

a perimeter around Twisp. Several helyaits sprawled on the wood-planked platform, grasping their throats and struggling for air. The sight was chilling, and Emerick wondered what tactics his mentor used to disarm them.

"Well, if it isn't Emerick Hammerthorne!" Another voice chimed from his left. "I was kinda hoping our next reunion was more fun, food, and drinks — not business."

"Phabien," Emerick said.

Phabien Krook greeted him with a mock salute, flaunting a blue-violet insignia with four diagonal black stripes on his tabard, indicating his rank as an honorary Firewraith. Only the top apprentices achieved this level; the rest were either placed in the Third Division chivalry or rejected from the Firewraith program to become regular soldiers and city guards. Emerick had graduated from the squirehood in the same year as the Firewraith standing before him, but while Emerick continued his apprenticeship into the fifth and final year, Phabien had completed it in just three years.

"I see the locals have treated you well during your vacation." Phabien pulled off his helmet, a wide grin plastering his face. Sweat dripped from his blond curls, and his face was slightly pink from sunburn. Just like Emerick, his body was unaccustomed to southern Holan's hot and humid climate.

Before Emerick could respond, a fist slammed into his sternum. The air left his lungs. He curled into himself, muscles spasming from pain. An elbow slammed into the back of his neck, and light flashed across his eyes. He collapsed to the ground, dazed. His assailant, Reg, was not finished and yanked him by the collar of his tunic, lifting him up before bringing his fist against the side of Emerick's head. The force rattled every bone in his face, as his neck snapped to the side. A copper taste filled his mouth. Blinking rapidly, Emerick rotated his jaw to make sure it was not broken.

Reg commanded Phabien to assist, and together, they dragged Emerick through the fallen helyaits, kicking anyone in their way and, sometimes, blatantly stepping on their convulsing bodies. A ping of pity trickled through the pain and confusion from Emerick's beating. Yet, he was in no position to confront them about their cruelty.

As they neared the jetty leading to shore, Emerick spotted the helyait matriarch and her guards attacking a Firewraith with whips of water through his lashes. He had anticipated the magic to dissipate upon contact with the Firewraith's armor, but instead, a wall of sand rose, forming a shield that blocked the attacks. Emerick's heavy-lidded eyes widened in astonishment. Had the Firewraith just used magic?

Before he could process the battle on the beach, Reg drew his attention back with his words.

"I had to beg King Bouldermaul for the task of disposing you. Yeah, that's right — me! Beg! Your brother was originally offered, after he killed your parents, but I lowered my standards and begged."

The worlds punched Emerick's gut harder than any fist or weapon. "What did you say?"

"Got cotton in your ears? I said I had to beg," he laughed before his face grew emotionless, looking down at Emerick with a knowing twinkle in his eye. "Or did you mean the bit about your parents?"

Emerick's chest heaved as he seethed. Strength returned to his limbs, and he dug his heels against the ground and twisted his body, yanking free from their hold. He rolled away until he hit a stack of crab pots, knocking the top cage over the side of the town's edge and sinking it into the water. A bucket of tools clattered by his head and spilled pliers, hooks, and shucking knives. One of the knives landed next to his hand.

Although he did not immediately grab it, not wanting to reveal its presence to the other Firewraiths, Emerick made a mental note of its location and pushed himself on his hands and knees.

Reg scoffed. "Well, there you go makin' even more messes!"

"Are my parents dead?" he asked, shakily.

"As dead as their maggot-riddled bodies can get."

"You're lying," Emerick gritted through his teeth.

"Am I?" A sinister grin revealed the blackened corners of his crooked teeth. "Kassian had no trouble with your old man. Granted, you once told me that your old man was a step in, not blood related. Must have been a no brainer. Now, your mother — I imagine that one would be tough, but from what I heard, your brother cut her down faster than you can blink — terrifying that one."

Arms quaking, Emerick lumbered to his feet, maneuvering his body to hide the shucking knife that he subtly grabbed, and he swayed as he faced Reg and Phabien.

"I find it hard to believe King Bouldermaul sent a squad of Firewraiths, one with a sorcerer, to dispose of a lowly, defective apprentice." Emerick paused to look past them. The Firewraith was definitely using magic. Matriarch Ira was right with her conclusion of his ignorance. Bile bubbled up Emerick's esophagus. Why had Reg spent the last ten years beating the evils of magic into him if Firewraiths blatantly practiced it? Judging by Reg and Phabien's nonchalance to the battle, they knew of the illegal use of magic. It was quite possible this Firewraith was given special permission. Regardless, this was Emerick's first time witnessing a comrade commit what King Bouldermaul was trying to purge.

"You're right, he does have an ulterior motive," Reg said. "So if you give me the answers I want, then I promise I won't kill you. I'll beat you only to the edge of your pathetic life. A prison rat, you'll be."

It was déjà vu of Emerick's interrogation with Matriarch Ira, except more crude. Dodge death for an even worse fate, the rest of his life subjected to starvation and cruel punishment. Now that Emerick thought about it, the only difference between his life now and prison are barred walls and locked doors. It was almost laughable.

"I will, however, be lenient if you tell me where the Elixir of Life is located."

"Why do you need it?" Emerick asked. "How did you find out about the potion?"

"Why is none of your business. We're following the king's orders. As for how, *heh*, your old man has loose lips when pressed."

"Prove it."

"Excuse me?"

"Your word is trash. Until I see physical evidence of my parent's death, I don't believe you."

A sly smile spread across Reg's face. "I had expected you to say that." He reached into one of the leather pouches of his belt and slowly removed an object wrapped in a velvet cloth. He tossed it toward Emerick, the cloth falling off as it hit the ground.

It was a severed hand.

Emerick gasped, bringing his hand over his nose. The flesh was gray and smelled of rust and slightly rotted eggs. The cut along the wrist was jagged as though someone had used a saw to dismember it. The sight was dramatic, and Emerick had not expected anything less from his mentor, but there was one issue: There was hardly any decay.

"That's a gift from your brother," Reg said.

Emerick shook his head. "There's no way that it would survive the trip to Twisp. Travelling takes months."

"Maybe for you, but we had proper transportation — only took a couple of weeks." He pressed a finger against one of his nostrils, blowing green snot out of the other. "But you're right — it should be all rot and bone." Reg shifted and pointed to the knight on the beach, who was currently in battle with Matriarch Ira. "Meet Malyse, an Elite."

Emerick's eyes bulged, shocked. There were only nine Elites, King Bouldermaul's personally selected Generals. They were the only Firewraiths allowed to meet the king in person, relaying his commands down the hierarchy of Firewraiths. Seeing one in the flesh was a rare occurrence — many Firewraiths going their entire career without being in their presence. For Emerick, though, this was the second Elite he had seen in his life.

The first was his older brother.

His gaze returned to the hand. He studied the flesh for any features that would indicate which parent it belonged to. Of course, he was hardly ever around his parents since his selection when he was five years old. Nonetheless, the hand was unrecognizable even with whatever means Malyse used to preserve it.

"This could be from anyone," Emerick said.

"You're too stubborn for your own good," Reg sighed. He dug through the pouch, again. "Your brother said you might recognize this."

Metal thumped the ground in front of Emerick. Sunlight reflected off of the polished gold disk of a tiny brooch, engraved with knotwork patterns and a dark ruby at its center. Emerick's lungs seized, unable to release his breath. His fingers shook as they hovered over the brooch. He was too afraid to touch it. Too afraid to lift it up and read the initials he had requested the jeweler to add. Too afraid to accept Reg's words.

The brooch belonged to his mother. It had been Emerick's

first gift to her as a Firewraith in training with the allowance given to apprentices — a symbol of the end to their poverty. Although his mother had scolded him for spending too much money on materialistic things, the twinkle in her eye and the loving stroke she gave the ruby told Emerick that she was pleased. Every time he visited, the brooch pinned proudly on her chest.

Emerick closed his eyes and, finally, picked up the brooch, thumbing the underside. He felt them instantly. MH. His mother's initials.

Somehow in his shock, his lips moved.

"How long have they been . . . " Emerick trailed off, unable to say their fate.

"Not even a fortnight into your defection. Do you forget that King Bouldermaul has means for monitoring his Firewraiths? The tattoo binds you to him."

Not even two weeks into his journey. Emerick let that knowledge sink in. He had failed his mission before he had even crossed halfway through Vroaevalon. An overwhelming wave of nausea churned his stomach, and he swallowed hot saliva coagulating in his mouth. He clenched the brooch until the pin dug into his palm, fighting the urge to throw it, the hand, and everything Reg had said into the bay. His aching body shuddered, and tears welled in his vision.

His mother was dead.

Through the ringing of his ears, a wail sounded through the air. Emerick felt as though he left his body and was standing between Reg and Phabian and himself, watching himself sob uncontrollably.

"Oh, don't be so overdramatic. Did you not expect consequences for lying to King Bouldermaul and deserting your rank? You forced him to make the order! King Bouldermaul had your brother carry out their deaths as a test to ensure he was not a part of your escape. Kassian, the heartless git, showed no hesitation — so unlike you. He swatted them like flies."

Emerick snapped back to reality. He cursed. Every dirty word that came to mind, he spat at Reg until his face was a red-and-blue patchwork from lack of breath. For the first time in his life, his contempt was not for magic, but instead for His Highness.

Reg laughed, turning to his partner and jutting his finger at Emerick. "He's like one of those yappy little dogs, ain't he?"

Emerick roared. He lunged forward with the shucking knife and stabbed Reg through his boot. His mentor screamed and bent over to dislodge his impaled foot. Phabien rushed around Reg to help apprehend Emerick, but the apprentice pushed the stacks of crab pots down between them. Out of sheer luck, Emerick sprinted to the edge of the platform and dove into the water.

Chapter Sixteen
Saving a Friend

A pathetic moan met Lotte as she sat Remi down at her kitchen table, the helyait still strong enough to hold himself upright. Grabbing a chair, she dragged it to the front door and shoved it underneath the handle, barricading them inside. Next, she retrieved the bathing tub, biting her lower lip as she tried to picture Remi's large frame crammed inside. Her friend required moisture to prevent from drying out. Already his skin had grown rough after the arrow imbedded into his abdomen, nullifying the rune belt he used for protection.

Unfortunately, the bathing tub was too small. Remi would have to fold himself in half to fit inside, and with his wound, that would cause more damage. He needed to lay flat as Lotte tended to him.

Another groan spurred her to rush to Remi's side. Her heart thumped at the sight of the arrow on the floor by his feet. Remi had pulled it out.

"What did you do!" Lotte cried, reaching out to cover the bleeding hole in his stomach. She needed rags.

Remi had shut his eyes and yet to open them since Lotte's arrival. His green-blue coloration was ashen from shock and blood loss. Somehow, he remained seated, but Lotte knew that any moment, Remi's body would rebel against him.

Draping his arm around her shoulders, Lotte coaxed him to stand, supporting the bulk of his weight, and they staggered to her father's room. Blood trailed behind them. When they reached the bed, Lotte carefully laid him on the covers and retrieved a cloth shirt from the dresser, folding and pressing it firmly against Remi's wound. The shirt was soaked within seconds.

Lotte packed another shirt on top before she fetched the hatchery's medical kit that had been left in her room. To her dismay, only a few square pieces of gauze remained. Emerick used most of their supplies while tending to her arm. Thinking about the Firewraith made her falter midstep, and a hot rage swelled in her chest. She had all but forgotten about him. Turns out, she was wrong to trust his word. He lied about the other Firewraiths, and he faked the promise of keeping the hatchery and Twisp secret from Bouldermaul.

She brought her injured arm to her chest, pressing hard against her sternum as she fought a panic attack. Everything she should have done when she first imprisoned Emerick weighed on her conscience. If she had told Healer Aklea the truth, then the inhabitants of Twisp could have evacuated in time. Instead, they lay either dead or at the mercy of the Firewraiths' hands. Gritting her teeth, Lotte scrunched her eyes shut as anger was replaced with a hollowing guilt.

She was responsible for Healer Aklea's death.

And quite possibly Remi's.

No. She refused the thought of bearing yet another loss of life, especially that of her best friend. Lotte shook her head to clear her spiraling thoughts and chose to focus on gathering what she could to save Remi. Her emotions could wait until later.

Swiftly, she gathered every clean article of clothing she could find, along with her bed sheets, which she cut into strips for makeshift bandages. She returned to her father's bedroom, replaced the folded clothing on her friend's stomach, and began searching under the bed and in the nightstand drawers for healing elixirs.

In Orm's wooden chest of venom vials, she found a rather potent pain elixir. It would do nothing for the actual healing process; however, a small dose would ease the pain and stop Remi from shifting and groaning. Lotte uncorked the vial and sniffed the dark brown liquid. While it was not the freshest elixir, it had yet to spoil. Good. Now her only dilemma was how much to give Remi.

Her mind flashed to her run-in with the pixies over a week prior. Now that she thought about it, her father had given her the exact same elixir. Just a small sip took all her aches and woes away. Perhaps its potency was why her father kept it under his bed instead of the emergency kit.

"C'mon, Remi. This will help." Lotte looped her arm under his neck to prop him up.

The helyait's eyes visibly moved side to side under his eyelids. The erratic sight unnerved Lotte. She quickly brought the vial to his lips as he parted them with a whimper, and she dribbled what she estimated as a spoonful into his mouth. A small drop fell out of the corner of his mouth, but the rest stayed inside. Remi instinctively swallowed, and soon his body relaxed.

With his pain now managed, Lotte focused her attention back on the wound on his stomach. The compression slowed the bleeding so it was no longer pouring out of him. However, a wet warmth met Lotte's fingers with each of his breaths, his wound leaking with every movement. This brought another issue to Lotte's attention: Remi's stomach was abnormally distended and rigid. He was suffering from internal bleeding.

Unless Remi received the right potion and surgery, he would

die.

Neither option was readily available, with Healer Aklea gone and the remainder of the healing potions in basement storage — of which she could not remember if they even had any potent batches left after her last delivery to the clinic. There was only one other solution, and she was lucky enough that it was nearly done — the Elixir of Life.

Lotte bandaged the helyait as best she could with the strips of sheets, packing as much shirt on top of the wound as possible. She managed to rouse Remi so he could sit up enough for her to wrap his midsection. Now with him settled once more in bed, she took the remaining clothes to the kitchen pump, wet them, and returned to drape them over Remi's body. That would have to do until she finished the potion.

Lotte left for the kitchen and to the cauldron still sitting on the stove. While there was only a soft glow in the charcoaled wood, the metal of the stove was still hot, and when she removed the lid to the cauldron, steam engulfed her face. The contents had cooled enough so it no longer simmered, but it was still hot enough for Lotte to continue with the current batch. Any colder and she would have had to start over completely, which Remi likely had not the time to wait for such a tedious process. She loaded kindling and smaller logs into the stove, then poked the hot charcoal until they ignited into flames. For a few more minute, she stirred the potion until it simmered again.

Judging by the thickness, the Elixir of Life still had half an hour left before she could add Scorn's venom. Lotte bit her lip. Did she even have that much time with the Firewraiths infiltrating Twisp? For all she knew, they could have found the stairs to the top of the cliff and were walking the trail to her house.

She never waited for Twisp to fully emerge, leaving the cliff's edge at the sight of the shipwreck emerging from the water, but it was possible that its surfaced presence bought her and Remi some time.

Lotte put the lid back on the pot and stood from her crouched position, scanning the table of empty dishes and leftover ingredients. Where was Scorn's venom? The jar was not with the other ingredients, nor was it anywhere in the kitchen when she checked the counters, cabinets, and every nook and cranny. She scoured her room, then her father's (checking on Remi momentarily), and even The Broody Room. Lotte turned the hatchery upside down and had no luck. Was it possible that it got left behind in Scorn's enclosure?

While she doubted it, remembering Emerick complimenting their success through her fog of delirium, Lotte still rushed outside to Scorn's enclosure and pressed her face against the glass as she studied the sand for the jar. Nothing. She doubted Emerick or anyone else had hidden it. There was only one explanation that Lotte could think of: Either Healer Aklead, Remi, or Emerick had the venom on their person.

She slammed her fist against the ground and spat a curse. Closing her eyes, she dropped her head back so the sun warmed her face. How strange it was that the worst moment of her life occurred on such a beautiful day. She expected the fall of Twisp to occur in the midst of the rainy season, when skies were black and raining in sheets, and the ocean waves were raging and beating the land. The atmosphere did not fit the Firewraiths' atrocities.

Lotte took several deep breaths, quelling the emotions swirling her thoughts into a depression. She knew her next step but was admittedly stalling. Her arm twinged like a child crying for her parent's attention. With everything that had gone on, she had forgotten about her injuries. She found it funny that the moment she remembered was the moment she decided to put herself into the same situation that got her hurt in the first place.

Back inside her home, Lotte gathered all the gear she had dressed in the day before and readied her second attempt at milking the most dangerous wyvern in all of Asoleenya. Every ragged breath of Remi acted like the tick of her father's pocket watch, and the seconds were winding down. Instead of fear, determination spurred her movements, and she shoved her hands into the very gloves that failed her before. Lotte then fetched twine from a workbench in The Broody Room and wrapped every possible opening around her wrists tightly and tied the string off. This time there would be no mistakes. She prepped another jar with a rubber lid and headed back out to Scorn's enclosure.

Halfway there, a brushing sound from behind made her turn her head.

"Nilka!" Lotte cried, spotting the wingless wyvern sliding on the grass in her shadow. "Where have you been? Never mind! You need to leave now. Go on a long hunt or something. Bad men are here, and you must stay out of their sight."

But Nilka persisted, following Lotte to the door of Scorn's enclosure. Lotte was too anxious to push anymore with the wingless wyvern.

She shot Nilka a stern glare. "Fine, you can stay, but out here — " she gestured to the area around the enclosure " — I have to handle this alone."

Nilka cocked her head and clicked her teeth together before anxiously rubbing her nose against the glass. The wyvern was more intuitive than Lotte gave her credit for.

"Okay." Lotte took several deep breaths. She lifted her

hooked stick and exclaimed, "Let's do this!"

She pressed her face against the glass door and cupped her gloved hands around her eyes to see inside clearer. Scorn habitually lounged on the platform next to the hatch for food and water, coiled and basking in a sunny spot, his slitted eyes fixating on Lotte.

With Scorn out in the open, Lotte found the process of catching him easier compared to the previous night when the wyvern had hidden. She approached the door, Scorn's head following her movements, and she unsealed the enchanted lock.

As Lotte stepped inside, Scorn, already in motion, opened his mouth and spat with territorial anger. Keeping her eyes on the wyvern, Lotte shut the door and maintained a sizable distance as she moved along the rounded glass panels. Holding the handling stick out in front of her, she was ready to ward off any strikes. They circled each other for a few seconds. Lotte's boots sank into the sand, slightly slowing her movements, but she remained focused and level-headed.

This time, dealing with Scorn, Lotte took the initiative instead of waiting for him to attack first. She inched closer, extending the hook and tapping Scorn on his tail. His body jolted away before he bluffed a charge, not biting but lunging at the stick. He then leaned back into a more defensive stance.

Lotte continued gently petting Scorn with the handling stick on different parts of his body, using it as a diversion as she slowly inched around his side. This technique forced a wyvern's hostility toward the stick instead of the wielder. Letting them wear themselves out was an effective method, one she and her father used to calm aggressive mothers during egg transfers to the incubator.

As expected, Scorn's constant dramatic movements fatigued him. Eventually, he realized his waning energy, turned away, and fled toward the rock-pile feature. Lotte gawked at how the once-terrifying wyvern had retreated after only a few minutes of the technique. She had anticipated more!

Scorn shot up the rocks before nose-diving into a crevice between two boulders, hiding out of sight. Clicking her tongue, Lotte approached cautiously. With the wyvern out of sight, she could not tell if he was gearing up for another attack or resorting to hiding. She hoped for the latter.

Lotte rapped the rocks, aiming to lure Scorn out. She was not dumb enough to stick her face over the spot where he disappeared. The noise and vibration of her hits would have to suffice.

A hiss from behind caused the hairs on her neck to rise. Lotte whipped her head around just as Scorn emerged from the sand, mouth gaping. He sprung, and Lotte screamed, falling backward. The wyvern had tricked her! After seeking refuge in the rocks, Scorn had burrowed into the sand and wormed his way behind her.

Landing on her rump, Lotte gasped at her vulnerable position. Her handling stick had slipped from her hands, falling somewhere nearby. A lightweight body slithered onto her leg and zipped up her abdomen. Lotte brought her hands together, clapping her hand around Scorn's head. He snapped, hissed, and spat at Lotte's face, saliva dripping in the sand dangerously close to her head. His tail slapped her covered neck, and had his stinger still been intact, she would have been dead. Lotte needed to move one hand up just a bit to gain control of its head, but she was afraid that releasing her grip would result in Scorn breaking free.

A loud bang from behind startled Lotte. She rolled her head back to find Nilka's massive body pressed against the closed door, trying to barrel her way inside. She retracted and tensed her body, hissing deeply. Lotte knew what was going to happen next.

"No, don't!" she cried.

Nilka crashed against the door. Screaming, Lotte turned her head to the side to avoid the glass as it cracked in half and flew off its frame. She recalled the tedious familiarity of the arachnea attack not even two days before. If Scorn or the Firewraiths did not kill her, then her father would do so, as two glass panels broke under her supervision.

Nilka shot forward, glided across the sand, and flashed her rows of serrated teeth at Scorn. The latter stopped struggling in Lotte's hands as he spotted the larger wyvern fast approaching. Using the distraction to her advantage, Lotte loosened her fingers and slid her hand up to his head, thumb underneath his jaw and index and middle fingers pressing down between his eyes, gripping hard. She got him!

Lotte jumped to her feet as Nilka appeared at her side to bite Scorn. She yanked the flailing wyvern out of Nilka's field of attack just in time, holding him high above her head.

"Enough, you crazy scales-for-brains!" Lotte wriggled her body when the wingless wyvern tried climbing up her legs. "You're gonna make me let go of him, and then we're all in danger!"

With the enclosure compromised, Scorn would attack everything that breathed within a kilometer's radius. A travel box would have to hold him until she readied a temporary enclosure inside The Broody Room. Oh, how she dreaded the thought of changing his water, food, and substrate in such small confines. That is, if the Firewraiths did not murder them all, first.

Time was sparse. Lotte could not dwell any longer. She let go of Scorn's lower body, but her hand still had an iron grip on his head, and fished for the jar in her pocket. Just like before, his tail wound her arm and prodded for an opening in her suit. However, the twine did its job and prevented a repeat of their previous encounter.

"Easy, Scorn. This will be quick, I promise." She brought the jar to his lips, massaged them open, and popped his fangs through the rubber. The venom exfoliated.

While this was happening, Nilka continued her attempt to reach Scorn, though her determination had dwindled. Lotte pivoted so her body was always between the two wyverns. Pride swelled in her chest at how she handled the most dangerous wyvern in Asoleenya.

Lotte kept Scorn attached to the jar as she left the enclosure, stepping out of the gaping hole in the glass. It was surreal walking across the compound and into her home with Scorn of all wyverns. She went straight for The Broody Room and to the workbench. On the table were leftover sacks and travel boxes from when she had originally gathered the mother wyverns for the safe house. Carefully, she jiggled Scorn's fangs free of the rubber lid and pinched his mouth shut. Setting the jar of venom aside, she grabbed one of the wyvern sacks and —

Lotte heard the front door to the kitchen slam open.

Her heart nearly exploded in her chest. Blood rushed from her face so quickly that it was painful. She staggered, her lungs hyperventilating. Subconsciously, she shoved Scorn into the sack, yanked away her arm, and tied the strings shut — the wyvern hissing and squirming inside. She caught herself on the workbench before her knees gave out and gripped the ledge until her thumb joints seared from strain.

What did she do now? What *could* she do? They wiped out an entire town of helyaits, including the town guards who were trained in both weapons and magic. This was not like before when Emerick was on his own. He was practically her age and had an incentive for keeping her alive. These were true Firewraiths, older and stronger and were using magic.

"Lotte?" a familiar voice called. "Lotte, are you here?"

"Emerick?" she whispered under her breath. Anger snapped inside her like lightning. She stowed Scorn into a travel box, before she whispered sternly, "Nilka!" The wingless wyvern snapped her head up, waiting for her command.

The Broody Room door opened, and Emerick poked his head inside.

Lotte whistled; Nilka pounced.

They wyvern bit the Firewraith's arm and coiled around him so tightly that his joints popped. She forced the strength from her legs, dropping him to the ground. The double doors were blocked from shutting by Emerick's body, and cooler air from the hallway rushed past Lotte as she approached. Although she did not have her blowgun or any other weapon on her person, she was not worried. There was no escaping Nilka's death grip.

"Stop," Emerick wheezed. "Please, stop."

The plea made Lotte hesitate. She studied him, noting his sopping hair and clothes and then, to her surprise, bruised jaw and crooked nose, broken and bleeding. His left eyebrow was three times its size and blocked his vision. A sliver of worry wormed itself past her contempt.

"What happened to you?" she asked bluntly.

Emerick rambled incoherently, gasping as he no longer had air in his lungs.

"Nilka, release," she commanded.

The wingless wyvern uncoiled her body, dropping Emerick to the ground, and slithered to Lotte's side.

The room was motionless. If it weren't for the rise and fall of Emerick's chest, then Lotte would have thought he was dead. After a few minutes, his shoulders began to shudder, and a choking noise came from his throat. Lotte inched closer. Had Nilka broken his ribs? Was one of his lungs punctured?

Lotte was shocked by tears leaking from the corner of Emerick's eyes.

"Why are you . . ." Lotte trailed off.

"They are coming," Emerick said gravely. "They are coming here for the Elixir of Life."

"You told them about it?" she screeched.

"No, th-they . . ." He cut himself off and brought his hands to his face and over his eyes, digging his nails into his skin. He was barely holding himself from breaking down. "They're dead. She's dead."

"Who? The helyaits?" Lotte asked.

Emerick shook his head, his body trembling. He whispered, "My mother."

Lotte froze.

"His Highness — no, *Bouldermaul* — " he spat the correction " — found out I lied about my whereabouts. My punishment was their fates." He paused, inhaling shakily. "My mother was already dead less than two weeks into my journey."

Lotte was stunned. All anger toward Emerick dissipated, leaving behind nothing but pity as tears seeped through his fingers, disappearing into his bloodied hairline. For the first time, she did not see him as a Firewraith, but as a victim of Bouldermaul and the society he created. He would not be here if he had not been, by luck, selected to be a part of the chivalry program. He did not hate magic by nature but instead was nurtured to believe it was the root of his problems. In reality, Lotte and Emerick were one in the same.

"I'm so sorry," Lotte whispered.

Emerick exhaled a sob, his rigid body shaking from strain.

In any other situation, Lotte would have offered consoling words. Losing her mother was unimaginable. Sure, she only saw her once a year or two . . . or five. Her only relationship with her mother was through letters. Yet, to lose her completely — to know she no longer walked and breathed in the realm of the living — the thoughts sent goosebumps down her arms.

Nonetheless, as Emerick had stated, the Firewraiths were coming.

"Emerick," Lotte said gently, "how much time do we have before they arrive at the hatchery?"

"They were in battle with Matriarch Ira when I escaped," he said, "so depending on the outcome, they could reach the hatchery at any time."

"The hatchery is hidden by the forest. It's almost imposs-ible to see from the bottom of the cliff."

Emerick shook his head. "If I spotted the roof of The Aviary from the beach, then they definitely will. Even if they somehow miss it, the Firewraiths have other . . . means." He finally removed a hand from his red-rimmed, watery eyes and lowered it to his left ear, folding it forward to reveal a hidden tattoo.

"What is that?" she asked.

"Every child is given one upon their recruitment into Firewraith training," he explained. "I thought it was a symbol of serving His Highne — *Bouldermaul* — but apparently, it's his way of tracking his followers."

"Tracking how? With magic?"

"Y-Yes."

"I always knew he was a hypocrite." Lotte snorted, unsur-prised. "How can they track you all the way from Guldkem to Twisp? Weren't you wearing armor that prevents magic from being used on you?"

"I didn't wear it all the time. The armor is impossible to sleep in, and there were some days that I wanted a break from wearing such a heavy uniform," Emerick said.

"So if you wore something to cancel out the magic, they can't track you here?"

He jerked a nod. "It would not stop them from scouring the area until they find the hatchery, but an anti-magic implement would buy you time."

Spinning on her heels, Lotte returned to the workbench and dragged the drawers open, rifling through all the tools and equipment. Her father had one anti-magic handling stick that he used in extreme cases of dealing with wyverns, and normally, he stored them in this particular workbench. However, after throwing everything to the floor, emptying the drawers' contents completely, it was likely that he took the handling stick with him, probably in case the basilisk egg hatched before reaching the sanctuary. Hopping over Emerick's body, Lotte checked the other workbench in the non-venomous wyvern hall before confirming her conclusion.

Frustrated, Lotte brought the base of her palms to her eyes. What could they use now? What else did she have in the hatchery that could stop magic from touching him, or at least keep him hidden? The only other enchanted manacore items that nulled magic were the shackles she had used on Emerick, but they were in the basement with the arachnea.

As she dragged her hands down her face, she winced at the dry blood cracking on her skin. Remi. Was he still alive? She lost track of time since Emerick's arrival. She needed to start the final step of the elixir and then check to see if the blood had slowed from the arrow's entrance wound.

Lotte froze. The arrow. That was a solution to their dilemma! Lotte could use the arrow's anti-magic properties. She left Nilka with Emerick and entered the kitchen, spotting the bloodied arrow where she had left it on the table. Taking it to the pump sink, Lotte scrubbed the blood off, a shiver running through her body as she watched her best friend's blood disappear down the drain. When it was clean, she dried it off with her shirt and spun around.

Lotte gasped at the sight of a blue, shimmering mist materializing through the front door and floating toward The Broody Room. Tracking magic. While it had been a while since she last saw it used, Lotte recognized it anywhere. The Firewraiths were searching for Emerick. If her plan with the arrow failed, then they had no chance. They would be discovered before she could formulate some sort of defense.

Lotte followed the mist to The Broody Room. It fully encompassed a grim-looking Emerick. He met her gaze and whispered, "They're coming."

"Take this," Lotte held out the arrow.

"This is — "

"We don't have time to talk! Take it, now!"

Emerick did. The mist dropped to the ground and dispersed. Lotte sagged with relief. Her plan had worked. Finally, something was going her way.

"The mist already showed them a general direction," Emerick warned. "This only holds off the inevitable for a little bit longer."

"Any extra time is better than nothing. I need a plan."

"You can't possibly fight them. These aren't your average Firewraiths. Malyse is an Elite! He is the best of the best, one of Bouldermaul's nine right-hand generals. And Phabien, he graduated his apprenticeship early. As for Reg . . . " Emerick paused, visibly trembling, "his crude appearance and manners should not be taken lightly."

Lotte tilted her head in thought. "You know them well?"

"Reg is — *was* — my mentor," Emerick said. "I was selected at the same time as Phabien. I know them well enough. This is my first time meeting Malyse and learning of his magic."

"But you know how Bouldermaul trains them — and the strategies they use when opposing their enemies?"

"Y-Yes."

Perhaps Lotte could save the hatchery, after all.

"Get up," she demanded, and Emerick looked at her with wide, slightly hurt eyes. He remained in his position, no doubt thinking she was about to kick him out. Holding out her hand, Lotte urged him. "Help me. You said they're coming. I can't transfer the wyverns in time. The only other option is to defend the hatchery. I can't do much on my own, but maybe, with you and your knowledge of the Firewraiths, we stand a chance."

Emerick gave a hollow laugh. "And go against everything I've been taught?"

"They had no trouble turning against you," she quipped.

He snorted and continued staring at her hand, contemplating. Next to him, Nilka slunk along his body, and to Lotte's surprise, he did not shy away from her. Instead, his hand inched toward her belly until his finger brushed her scales.

"Please," Lotte said.

Emerick locked gazes with her and gave a firm nod. Shakily, he propped himself up and took her hand, a look of determination on his face. Once on his feet, Emerick growled, "Let's burn these swines."

Chapter Seventeen
Retrieval Mission

Lotte ladled the simmering contents of the cauldron into a measuring cup, stopping where her father had etched a line into the carved wood. Steam tickled her nose as she sniffed for a skunk-like odor that told her the potion was ready. At last, their efforts were a success. Now it was time to add the final ingredient.

Emerick watched from his seat across the table, too battered to do anything more than provide an audience for Lotte's work. He had been abnormally silent since agreeing to help fight his former comrades. It was obvious his decision weighed heavily on his conscience, but vengeance against his mother's murderers solidified his defiance of his society's beliefs. Lotte knew they would have to formulate a plan soon. They had less than an hour, quite possibly any minute, before the Firewraiths arrived. However, Remi was in his final moments — unconscious, pale, and struggling to intake air. If the Elixir of Life could not heal him, then nothing would.

Lotte brought the measuring cup to the table, next to a dropper and the jar of venom. Still gloved and with her body completely covered, she removed the rubber lid and used the dropper to extract half of the venom, tapping any remnant droplets off on the glass lips. Her hands shook as she hovered the dropper over the measuring cup. Lotte inhaled, counting to three, before exhaling. She continued the breathing exercise until her hand steadied.

Lotte pinched the rubber end of the dropper, and the venom squirted out. The potion fizzed where the stream landed but stopped after a second. Lotte stirred the potion with a thin iron rod, and the liquid turned a red-black iridescent.

"It's done," Lotte whispered.

Emerick leaned forward, his voice solemn. "So this is the Elixir of Life."

Her eyes flickered to him as she retracted the iron rod and licked the potion off, testing it. She wondered what he was feeling, finally seeing the guerdon of his efforts, only to know he had failed from the start. Scrunching her face from the revolting taste, Lotte carefully lifted the measuring cup and headed toward her father's room.

A faint, labored whine from Remi's lips was the only indication he was still alive. As Lotte approached, she wanted to cry at his motionless body. She kneeled on the ground next to his head and shoved her free arm under his neck to prop him up. Unfortunately, his lips were dried shut, and Lotte doubted she could angle the measuring cup correctly without sloshing the potion out. She tried lifting him up, but his dead weight was too much for her. Lotte huffed with frustration. How was she going to do this?

"Is there anything I can do?" Emerick said from behind.

Lotte jumped, whipping her head around. "You followed me!"

"Was I not supposed to?" he shifted, rubbing his arm uncomfortably.

"It doesn't matter." She stood up and beckoned Emerick forward. "Can you push push him into a sitting position?"

"Yes."

Emerick took her place at Remi's side, gently folding the helyait until he was sitting. Working around him, Lotte pinched Remi's lower lip to open his mouth and brought the Elixir of Life closer, holding her breath as she drizzled a small portion of the thick liquid onto his sharp teeth. She watched the potion disappear past his gums and heard a gurgle as he breathed. Lotte massaged his neck, successfully encouraging him to swallow before she repeated the process until the measuring cup was empty.

The effects were instant. Remi inhaled deeply, and a bright light seeped through the makeshift bandages from the arrow wound. Black eyes snapping open, he blinked at the ceiling in confusion. The glow on his abdomen ended, and his scales had returned to their vibrant color. Slowly, he turned his head toward Lotte, mouth opening and closing like a fish.

A sob tore from Lotte, and she launched herself onto the now-healed Remi. Helyait customs regarding touching aside, she hugged her best friend with all her might, rocking him side to side as she cried into his shoulder. She was mildly embarrassed about the tears and snot pooling on his shoulder but pushed aside her worries as Remi embraced her back.

"What happened?" he asked.

She leaned herself back, wiping her nose with the back of her hand. "Don't you remember the Firewraiths on the beach? Or getting hit with an arrow?" She reached out to clean the slimy mess she left behind on his skin, but he swatted her hand away.

"I remember the Firewraiths, but only bits and pieces after that." Remi sat up, a harsh look crossing his face as he noticed Emerick in the bedroom with them. "What is *he* doing here!"

"It's a long story that we don't have time to explain," Lotte said. "He's on our side, though."

"I find that hard to believe," he growled.

"Trust me, please," she urged.

Scowling, Remi dropped his attention from Emerick and slowly sat up until his back propped against the headboard, dorsal sail folded in on itself. Wet pieces of cloth fell onto the blankets from when Lotte had soaked and placed them on his scales. He felt the bandages on his belly, eyes widening at the blood stains not only on the strips of sheets but also on the bed and all over Lotte.

"You were dying," Lotte filled him in. "I gave you the Elixir of Life."

"Is that why you are in your gear? Father took the venom. Did he give it back? Where is he?"

Lotte froze.

Remi recognized her distress and asked, "Where is my father?"

Lotte swallowed, her throat becoming dry. Her heart physically hurt as she turned her head away, unable to look him in the eye, silence speaking louder than words.

"Was he captured by the Firewraiths?" he asked.

"No," Lotte said, more tears filling her eyes. "He stayed behind so we could escape. When I checked on him from the top of the cliff . . ." She lacked the heart and the stomach to finish.

"Is my father dead?"

She jerked a nod. "I'm sorry."

Remi inhaled sharply, closing his eyes and dropping his head backwards. He swayed to the side, and Lotte resisted the urge to reach out and place a hand on his shoulder. His breathing became erratic, a tremor sweeping through his body, but he did not cry — or rather, he could not cry in the same way as humans, considering helyaits did not have tear ducts. Instead, he pressed a hand on his chest, over his beating heart.

Lotte was at a loss for words. She wondered if telling him was the right choice, or if she should have waited. The latter ignited a maelstrom of guilt in her stomach, though. After all, she caused this mess for striking a deal with Emerick instead of telling Healer Aklea. If Twisp was given enough time to prepare, perhaps none of them would have met such a gruesome fate. Healer Aklea would still be alive, too.

Emerick spoke urgently for the first time since Remi's awakening, "The Firewraiths are coming as we speak."

Lotte wanted to smack him for disrupting Remi's despair. Yet, Emerick was right. Neither he nor the helyait had any time to grieve their losses. It was unfair and downright traumatic for both of them to set aside the deaths of their parents, but there was no other choice.

"This is so sudden, and I can't imagine how you must feel right now, but," she paused before asking Remi, "will you help us?"

"With what?" he barely choked out.

"I need to defend the hatchery. With yours and Emerick's help, we might stand a chance."

He exhaled loudly, gills fluttering, and shook his head. "We are better off fleeing."

"I'm not leaving my wyverns behind. You know I can't."

Remi fell silent.

Stepping past Lotte, Emerick crouched until he was eye level with Remi, ignoring how the helyiat tensed and clenched his fists. He spoke in a low and chilling voice. "Do it for your father. Avenge him. Avenge all the helyaits they have hurt."

Lotte opened her mouth to deter his rather violent word of encouragement. She was shocked, though, when Remi swung his legs over the side of the bed and stood, tugging on the bandages until they fell off. Determination glinted in his eyes.

"How do we stop them?" he asked.

"We planned on figuring that out after we healed you," Lotte said, then turned to Emerick, "What did you have in mind?"

"The same thing we did with the entelodont," he said. "We distract them — " he gestured between himself and Remi " — while you hide somewhere with your blowgun. When the time is right, you fire at Malyse, the Firewraith using magic. He is the most dangerous one out of the squad and should be neutralized first."

"What about the other Firewraiths?" She crossed her arms.

"They have armor that cancels magic," Remi said. "I fear that my abilities would be useless toward them."

"Perhaps if the attacks are an indirect result of magic, they might work," the former Firewraith mused. "Can you use anything other than elemental water magic?"

"Innately, no. I do know a plethora of incantations if we have any manacore present." Remi tilted his head in question at Lotte.

She clicked her tongue. "I have some torches you could use, but nothing with enough manacore to produce more than your average oil lamp. We could gather all the runes on the property and then you might have enough magic, but I doubt there's enough time," she said.

"No, he doesn't need to. His elemental magic will be fine enough. If you can somehow use it as a pendulum or mimic a long-distance weapon, you could use anything from rocks to kitchen knives as projectiles."

"I can easily create enough force." Remi brought a finger to his chin, thoughtfully. "But what of their enchanted weapons to cancel magic? I am afraid I will fall into the same circumstance if I am hit with another arrow."

"That's why we must be quick to dispose of Malyse. Then Lotte and I can take on the other two Firewraiths."

"Can you overpower what my people could not?" If Remi had eyebrows, Lotte imagined one of them being raised with doubt.

"They did not have Nilka," Emerick said.

Lotte jolted. "She can't fight."

"Yes, yes she can. She can neutralize one of the Firewraiths for us. Basically, we need to separate them — prevent them from working together. That's when they are dangerous."

"Let me repeat myself — Nilka can't fight. I won't let her."

"Well, you're gonna have to. The fate of not only us and the hatchery but also everyone in Twisp depends on this plan working," he said. "Plus, I doubt she would stand by and not let anything happen to you. She's awfully protective."

"I could lock her up." Lotte lifted her chin with defiance. "She would be safe and not able to get to me."

"She will be safe until we fail."

Lotte snapped her mouth shut. She glared down at her boots, wanting nothing more than to demand Emerick to scrap that idea. Nilka was a rescue. She had already suffered so much in her lifetime.

"You need to make your decision now. Otherwise, we need to consider a different, less effective plan."

"Fine," Lotte grated. "You are putting a lot of faith in our abilities. I still do not know if we are capable of fighting the mage. You expect me to hit him with a dart, but what if I miss? We should have a second plan."

"Have you realized the weakness of Malyse?" Emerick asked.

"He's using magic," Remi hummed in thought. "He is not wearing or using weapons that have anti-magic enchantments!"

"Exactly." The former Firewraith held up the enchanted arrowhead. "Remi and I just need to hit him with something that cancels magic, and then he will be incapacitated. That's when you'll strike."

Lotte's heart raced, adrenaline rushing through her veins. Listening to Emerick's strategy gave her hope. They might actually be able to save the hatchery!

"There's just one thing, though." Emerick cut through her thoughts.

She shifted with jitteriness. "What's that?"

"We need to retrieve my sword."

Cracking the basement door ajar, Lotte peeked through the opening with a torch in hand, the glow reflecting off a tunnel of thin, white silk. Webs. Somehow the arachnea survived and created a burrow. Some of the webs clung to the door, and the slightest movement sent a tremor down into the darkness of the basement.

Skkrrt.

Lotte snapped the door shut, breathing heavily at the fresh memories that sound caused.

"How is it still alive?" Emerick asked, standing behind her. "The way it began melting from the venom, I was sure it would be dead."

"Me too."

"And don't remind me of the entelodont," he continued. "Are you positive you used the right venom?"

Lotte's eyebrow twitched. "Of course, I did." Who did Emerick think she was?

"Do you have any ideas on how to get the beast out?"

"We could leave the door open and see if it wanders out. I'd say we should try and lure it, but I don't think any of us want to be bait," Lotte said, then smirked at the former Firewraith. "Unless you want to volunteer."

"No, thank you."

"If we had enough water, I could flood the basement," Remi offered from the kitchen.

"Drown the arachnea?" Emerick scratched his chin in thought. "Barbaric but effective."

"We are not drowning the arachnea!" Lotte exclaimed.

"That thing is a monster."

"It can't help its nature."

"You are the most naive and delusional person I've ever met."

"How dare yo–"

"Quiet, you two, and I will explain," Remi said, sounding so similar to his father that Lotte's heart tugged. "We leave the basement door, as well as the front door, open and draw the creature out with a strong current of water."

"I still think we should kill it," Emerick muttered.

Lotte smacked his arm. "Enough!" Then to Remi, she said, "Our pump sink is hooked to a well. Will that be enough water?"

"We will see," he said. "In the worst-case scenario, I can draw upon the water in the soil and plants."

Nodding, Lotte led Remi to the sink while Emerick positioned by the basement, hand on the doorknob as he waited for the warning. The pump handle shuttered when Lotte lifted it up and down as fast as she could. Water soon trickled out, splattering against the basin, before turning into a heavy flow. Remi raised his hand, palm flashing with magic, and the water stopped in midair, collecting and growing into a wobbly orb. Lotte's arms strained from the constant movements and pressure that fought gravity. To her dismay, she began to slow.

Before she could ask Emerick to take over, Remi declared, "I can pull it now that there is a steady stream. You may stop."

"Thank Asoleenya." Lotte let go of the handle, hands

shaking.

The orb of water expanded across the kitchen and forced Lotte to take a step back. Eventually, Remi raised it above their heads and into the rafters.

"How deep is the well?" Remi asked after a few minutes.

"About fifty feet," Lotte said.

He clicked his tongue. "The water is slowing down."

"Does that mean this is all the water you can draw upon?" Lotte pointed above their heads.

"It will not be enough to flood the basement," the helyait said. "I will have to improvise."

"What do you have in mind?" Emerick called, still by the basement.

Remi was quiet as he breathed deeply. Hand now raised above his head, he walked toward Emerick. "Arachnea are native to warm temperature regions. They detest the cold."

"You plan on freezing the basement." Lotte trailed after him.

"Something of the sort." He looked to Emerick. "Open the door."

The former Firewraith obliged. Remi wasted no time shooting the water down the tunnel of webs. Closing his eyes, he made a swirling motion with his hands, brow ridges twitching every now and then.

"The arachnea is on the ceiling," he said monotonously. "She has made a funnel-like nest. Manipulating the temperature may not work as the webs act as insulation."

"How do you know this?" Emerick asked, mildly impressed. "Can you see down there?"

"I can *feel* the resistance against the water," Remi said.

"What can be done now?" Lotte felt their options slipping.

Remi surprised her when he said, "This might be the best-case scenario."

"How so?"

"You will see." His hand movements quickened until they stopped, slowly and with great strain closing into a fist and holding still. Remi exhaled and sagged, looking fatigued. "Hurry, I don't know how long the ice will hold her."

"Right." Lotte swallowed. To Emerick, she said, "You're coming with me."

"Planned on it." He took the first step down the stairs.

Lotte shivered as she placed her hand on the rail, the damp, sticky strands clinging to her fingers. Her boots squeaked with each step, and the stagnant air grew more pungent of dirt and mold. It was abnormally cold, too, a result of Remi's magic. The light of the torch brightened only enough to show a couple meters ahead of them. Other than the faint dripping sounds, the basement was silent. Eventually, they reached the bottom of the stairs.

Every inch of the room — shelves, boxes, and furniture — was covered in the same silk, except for the quarantine enclosure. The now panel-less space was dark and vacant, pale reflections off the glass shards skewing across the rocky floor and into the shallow pool. Before Lotte could search the ceiling for the arachnea, Emerick gasped and stumbled backward, his elbow knocking painfully into her diaphragm.

"What's your problem?" she wheezed.

Emerick pointed ahead, "Look!"

Lotte followed his hand with her torch. Her heart raced at the sight in front of her. What she had originally thought was a piece of furniture under a thin layer of webs was actually the arachnea! At least, the collapsed exoskeleton of it. The human-like lure was split in half and behind it was a hole where the arachnea had wiggled out. The thorax was partially melted.

"So it did survive by shedding its exoskeleton," Lotte said. "It shed its exoskeleton."

Emerick brought a hand over his mouth. "I might throw up."

She looked to the ceiling, finding a massive knot of ice. Remi had encased the arachnea in her cocoon. She commended his temporary solution, though she agreed it would not hold the arachnea forever.

"Follow me." Lotte tugged his arm to the incubator in the space underneath the stairs. She began ripping off the webs, and soon Emerick joined her. Lotte grinned as the stone chest was still warm to the touch and a glow emitted from the lid's seal. The incubator was untouched, and the wyvern eggs were okay.

"Where is my sword?" Emerick asked.

"Behind this." Lotte patted the top of the chest.

Craaaacccckkk.

Both Lotte and Emerick snapped their heads toward the frozen casing on the ceiling. The terrifying noise had come from it.

"Hurry." Emerick bounded around the incubator, ripped the last of the webs, and made a noise of happiness at the sight of his sword, sheathed in its carrier. "Finally!" He snatched it up and cradled it in a tight hug, like a long-lost friend.

A silver glint on the ground caught Lotte's attention. It was the rune necklace she had found in the Firewraith's pocket while stripping him of his armor. She wondered where he had gotten it, suspecting he likely stole it from either the farmer or the helyait he attacked when he first arrived at Twisp. The rune faced up, the helyait characters revealing the words spoken when conjuring its magic: *Lycka Amat.* Technically, it translated to "push forward." However, it was more of a defensive enchantment, meant to create an energy blast to ward off attackers.

Noticing her distraction, Emerick followed her gaze to the

necklace. He reached out shakily and took it, too.

Craaaacccckkk.

The arachnea was breaking free.

"Let's get out of here." He tucked the necklace into his pocket. He moved toward the stairs.

"Wait!" Lotte said. "We have to get the eggs out of here." She spoke the unlocking incantation, and the chest's seal flared. She lifted the lid to reveal the first crate of eggs. The other crates stacked underneath.

"We don't have time for this!" he argued.

"They can't be left down here with the arachnea. If they hatch, they'll have no food or water."

"We have bigger problems right now, you fop!"

Lotte's eye twitched at the insult. "Just grab a crate," she growled.

Craaaacccckkk.

Emerick strapped his sword to his back before he held out his arms. "Stack them, hurry!"

Giving him a thankful nod, she carefully lifted the first crate and placed it on him. The soft eggs clung together on their bed of clean wood shavings, undisturbed by the movement. They would survive outside of the incubator for several hours, possibly even a day or so, depending on the breed of wyvern, thanks to Holan's heat. It was the humidity that could ultimately hurt the eggs. Too little could dry them out; too much would promote the growth of mold. Thankfully, the kitchen would suffice as temporary housing.

Together, they managed to hold three of the four crates when another fissure sent a shiver down their spines. Emerick labored to the web-covered stairs, sweat crowning his hairline. Awkwardly carrying a crate while providing light with the torch, Lotte impatiently demanded the former Firewraith to pick up his pace. Her eyes darted between the incubator where the fourth crate of eggs remained and the ice capsule on the ceiling.

Craaaacccckkk. Craaaacccckkk! THRAWP!

Lotte screamed as a massive chunk of ice shattered against the ground. A long segmented leg emerged from a hole. It was much too small for the arachnea to fit through, but it was only a matter of minutes before it broke free completely.

Finally, they arrived at the top of the stairs, Remi waiting with wide, horrified eyes. Lotte shoved her crate into his hands, spun around, and descended into the basement again.

"What are you doing!" Remi called after her, just as Emerick exclaimed, "Is she insane?"

Ice flakes trickled around Lotte as she approached the incubator. Glancing up, she found another leg had broken free. A large crack revealed the arachnea's ring of glinting eyes — all staring directly at Lotte. She swallowed back a scream and forced her attention back on the remaining crate. Hands shaking, she reached for the handles, standing on her tiptoes, stretching her arms and back as far as they could go. The incubator's ledge dug painfully into her gut as she tried yet failed to gain a good grasp. Curse it all! She was too short!

The noise from the ice grew louder and more frequent. Chunks rained down behind Lotte, and a quick glance back revealed the arachnea was halfway out. The lure on the top of its head, which had once resembled a woman, was now just a gray mound that would eventually re-grow into the preferred prey of the arachnea's diet. Lotte was out of time. She would have to leave the crate or risk being eaten. And if she died, there would be no one left to protect the hatchery.

With a heavy heart, Lotte retracted her hands, fingertips glossing over the top eggshell. It was soft like fine sand and squished under the slightest pressure. If only she could pinch the top and — that was it! Lotte fastened the egg's shell between her thumb and forefinger, and she slowly raised the entire clutch, sticking together with natural adhesive coating, out of the crate. When high enough, she scooped the eggs with her other arm and hugged them to her chest, pushing her abdomen off the incubator edge with a long-winded exhale.

Lotte turned and sprinted to the stairs. She refused to look behind her, even when an enormous thud reverberated the floor. Both Emerick and Remi beckoned her frantically, shouting for her to hurry. At the top step, hands grappled her tunic and pulled her into the hallway. The basement door slammed shut.

Legs quaking, Lotte closed her eyes and breathed heavily. Creaks from below the floorboard told her how close she was to being the arachnea's lunch. An arm wrapped around her shoulder, and she was guided by Remi into the kitchen where the rest of the incubator crates rested on the table. Lotte gently pushed aside one of the clutches to make room for the one in her arms.

She stepped back and faced Emerick, who was glaring at her half-heartedly. Risking her life to save the eggs obviously perturbed him. He would likely never understand her protectiveness toward the wyverns. He shook his head, pinching the bridge of his nose.

"Can we proceed with our plan, now?" Emerick demanded.

Stomach churning with anticipation, Lotte nodded. It was time to deal with the Firewraiths.

Chapter Eighteen
DEFENDING THE HATCHERY

Finding the densest and tallest tree along the hatchery's perimeter, Lotte tugged on the thick, woody vines and then leaned back, testing their strength with her weight. They slithered up the smooth trunk and draped off the branches like hundreds of snakes. She lifted her legs and swung side to side in one final assessment, mentally cheering as they tightened but did not snap. Other than dust and pieces of moss trickling down, the vines remained firm enough for her to scale.

This tree would hide her from the Firewraiths.

Next to her feet, Nilka lifted her head as if observing the tree for weaknesses. From Lotte's body cues, she likely thought they both were about to climb it. However, the wingless wyvern was to stay on the ground with Emerick and Remi, hiding out of sight until Lotte gave the command to attack. Hopefully, she would listen this time. Her disobedience when milking Scorn had cast some doubt on Lotte's confidence in the plan.

"Come, Nilka," Lotte said, releasing the vines and then starting toward one of the raised vegetable beds in front of her home. It contained large, leafy plants and would be Nilka's hiding place.

Kneeling down next to the log-perimeter, she watched with

teary eyes as Nilka approached dutifully. She almost lost her composure when the wingless wyvern, who must have sensed the fear and sadness in the air, wound up her leg and torso before stopping with her head on Lotte's chest — as though she was offering a hug.

"I promised my father to always look out for you." Lotte rubbed the base of Nilka's head. "You have come so far since living with those monsters. I don't want to lose you today — or ever."

Despite her missing wings, Nilka was the fiercest creature she had met. Even the arachnea could hardly compare to Nilka's cooperation and loyalty. She would sacrifice herself to save Lotte, and that's what was scary.

"You must help me fight, but — " she looked around to make sure neither Emerick nor Remi was listening " — if things become too dangerous, I want you to hide in the forest. Wait there until I find you. If by tomorrow I'm no longer . . . *here*, go deep into the forest. You're large enough that most predators won't attack you. Just avoid giant spiders and entelodonts. Eat plenty of howler monkeys, deer, and pixies."

Her voice cracked as she spoke. Despite the dire circumstances, she believed in her plan. The thought of dying today was daunting, but she dismissed any notion of abandoning her mission. She could not break the promise she made to her father, to protect the wyverns and their home. With renewed determination, she resolved to see her plan through.

She already lost her first home in Urtica, and she was not going to lose this one.

Lotte stood, gently unwinding Nilka, and instructed her into the vegetable bed. She walked around each corner and tucked any of the wingless wyvern's body under the leaves. Soon, a bypasser would have no idea that a 130-kilogram wyvern was lurking nearby.

With a huff, Lotte examined the compound once more: her home, the sheds, and The Aviary. Everything felt surreal, as though she was saying goodbye.

"Enough!" Lotte exclaimed. "This is not the end!"

Commanding Nilka to stay, Lotte marched back to the tree and snagged the vines. She placed her boot on the trunk and leaned back until her body was at an angle, just as she had done hundreds of times during her childhood, and took a step up.

"Lotte, wait!"

What now? She had finally mustered the courage to complete their trap. Lotte exhaled, allowing her legs to fall and feet slap the ground. She pinched her lips together as she turned. Remi rushed toward her, carrying the relic he had given her days before. Why did he have it with him?

"You still never opened your gift." He stopped before her and held out the kelp-covered pole. Since Lotte had received it, the leaves of kelp had dried. However, they were rehydrated and no longer flaking off. Remi must have used his magic.

"Is now a good time?" Lotte asked but took the gift anyway. She began to peel away the layers. Remi attempted a grin, but it came out as a grimace. "If there's ever a time to use this relic, it's now," he said.

The relic had a six-foot-long, metal shaft with a handgrip in the middle and a mouthpiece on one end, made of manacore. Runes as tiny as ant larvae engraved in a ring where the stone connected with the metal. It was in a language not of her own or Remi's.

"It's a blowgun!" Lotte gasped.

"Made in Kullusk," he said.

She whistled, balancing the relic in her hand. It was surprisingly lightweight and easy to carry. If only she were a bit taller, then it would be perfect for her. But even in her current state, it was leagues better than the one she had whittled herself.

The blowgun could give her the upper edge on the Fire-wraiths.

"The capital of Kullusk, Drovinbog City, is one of the most advanced cities when it comes to their technology," he explained. "They have balanced science and magic, not only with their weapons, but also into their everyday life."

"What does it do? What words must I say?" She brought the mouthpiece to her lips and blew air through for practice. The runes glowed immediately.

"You do not say anything. It registers air fluctuation inside the shaft. When the other *Idateori* and I tested it, we discovered it utilizes wind elemental magic to increase the dart's speed and ensure it stays in a direct line without the elements outside the blowgun influencing its trajectory."

"Where is the energy source?" Lotte asked. "The mouth-piece?"

"The shaft," he corrected. "They melted manacore minerals into the material used to make it."

"This is amazing!" Lotte all but hugged the blowgun. She could not believe she had received such a gift.

A whistle from the treeline east of the compound broke their conversation. Emerick's head popped out of the bush, and he pointed down the path that led to the cliff-stairs. Even with their distance, Lotte could see the tremor in his hand.

The Firewraiths had found the hatchery.

Lotte moved before her mind could process her actions. She was halfway up the tree in what felt like a blink of an eye. After another dissociated moment, she was hidden among the branches. Remi returned to his position behind the shed, a wall of flowering shrubs curtaining him.

The Firewraiths arrived with the quietness of an ocean storm in the midst of her rage. They all wore chainmail armor and helmets identical to Emerick's. Though, they each had a violet-blue tabard with a different number of black strikes on them. Lotte was unsure of what they meant. Thankfully, Emerick at least taught her and Remi the names of these three Firewraiths, as well as their descriptions so they could decipher who was who.

At her house, the Firewraith with long black hair, Malyse, lifted his fist as if to knock. He said something to the other Firewraiths that made them chuckle, then flexed his palm, causing the front door to blow off its hinges and crash loudly into the kitchen. Malyse hollered a sarcastic greeting and lifted his foot to step inside —

Remi cast a whip of water directly at Malyse's face, sending him flying to the side. A battle roar from the bushes caused the other two Firewraiths, Reg and Phabien, to whip their heads toward Emerick rushing out from his hiding spot with his sword raised above his head. They drew their weapons to disarm him, but before they could, Lotte whistled sharply.

Nilka sprang from the vegetable beds, hissing shrilly. The Firewraiths barely had time to turn their heads before she wrapped around the taller of the two men, coiling so tightly that his scream was cut short into a squeak. She knocked him off his feet and bit into his neck. He somehow managed to free a hand to catch himself and scrabble at Nilka's body.

"What the — " exclaimed Reg, identifiable by his indecent appearance. Distracted by the wingless wyvern, he failed to notice Emerick quickly gaining ground. By sheer luck, Reg raised his sword in time to block the attack.

On the ground nearby, Malyse pushed himself to all fours, but a rush of water formed up his arms and legs. The water froze, imprisoning him to the ground. This was it. This was the moment Lotte needed to strike. This was her chance to save the hatchery.

Lotte loaded the relic blowgun dipped in Scorn's venom,

brought it to her lips, and aimed.

"It registers air fluctuation inside the shaft," Remi's words played through her mind. *"It utilizes wind elemental magic to increase the dart's speed and ensure it stays in a direct line without the elements outside the blowgun influencing its trajectory."*

She hesitated, blowing her breath through her nose instead of her mouth to avoid a premature release. Did that mean she could fire directly at him, instead of aiming higher to account for gravity and slightly to the side for wind resistance? Lotte shook her head to clear her thoughts. Remi had said to aim directly, so she would do just that.

Inhaling until her chest strained, Lotte blew. The runes on the mouthpiece flared with light, and the blowgun jerked back from the force. Unlike water and fire elemental magic, wind magic was silent and scentless. Lotte recovered from the ricochet quickly and looked to Malyse to see how he reacted to the effects of Scorn's venom. To her surprise, he was staring directly at her, completely unfazed. A glint above his head on the exterior of her home caused her stomach to sink.

The dart was impeded in the wood.

Lotte had missed.

An invisible force grasped Lotte's body, locking her limbs in place, and she was yanked from the branch she crouched on. Scream torn from her, she sailed through the air and across the compound, the world blurring past her. She stopped abruptly not far from where Emerick engaged with Reg in trading blows with swords, before she collapsed to the ground in a disheveled pile of crooked limbs. She blinked several times at the cloudless sky. Her mind struggled to process that not only had she failed at hitting her target, but also she had been caught by the mage and magically pulled toward him.

Out of the corner of her eye, Remi emerged from where he

hid, wielding a spear of ice, no doubt coming to Lotte's aid. He charged Malyse. The Firewraith's hands glowed in their bindings, and the ice bindings melted away. With a roar, he jumped to his feet, barked an incantation, and held his palm to face Remi.

The helyait managed to stop midstep and bring his arms up in defense, before the same invisible force knocked him backwards and off of his feet. He landed on his back with a yelp, his spear dissolving back into water.

The sight of her fallen friend brought Lotte back to her senses, and she eased herself into a sitting position. Her gaze flickered to Nilka, specifically at the knife embedded in her side, blood painting her white scales scarlet. They wyvern continued her hold on Phabien despite the wound.

Lotte began to tremble as fear and anger swirled in her chest. Profanities filled the compound, and it took Lotte a moment to realize they were coming from her. Malyse hardly noticed her, too focused on Remi — same with Emerick and Reg, the latter of which was gaining the upper hand on Emerick.

Rage clouding her vision, Lotte staggered to her feet and rushed toward her home, hopping over the fallen door as she entered the kitchen and headed to The Broody Room. She stopped in front of the work bench where Scorn's crate rested, shoved gloves on her hands, tore off the lid, and seized the sack by the tie. Fear of the wyvern biting her through the fabric was non-existent. Instead, only the pulse of her desperation sounded in her ears.

Gritting her teeth, Scorn carried him out of The Broody Room and back outside, where no one had noticed her brief absence. They were losing, and this was the only solution Lotte could think of. She unfastened the strings and reached inside, swiftly grasping Scorn by his body and yanking him out.

Before he had a chance to bite — let alone hiss — Lotte threw him toward Phabien and Nilka, whistling her command for the wingless wyvern to release the Firewraith. Just as she uncoiled, Scorn landed on Phabien's head. His mouth opened and fangs sunk into the Firewraith's cheek.

A blood-curdling scream silenced the compound. Malyse turned, and Reg and Emerick jumped away from each other before they, too, watched Phabien claw at Scorn. The Desert Deathbite Wyvern encompassed Phabien's head, toxic scales scraping his bare skin, and he injected deadly venom into the Firewraith's bloodstream.

Chapter Nineteen
SAFETY IN SWARMS

Phabien's skin visibly melted when Scorn finally retracted his fangs from the Firewraith's face. The wyvern fixed its gaze upon its next target, Malyse, and Lotte had a sick sense sense of pleasure imagining the Desert Deathbite Wyvern attacking the Firewraiths one by one. Of course, that would mean Scorn would eventually turn on Lotte and her companions, his aggression not caring even for the hands that fed and tended to him.

Scorn slid off of Phabien and onto the grass. He bared his open mouth and let out a deep, windy hiss. Tensing his body, Scorn coiled back on himself before he sprung toward the Firewraith mage.

Malyse raised his hand, incantation spilling from his lips. Fire surged from his palm and encased the Desert Deathbite Wyvern. He dodged Scorn's fully inflamed body, and the wyvern fell against the ground and began to wither.

"NO!" Lotte screamed, running toward Scorn despite Malyse looming beside her. She patted the flames in an attempt to stop them.

On his feet again, Remi roared and attacked Malyse with another spear of ice. This spurred Emerick and Reg to resume their fight, all while Phabien's blood-curdling wails echoed through the forest. Both fights quickly ended, though. Reg disarmed Emerick's sword, causing it to fly through the air and land in a vegetable bed, and Malyse enchanted vines to catch Remi by his ankles and climb up his body, immobilizing him. Heavy panting from all parties followed as their efforts came to a standstill.

Reg touched the tip of his sword to Emerick's throat. "Why don't we all just calm down for a bit?"

Lotte hyperventilated as she finally put out the fire on Scorn. To her horror, his body was completely charred. The stench emitted from him was overpoweringly bitter, and Lotte covered her nose and mouth as smoky fumes curled around her face. Tears spilled down her cheeks. Scorn was dead.

"I'm actually impressed that you lasted this long, though your fish-headed friends gave us a nice workout earlier." Reg wiped his arm across his sweaty forehead. His eyes narrowed on Emerick. "And you! Traitorous scum!"

"My mother was dying," Emerick reasoned.

"Everyone's mother dies!" Reg spat. "Death is inevitable. You simply sped up the process by disobeying the king. And look!" He gestured to Phabien whose noises dwindled to gurgles and face globous with strings of bloody fat and skin. His right cheekbone, teeth, and lower jawbone were visible. "You wasted a perfectly exceptional Firewraith! What a shame!"

"Why did King Bouldermaul pinpoint his efforts on me!" Emerick cried. "There are dozens of Firewraiths he could be fixated on! Why me?"

"'Cause you're the one dumb enough to use magic!"

"He's using magic!" Emerick nodded to Malyse. "How is that not treachery?"

"King Bouldermaul isn't naive enough to believe magic can fully be vanquished by mere might and weaponry. He authorized a select few — his Elites — to use magic in extreme situations," Reg said.

Emerick scoffed, "So King Bouldermaul is allowed to break his own laws?"

"King Bouldermaul *is* the law."

"Enough," Malyse cut their conversation short, sounding bored. He approached Lotte and nudged Scorn's body with his boot.

It took all of Lotte's willpower not to slap his foot away and cradle the wyvern to her chest. She risked a glance at Nilka, remembering the knife embedded in her side. The wingless wyvern had somehow removed the weapon, and she was nosing the door to their home, trying to get inside as her wound leaked onto the grass. Frankly, Lotte was surprised that Nilka had not sought shelter in the jungle.

"Girl!" the Firewraith mage barked. "What is your relation to Orm Skale?"

Fear gripped Lotte's lungs. She couldn't bring forth the breath needed to form words.

Punishing her hesitation, Malyse flicked his wrist at Remi, and the vines began binding around him, looping around his neck and over his mouth. Her best friend's wide, black eyes met Lotte's with terror.

"My patience is waning," Malyse said.

Lotte gulped. "Orm Skale is my father."

"Don't tell him anything!" Emerick hissed as Reg applied more pressure to his jugular with his sword.

"Where is your father?" The Elite continued his interrogation.

Another glance at Remi told Lotte she had no other choice but to answer.

"On a trip. He left me in charge," she said.

"Is that so?" he asked skeptically. "A young girl such as

yourself is put in charge of such a big facility?"

"Yes," Lotte was too stunned to feel any irritation.

"Where did he go?"

"North. He won't be back for another two weeks."

Malyse watched her without speaking. Each second that passed felt like an eternity, leaving Lotte wondering if they would kill her, Remi, and Emerick right there and then wait for Orm to return. That certainly would be easier than interrogating them. Yet, the Firewraith mage crouched to her level. The slits in his helmet were too shaded to see his features.

"You've seen what the power of King Bouldermaul can do," Malyse said lowly. "And you have seen what *I* can do. All I need is a little cooperation, and maybe you can walk away from this altercation."

"I know what you came here for." Lotte ducked her head, bangs falling into her face.

"You do?"

She nodded, more hair shrouding her gaze. She subtly searched the ground around her for something that could help with this situation. If she could stall him long enough, then perhaps she could devise another plan of defense. Maybe she could even retrieve another dart from her canister, though she did not move her hand toward her belt with everyone's attention on her.

"Tell me, then, the name of what I seek."

"The Elixir of Life."

"Lotte!" Emerick growled.

Malyse removed his helmet, revealing his remarkably fair complexion. He had a sharp jaw, wavy black hair, and slanted green eyes — younger than Lotte had expected, no older than his mid-twenties. His soft features reminded her of a Prairie Snap Wyvern: small and harmless-looking until its sting left its victim in white-hot, feverish agony for three days, the toxins attacking every nerve around the puncture site. It was always the small and insignificant looking wyverns that packed a wallop. That made Malyse terrifying. He was right — Lotte knew what devastation he could commit.

"Do you have the Elixir of Life?" he asked.

Lotte bit her lip and nodded.

"*Lycka Amat!*" Emerick shouted.

Malyse was knocked off his feet and flung backward, colliding with the vegetable bed. He groaned, grabbing the back of his head and rolling to the side. Reg, caught off guard by Emerick's swift actions, lost his grip on his sword and was disarmed by his former apprentice.

Lotte's mouth opened and closed like a fish, amazed. Emerick had used the rune necklace; he had actually used magic! How in Asoleenya did he even know the incantation?

Emerick pulled the arrowhead from his pocket, which they had tied to a thick stick to create a handle during their preparation to fight the Firewraiths, and rushed toward Malyse. His efforts were beyond foolish — suicide, even — and Lotte watched in horror as Malyse lifted his palm and blasted Emerick with enough force to catch the flowerbed next to him, sending the former Firewraith and debris flying through the air and slamming into the side of The Aviary. The glass panel shattered.

Lotte's distraught shouts mixed with the dozens of beating wings as the vibrant bodies of wyverns streaked out of the glass dome and to the sky. Some wyverns circled the compound in a frenzy, while others fled to the forest canopy — likely never to be handled by Lotte and her father again.

Malyse tilted his head to observe the wyverns, taking his attention fully off Lotte for the first time since his questioning began.

Praying that Nilka still had strength left over, Lotte whistled. The wingless wyvern snapped her head into attention and, despite her wound, charged toward Malyse. Nilka wound around his body and brought the Firewraith to his knees like she had done with Phabien.

Lotte roared as she leapt from her position on the ground. She retrieved a dart from her canister, gripped it in the middle, and charged the wyvern-bound Firewraith. He opened his mouth, but the air had been squeezed out of him. Lotte stabbed the dart into his eye.

There was a pop, and then her gripping fist hit his skull from the force. She would have aimed for the soft flesh of his neck if not for the steel garget. The dart was painted blue, indicating it had been dipped in paralysis venom — the same kind used on Emerick. It was not deadly. However, at least five inches of the dart disappeared through his spurting eye and into his brain. Malyse's body shuddered, his head rocking side to side, teeth grinding. The bones of his ribs snapped as Nilka increased the pressure.

Bile rose in Lotte's throat, and she turned away.

The vines around Remi visibly dried and cracked. The helyait wiggled his hand free and began ripping them off. The bramble of vines was thick and tangled, and it would likely take him time to break out of them. However, he was alive and mostly well.

Lotte flickered her eyes to The Aviary. Could the same be said about Emerick?

"You filthy wench!"

Somehow, Lotte spotted the shadow of Reg and his raised sword just in time to dodge a fatal swing. The tip caught her sleeve, and she cried out as it cut her bicep. She gripped the spot, hot liquid glazing her fingers. Now she had two injured arms, yet adrenaline saved her from feeling the pain. Reg swung again, but Lotte ducked and sprinted toward the forest.

Leaves and branches whipped Lotte's face, as she slunk deeper and deeper into the lush jungle. Boots drummed in her wake, the Firewraith spewing profanities. She had another sense of déjà vu regarding how many times she had run for her life over the past couple of weeks. The first time with the pixies was once too many.

Pixies.

The fiendish pests gave her an idea!

With a rage-filled Reg wildly hacking vines and foliage, he was oblivious to where they were going — or of Lotte gazing toward the sky, finding the sun through gaps in the canopy to gauge their direction, and making a sharp turn so they were heading west. He never noticed as the ground became muddier, nor the growing stench of rotting leaves, nor the increasing buzzing sound that began drowning out the rest of the forest.

"I refuse to let a brat like you be the reason I fail King Bouldermaul's orders!"

The trees cleared ahead of them, and in their place grew fragrant ginger lilies. Beyond their large leaves and beehive-like flowers, Lotte spotted the bank where the pixies had built their underground dwellings. Gray bodies flew aimlessly above the pond. While their numbers were considerably less than Lotte's last visit, as her father had captured enough to keep their population from infesting the inhabitants of Twisp, there were still enough pixies to consider this swarm dangerous.

Lotte headed directly toward them.

"You can't run forever!"

Pixies shrieked as Lotte burst from the foliage. She stomped on their nest, aggravating them even further. One landed on her arm, but she swatted it away. Just as they began to horde, Lotte waded into the pond before inhaling deeply and diving into the murky waters. She swam to the bottom and gripped the roots of plants to keep her from floating back up. Kicking her feet, Lotte crawled her way along the floor of the pond, weaving in different directions to throw off both Reg and the pixies.

She waited until her lungs begged for air before stopping at a pocket of mud, grabbing handfuls, and bringing them to the surface. Eyes still closed, Lotte smeared the mud all over her face and arms. Ginger lilies and cattails surrounded her, blocking her view of the bank. However, she could hear cries from Reg and screeches from the pixies. Judging by how he did not follow her into the water, Lotte considered calling her plan a success.

There was only one way to confirm, though.

Lotte pushed aside the leaves until she had a clear view of Reg. He flailed as pixies clung to his body, swarming around his face, the only exposed part of him. He swung his sword blindly, hoping to ward them off, but they easily zipped out of the way. Eventually, he lost his grip, and the sword fell into the pond. He scrambled to throw off the pixies stripping his flesh, but there were too many. Howling, Reg bumbled away into the jungle, attempting to distance himself from the swarm, but his efforts were futile as the pixies followed.

Lotte spent the next few minutes simply breathing. She leaned back in the pond, her back catching on dozens of hardy stems as she allowed herself to float. If not for the young pixies chirping from their nesting mounds, Lotte would have dozed off. Reg could still be heard, but it would not be long before he succumbed to his fate.

She did it. *They* did it.

Relief exploded in her chest. She brought a hand over her mouth as she sobbed. Only now did her mind catalog all the bumps and bruises on her body.

The cut on her arm throbbed, and the pond water threatened infection. Lotte knew she should get out and return home to help Remi from the vine restraints and to tend to Emerick's and Nilka's injuries, as well as salvage whatever she could of The Aviary. But her body needed a moment to process the emotions brought upon by one unbelievable thought: They had saved hatchery.

Chapter Twenty
AISLA NENIN

A cool breeze swept through the door of The Aviary, offering a gentle reprieve from the heat inside. Lotte crouched on all fours, carefully picking up the last few pieces of glass, each one a small triumph in the process of rebuilding. The larger shards were already propped against the shed outside, and she knew the smaller glass dust would be raked and packed into the dirt soon, ensuring the safety of future wyverns once The Aviary was restored.

Despite the challenges, her chest held a quiet determination. Most of the wyverns had fled the compound, but some had stayed, finding solace in the crevices of The Aviary's habitat, and others had even returned, drawn by the familiarity of home. Lotte had managed to catch a few and store them safely in the enclosures of the Broody Room. Though many were gone, she still had hope.

She knew it could have been much worse. She could have lost all the wyverns, the hatchery, and even her own life. Yet here she was, still standing, with some of the mothers and the precious eggs she had saved from the basement. Nilka was alive and healing, basking in the sun outside with her wound treated and wrapped in strips of cloth. Lotte could not help but think how different things might have been if she had told

Healer Aklea about Emerick sooner. Perhaps they could have predicted the arrival of the three other Firewraiths, but dwelling on the past would not change the present.

Lotte shivered at the thought of Malyse and his partners. After working with Remi to create enough potions to heal the helyaits who had not succumbed to the poison, they worked together to drag Malyse and the unrecognizable remains of Phabien into the jungle, burying them in shallow graves — but not before removing their armor, weapons, and anything else on their person. Taking things from the dead seemed wrong, but Remi had disagreed.

"*We can use these to learn from our enemy,*" he had said, devoid of emotions, the loss of his father weighing heavily on him.

Lotte leaned back on the balls of her feet and wiped her sweaty forehead. She stared at the sky through the missing glass panel. Though the sun heated southern Holan until it was stifling, wisps of clouds appeared overhead and announced the impending end of their dry season. Soon they would grow bulbous and gray and heavy with rain, occasionally streaking with lightning. In fact, Lotte would not be surprised if the wet season started tomorrow. She hoped it would wait until after her father returned. Two weeks left to go.

Lotte perked at the sound of footsteps. "Who's there?" she called out.

"Me." Remi poked his head around the missing glass. "The ceremony is starting."

She took a deep breath and stood, lifting the bucket of glass with her. She carried it out of The Aviary and to the shed where the rest of the broken glass waited for Orm to decide what to do with them. There was a chance they could be re-melted to make another panel.

"Let me change my clothes," Lotte said, and Remi nodded

and waited by Nilka.

Inside, Lotte stripped off her gloves and tossed them onto the kitchen table, now vacant of wyvern eggs. The helyait guards had drawn the arachnea out of the basement, allowing them to retrieve the stored potions and gather the ingredients needed to brew more antidotes. With the threat gone, the eggs were returned to their snug incubator.

Down the short hallway, she glanced into her father's room, the door ajar. On the bare mattress lay Emerick, facing the wall. He had not spoken since Lotte had used the last of the Elixir of Life on him, as the force of Malyse's magic and the fallen glass had proven near fatal.

A plate of food lay on the nightstand, once again uneaten. The pang in Lotte's chest made her almost push the door open and engage him in some sort of conversation, but the last few times she tried consoling him were fruitless. She knew any further efforts would garner the same result. It was best to give him space.

In her room, Lotte changed into her last set of clean cloth — a sleeveless tunic and cotton pants. Laundry had been the last thing on her mind with everything going on. All of her cloaks, scarves, and normal apparel were soiled with dirt, sweat, and blood. Surprisingly, Lotte did not feel insecure without covering up. In fact, she preferred being out in the open, no longer hiding. She existed, and so did the hatchery. Those who had a problem with her or her wyverns would meet the same level of ruthlessness that she showed the Firewraiths. Lotte just hoped this was the last of dealing with Bouldermaul.

Lotte clipped her belt and adjusted the canister of darts and her whittled blowgun. She left the relic Remi had given her next to her bed. On her way out, she grabbed a canteen of water and a handful of dried, pitted dates, tossing them into her mouth and chewing until her jaw hurt. Her stomach growled fiercely for something fuller than the meager snack, yet it would have to wait.

"I'm ready," Lotte said, emerging from her home.

Remi lowered his chin in acknowledgment and headed toward the path without a word, shoulders slumped and feet dragging. Frowning with pity, Lotte trailed behind him.

They continued walking in silence until they reached the stairs down the cliff. On the beach below, nearly half the helyait population of Twisp lay wrapped in kelp on the sand. Their loved ones surrounded their bodies, mourning the needless loss of life. A lump in Lotte's throat formed, and a wave of nausea hit her. She wished she had not eaten anything before coming.

One by one, the friends and families summoned a wave large enough to lift each body and carry it to the water. The helyaits' loved ones then followed, guiding the kelp-wrapped bundles. Eventually, they swam out of the bay and disappeared from sight. Lotte and Remi descended the stairs, joining the others in *Aisla Nenin*, the Final Swim.

"Where are they taking them?" Lotte asked softly.

"To a reef three kilometers east of here," Remi said, voice hollow. "That way they remain at a part of the sea, even after death."

Lotte swallowed, no longer trusting her voice.

They approached the pod, and Remi wove around the parties of helyaits until coming across his father. He too was wrapped in kelp and waiting for his turn. Matriarch Ira watched over him, greeting Lotte with a curt nod as Remi dropped to his knees and lay his head onto Healer Aklea's chest. The helyait matriarch was mostly recovered from her battle with Malyse, thanks to a healer from a transient pod. Her voice echoed over the lapping waves as she called out each fallen helyait's name.

The ceremony lasted well over an hour, possibly even two. Lotte sat in the sand on the other side of Healer Aklea. She rested her hand on his abdomen. Her mind drifted through the years of memories she had of supplying his clinic with potions, joining him and Remi for a meal, and receiving his bountiful kindness. He was more than just a friend to Lotte—more like an uncle. Her father had known Healer Aklea since his time in Urtica. Lotte was not looking forward to telling Orm the tragic news.

Healer Aklea was one of the last to be called. Before them was the mother and infant that they had saved from the Firewraiths' poison. They swam with two other adult helyaits while pushing a smaller body — most likely a helyait child. She forced herself to look away.

Both Matriarch Ira and Remi spoke the incantation, and like with the others, a wave came forth and lifted Healer Aklea. Not wanting her friend to swim alone, Lotte kicked off her boots and walked alongside them. The waters were back to their calm, pristine norm, and she could see the plumes of white sand with every step they took. Healer Aklea bobbed in the waves, but he remained afloat with their hands on his chest.

"I will take him from here," Remi said, once they reached waist-deep water.

"You shouldn't do this by yourself," she countered.

"From here on out, the waters grow more dangerous for landwalkers," he said. "I must focus."

Lotte understood his unspoken plea: He needed to put his energy into grieving, not protecting her from both predators and the elements. Looking down at Healer Aklea's kelp-encased body, she wished she could see his face one last time. The water was now to her chest, so Lotte bent forward and hugged him.

"I'm so sorry," she whispered. "Thank you for everything." Her hand slipped off of him, and she took a step back.

Remi spared her no glance as he continued forward. Lotte frowned but chalked it up to the tragic task at hand. Turning around, she trudged to land. The final group passed her along the way, and the ceremony was officially over.

Only Matriarch Ira and a few stragglers remained on the beach, waiting for the others to return. Lotte decided to do the same for Remi, sitting cross-legged right before the dry sand met the damp. The sun shifted toward its descent, and Lotte's thoughts faded to an open-eyed doze. It was an hour before the first helyait group re-emerged.

After what felt like an eternity, Remi's head popped up into view. Lotte jumped to her feet, her legs straining from sitting in one position for so long. Her clothes were damp, but no longer soaking. Remi approached her, holding out something in his hand.

"I should return this to you." His voice cracked as he revealed a small glass vial.

Lotte gasped, recognizing the venom inside. It was Scorn's! This was the venom from when she and Emerick had milked the wyvern. This was likely the last dose in all of Asoleenya. She tucked it into her belt pouch, before returning her attention to Remi. She wanted to thank him, but he spoke first.

"I plan on joining my mother's pod," he announced. "I will not be returning."

Her heart thumped heavily in her chest. "What?"

"There is nothing left for me here," he said. "But Matriarch Ira has already spoken to the survivors. In one month, we will guide a ship to Port Labree and then to northern Holan. Any landwalker may board if they wish to migrate. I recommend you and Orm do this, as Bouldermaul is likely to send more of his Firewraiths. There will be enough room on the ship for your wyverns."

"Remi, I —" Lotte reached out to place a hand on his wrist, but Remi jerked away. For the first time since meeting the helyait, Lotte found herself at the receiving end of his glare. It stung, but she understood.

"I wish . . ." Remi snapped his head away, fists clenching. "I wish you had told someone about the Firewraith when he first arrived. Maybe then . . ." He turned his back to her.

Lotte froze, her mind blank. Her mouth remained rigid as Remi returned to the water and disappeared from sight and, most likely, her life. The weight of the recent events — of each death — nearly swept Lotte off her feet. She wished the beach would turn into quicksand and swallow her whole.

Someone cleared their throat behind her, and she jumped. Spinning around, she found Matriarch Ira giving her an unreadable look.

"Forgive me, but I have overheard your conversation," the pod's matriarch began.

"Remi is right," Lotte swallowed, thickly. "This is my fault."

"You are not to blame for the actions of the Firewraiths. Whether or not you had spoken up sooner would not have prevented their arrival. We received reports they were in the area even before the Firewraith named Emerick attacked the Gibbs family."

"You cannot deny, though, that me telling you about Emerick would have prepared you for a possible attack."

Matriarch Ira inclined her head. "Why is it that you withheld such information?"

"It's complicated," Lotte shrugged. "I thought I could protect the hatchery on my own, but . . ." She brought her palms to her eyes to physically stop the tears from falling.

"But?" the helyait urged, gently.

"If I could go back in time, I would change everything." Lotte closed her eyes when tears threatened to spill.

"While I agree you should have spoken up instead of taking on such a huge responsibility by yourself, there is still a likelihood of the same or similar outcome. We are a small pod. Even our guards are not given the training on the same level as Bouldermaul forces his Firewraiths.

"Based on what Remi has informed me, the Firewraith you are sheltering has deserted Bouldermaul and no longer intends to cause harm to Twisp. He had not known there was a tracking spell in the mark behind his ear, nor had he known Bouldermaul was actively looking for Orm Skale and the Elixir of Life. This does not excuse him from the crimes he committed toward the Gibbs family, nor the unknown crimes that time will only tell, but if there is anyone to blame, it is Bouldermaul."

Lotte shook her head, not believing her sincerity.

Matriarch Ira noticed and continued. "Our fates would be much worse had you three not stopped those Firewraiths. Furthermore, you prevented Bouldermaul from obtaining the Elixir of Life. Who knows what he planned on using the potion for. It is for that reason, as well as the lack of resources and people, that I am not actively pursuing Emer-ick," she paused, her eyes narrowing. "But he is forbidden from interacting with this pod. He must leave the area immediately."

Though Lotte worried for Emerick, she nodded her head in agreement. He had still assaulted the Gibbs family and burnt down their farm. He should be imprisoned for that alone, so the fact that Matriarch Ira was letting him walk free with only a banishment slapped on his wrist shocked Lotte.

"I must return to my duties," Matriarch Ira said, as the helyaits returned from the *Aisla Nenin*. "And Lotte, I have told my people that Emerick perished in the fight. I expect the truth to stay between me, you, and Remi. Do you understand?"

"Yes, Matriarch," Lotte whispered.

"Good." The helyait leader took a deep breath as she stared at something in the distant horizon. "Grief often puts blame on the wrong people. Dire situations cause for dire decisions. One day, your friend Remi will come around. Until then, focus on preparing your wyverns for the journey ahead. Has Remi shared the news of our migration?"

Lotte nodded, feeling a small spark of hope in her chest. Perhaps there was still a chance to mend things between them.

The matriarch's next words stole her breath.

"I sent a messenger to your mother. She will be expecting you and your father at the sanctuary. We leave in one month." Matriarch Ira stepped lightly toward the waves. "Goodbye, Lotte Skale."

As Matriarch Ira dove into the water, the air pulsed around Twisp. The dock and the shipyard shuttered before the town began its final descent into the depths of the bay. Lotte waited as the steel port sank, and disturbed swells were all that remained.

She felt a quiet sense of excitement. After years of longing and countless dreams, she was finally going to join her mother at the sanctuary. She should be overjoyed, and part of her was. But a nagging doubt lingered in the back of her mind. Was the cost of this dream coming true too high? Had she truly earned it, or was it overshadowed by what had been lost? The mixed emotions left her feeling uncertain, caught between anticipation and unease.

For the first time ever, Lotte was truly alone. Two weeks ago, she would have relished this sort of independence. Now, she was painfully aware of the safety in numbers. Surviving meant increasing her odds in any way she could, not sabotaging herself with ignorant refusal for help.

With one final glance around the beach, and at the few remaining cloudless skies, Lotte began the trek home to her wyverns.

GLOSSARY

Aisla (ah-eye-slaw)
The helyait word for "swim."

Aisla Nenin (ah-eye-slaw nee-nin)
The helyait tradition of guiding dead loved ones to a reef where their bodies become part of the coral. Translated to Lotte's native tongue, it means "Final Swim."

Alsum (all-soom)
The helyait word for "open."

Aksman (ah-x-man)
A bovine-humanoid race.

Akeltic Sea (ah-kell-tick)
The body of water that borders Asoleenya's west coast.

Amat (ah-mah-t)
The helyait word for "forward" in terms of motion.

Arachnea (ah-rack-nee-uh)
A massive spider-like beast, native to the Immorthial Forest, with a shapeshifting lure on its back, meant to attract its prey.

Asoleenya (a-so-leen-ya)
A continent that consists of five countries — Ceris, Endlor, Holan, Kullosk, and Vroaevalon — and three major territories — Gruik Territory, Immorthial Forest, and Shattered Islands.

It is bordered by the Akeltic Ocean, Etisa Sea, and Slokyl Ocean.

Ceris (seer-is)
The furthermost country apart of Asoleenya's mainland. Its southern borders connect with Vroaevalon, the Immorthial Forest, and Endlor.

Endlor (end-lore)
The northeast country next to the Immorthial Forest and above Holan. It is the smallest country in Asoleenya.

Entelodont (Ehn-tell-ih-doh-nt)
A massive pig-related beast.

Etisa Sea (eh-t-sah)
The body of water that borders southern Asoleenya.

Firewraith
The name of King Bouldermaul's selected chivalry.

Galm (g-ah-lm)
The helyait word for "slow" or "slowly."

Gruik (groo-ick)
A sentient race born with magic. They seemed to have vanished fifty years ago.

Gruik Territory
The southern most peninsula of Asoleenya. Once the home of gruiks, its harsh desert climate has left most of the territory uncharted.

Holan (hall-in)
The eastern-most country of Asoleenya's mainland. It borders Endlor, the Immorthial Forest, and Gruik Territory.

Idateori (Eye-dah-tee-or-ee)
Translates to "theory knight." A helyait chivalry class of researchers.

Kullusk (k -oh-luh-sk)
A foreign island country northeast of Asoleenya. Its capital is Drovinbog City.

Lupa (loo-pah)
The helyait word for "wind."

Nebbin (neh-bin)
A form of helyait currency made of whale-bone beads.

Nenin (neh-nin)
The helyait word for "end" or "final."

Nerla (n-ehr-lah)
The helyait word for "lower" or "descend."

Parin (p-ehr-in)
A helyait diety.

Phyra (p-hi-rah)
The helyait word for "poison."

Riv (r-ih-v)
The helyait word for "stop."

Sfavatt (s-fah-vah-t)
The helyait word for "levitate."

Vroaevalon (vroh-aye-vah-lah-n)
The largest country of Asoleenya, ruled by King Bouldermaul
and his Firewraiths. Guldkem is the capital.

ACKNOWLEDGMENT

First and foremost, I extend my deepest gratitude to everyone who has dedicated their time and effort to help me edit and perfect *Lotte Skale and the Wyvern Hatchery*. Your invaluable feedback, encouragement, and insights have been crucial to bringing this story to life.

A heartfelt thank you to the fantastic community at Tally Ink. Your support and camaraderie have been a constant source of inspiration. The 60 Day Novel Writing Challenge has been an incredible journey, and I am grateful for the shared experiences and motivation from fellow writers.

To my husband, Gordon, and my son, Morgan: Your unwavering love and patience have been my bedrock. Thank you for believing in me and for giving me the space and time to pursue my passion. This book would not have been possible without your support.

ABOUT THE AUTHOR

Growing up, Shanna P. Lowe desperately wanted a pet snake. When she was ten years old, she caught a bull snake at a creek in Colorado, USA. She set up a tank underneath her bed with everything the snake would need, even going so far as to buy frozen mice at the pet store without her parents knowing. Her secret was safe until her loose-lipped brother discovered it and ratted her out three days later. Grounded for what felt like eternity (a week), Shanna decided to wait until she had moved out to get a snake.

However, she then met her snake-phobic husband, who also denied her a pet snake. No amount of begging could sway him. In her disappointment, Shanna channeled her desire into her writing, creating a character who could have what she could not, with a twist. She is a fantasy author, after all, her debut book called *Candy Sky Tells A Lie*. So the snakes in her fictional world evolved into wyverns. From their bred the plot of *Lotte Skale and the Wyvern Hatchery*.

The good news? Seeing that his wife would go so far as to write an entire book about python-inspired wyverns to satisfy her desire for a snake, Shanna's husband finally granted her wish.

>>>

Connect with Shanna P. Lowe

Website: www.shannaplowe.com

Instagram: @author_shanna.p.lowe

www.ingramcontent.com/pod-product-compliance
Lightning Source LLC
Chambersburg PA
CBHW051508150726
47997CB00001B/158